THE MYSTERIOUS AFFAIR OF JUDITH POTTS

ROBERT THOROGOOD

ONE PLACE. MANY STORIES

HQ
An imprint of HarperCollins*Publishers* Ltd
1 London Bridge Street
London SE1 9GF

www.harpercollins.co.uk

HarperCollins*Publishers*
Macken House, 39/40 Mayor Street Upper,
Dublin 1, D01 C9W8, Ireland

This paperback edition 2026

1
First published in Great Britain by
HQ, an imprint of HarperCollins*Publishers* Ltd 2026

ISBN: 978-0-00-856742-2
Indie edition: 978-0-00-884135-5

Set in Bemo by Type-it AS, Norway

Printed and bound in the UK using 100% Renewable
Electricity by CPI Group (UK) Ltd

Robert Thorogood is the *Sunday Times* and *USA Today* bestselling author of *The Marlow Murder Club* mystery novels, which have been adapted into a major TV series starring Samantha Bond as Judith Potts. Robert is also the creator of the hit BBC One TV series *Death in Paradise*, he has co-created the spin-off shows, *Beyond Paradise* and *Return to Paradise*, and has written a series of *Death in Paradise* novels featuring DI Richard Poole.

When Robert was ten years old, he read his first proper novel – Agatha Christie's *Peril at End House* – and he's been in love with the genre ever since. He now lives in Marlow in Buckinghamshire with his wife, children and two whippets called Wally and Evie.

Follow him on Bluesky @robthor.bsky.social and Instagram @robertthorogoodwriter

Also by
ROBERT THOROGOOD

The Marlow Murder Club Mysteries
The Marlow Murder Club
Death Comes to Marlow
The Queen of Poisons
Murder on the Marlow Belle

The Death in Paradise Mysteries
A Meditation on Murder
The Killing of Polly Carter
Death Knocks Twice
Murder in the Caribbean

For Leslie Breathwick

Prologue

Mrs Judith Potts looked at the woman standing outside her front door and didn't say a word. She didn't dare say a word. Her heart was racing. Her thoughts were in freefall. The woman, for her part, stared straight back at her, refusing to back down.

'Who are you?' Judith eventually managed.

'You know who I am,' the woman said. 'You killed my father.'

'How can you say that?'

'You're Judith Potts, aren't you? Philippos Demetriou's wife.'

'Philippos died forty-nine years ago.'

'So you admit it?'

'I don't know what you're asking me to admit.'

'Ha!' the woman said, tossing her head back. 'Grandma Sofia was right about you.'

The woman pushed past Judith and entered the house.

'You can't go in there!' Judith called out before scurrying after the intruder, her sense of panic now almost completely overwhelming her. Only an hour ago, she'd managed to catch a killer. This was supposed to be her night of celebration. How dare this stranger barge into her house like this?

'What's this?' the younger woman said, pointing to the photographs of suspects and various index cards of clues and evidence that were pinned to the wall behind Judith's desk. 'Are you planning another murder?'

Judith strode over and started to pull down the crime-scene photos that had been her constant companion for the last few weeks: Oliver Beresford's dead body; the pistol that had been used to kill him; the *Marlow Belle* boat and, of course, headshots of all of the suspects in the case.

'I don't know who you are,' she said as she stuffed the printouts into the bin. 'Or what you're talking about. But I'd like you to leave at once.'

'My name is Eleni Paphides, daughter of Michaela Paphides and Philippos Demetriou.'

'You're *Michaela's* daughter?' Judith said before she could stop herself.

'I am,' Eleni said proudly. Judith's legs buckled and she slumped into the chair by her desk, the dam on her memories bursting: the times Philippos had told her that he could be trusted; that she was being paranoid; that she couldn't smell the scent of another woman's perfume on his clothes.

'W-when were you born?' she stammered.

'Seven months after you killed my father.'

'Please stop saying that.'

'You made him go out in a storm.'

'I tried to stop him.'

'So now you admit it?'

'The forecast was atrocious, everyone in the village knew it. But he wouldn't be told. He was too proud. I begged him to stay.'

'And you told the police you went to the church to pray for his safe return.'

'You've got to slow down. How do you know all of this? It happened before you were born.'

'Admit it. You didn't go to the church after my father left on his boat. You never went to the church. That's what my mother says. You weren't a believer.'

In an act of sheer will, Judith forced herself to look properly at the woman who was standing in front of her. In the shape of Eleni's jaw, and her brow and thick hair, Judith could see her ex-husband Philippos so clearly. Even in how she stood, her broad shoulders thrown back. But her eyes? They were her mother's. The olive-green eyes of Michaela Paphides. The prettiest girl in the village. The girl who Philippos had been supposed to marry.

Judith would never forget the first time Philippos had taken her back to his village on Corfu. How she'd baked in the midday sun as she'd met his parents and wider family, all of them barely concealing their discomfort at meeting Philippos's English wife. But he'd been impervious to his family's disapproval. That had always been Philippos's strongest suit. His self-confidence. How he expected everyone to be swept along by his exuberance. But Judith knew to her cost, his enthusiasms had been those of a child. He soon lost interest and wanted something new. And he got angry when he didn't get it.

'You went out on my father's boat that day,' Eleni said.

'I went through all of this with the police.'

Eleni took a step towards Judith and clenched her fists.

'You went out on his boat and you killed him,' she said. 'You then swam back to shore to make it look like he died at sea.'

'No, I'm not having this,' Judith said, rising from her chair. She had to stop the conversation before it went any further. 'You can't come in here and make wild accusations – you could be anybody.'

'You know I am who I say I am.'

'Can you prove what you're saying?'

'Back at my hotel, of course.'

'Get out of my house,' Judith blurted. She had to stop Eleni from talking. 'Leave at once or I'll call the police.'

A sly smile slipped onto Eleni's face.

'You won't do that. We both know you won't. But I'll go. It's a lot for an old woman to take in. I'm staying at the Tollgate. I'll confirm my identity any time of your choosing. But come and see me soon. If you don't, I'll take all of the evidence I've got to the police.'

Eleni left and Judith realised she'd stopped breathing.

She didn't doubt for one moment that Eleni was who she said she was – Judith's words to her had just been a delaying tactic to get her out of her house. But what on earth had Eleni meant when she'd said she had evidence that Judith had been on the boat that day? It wasn't possible. The Corfu police had tried every trick in the book to prove that she had been behind her husband's death. Even though, when his body had washed up two days after the storm, there'd been no evidence of foul play. As the coroner later reported, he'd died from drowning. It was the same when the police eventually recovered his boat. It was found smashed to pieces in a nearby cove and all of the physical evidence confirmed that he'd gone out to sea on his own, got caught in a storm, and then drowned when the boat sank.

Judith went over to her drinks cabinet and poured herself a small glass of whisky. Her hand was shaking and she stiffened the drink with another splash before she downed it in one.

She glanced at the gold ring she wore on her wedding finger. She'd continued wearing it every day since Philippos's death. It was the symbol of the choice she'd made that day, and she knew she'd never take it off.

Chapter 1

Suzie Harris was in her kitchen, keeping an eye on the television in the corner of the room while she put a fresh bowl of dog food down on the floor.

'Any second now,' she said to her Doberman Pinscher, Emma, who skittered across the linoleum and started to wolf down her breakfast.

Suzie was a dog-walker who had a sideline presenting a phone-in programme about pets once a week on the hyper-local radio station Marlow FM. But the night before, along with her friends Judith and Becks, she'd helped catch a killer, and she was convinced it would make the local TV news. It had been so dramatic. So thrilling. As the weather update finished, she turned the volume up on her remote control.

'Here we go,' she said to Emma, as the picture cut to a fresh-faced news anchor sitting behind a desk.

'This morning's top story,' the woman said. 'In a further development in the "cash for questions" scandal, Lord Harleyford has announced he's giving up his seat in the House of Lords.'

'What?' Suzie asked the screen.

'This follows days of speculation following accusations in the press that Lord Harleyford has been selling access to government ministers. An accusation he strenuously denies.'

Suzie grabbed up her phone and pressed a speed-dial number, as the picture on the screen cut to a ruddy-faced man in his sixties standing in front of the Houses of Parliament.

'I'm an innocent man,' the man said in an upper-class drawl that oozed self-confidence. 'And I welcome the government inquiry that I know will clear my name. In the meantime, I have to protect my family from the constant intrusion of the press. It's for this reason that I've decided to resign my seat in the House of Lords with immediate effect.'

'We're not top story!' Suzie bellowed into her phone when the call was answered.

'Good morning, Suzie,' Becks Starling said with a smile.

Becks was the wife of the vicar of Marlow, and she was well used to her friend's passion.

'They're leading with that stupid Lord Harleyford story.'

'But he's just resigned, hasn't he?'

'So what?' Suzie said indignantly. 'Who cares what a lord gets up to? Last night we actually caught a real-life killer!'

'I'm not sure the press will have had time to pick up on our story just yet.'

'All he's done,' Suzie said, wafting her hand in the general direction of the TV, 'is get involved in corruption. Just like happens every day. But how many times have three women caught a killer in the middle of a performance of *The Importance of Being Earnest?*'

'I agree it was dramatic,' Becks said tolerantly. 'Oh, hold on, I've got a text message.'

In the silence that followed, Suzie glared back at the TV screen. Lord Harleyford was still reading from his prepared statement.

'Pompous arse,' Suzie muttered as her phone chimed loudly in her ear. 'Wait up,' she said to Becks. 'I've got a text as well.'

'If it's the same as the one I just got,' Becks said, 'I think you'll like it.'

★

At the same time that Becks and Suzie were receiving their texts, Judith was sitting in her nightie and dressing gown by the dying embers of her fire, fast asleep.

She'd had a terrible night.

She'd drunk a few more whiskies than planned while having a long bath, but she'd not been able to stop her thoughts from spinning. When she'd got into bed and turned the lights off, her heart had started pounding again as the darkness of the room engulfed her. So she'd turned the lights back on and tried breathing exercises to calm herself. She'd not been sure what a breathing exercise was, but she'd figured that slow breaths in and out would probably cover most bases. She'd then become so desperate that she'd even got the tube of magnesium cream that Becks had given her for her birthday and rubbed it into her feet and ankles. It had made no difference.

And as much as she couldn't stop thinking about Eleni and the past, her thoughts also kept reaching for the little suitcase she kept in the box room. It was something she hadn't dared tell Becks and Suzie about when they'd cleared – and then burned – her vast archive of old newspapers after they'd caught the mayor of Marlow's killer a few years before. But then, if her collection of old newspapers had been the secret that she'd kept from the outside world, the case in the box room was the secret she kept even from herself. In truth, she hadn't thought about it in years, so deep was the memory buried. But Eleni's arrival had forced her to think about it and what it contained.

By 3 a.m., Judith had admitted defeat and got up. Even two rounds of toast dripping with butter and honey and washed down with a large cup of tea hadn't improved her mood. So she'd gone to her card table and turned her attention to the thousand-piece jigsaw of Burgh Island in Devon that had been sitting there untouched since the start of the Beresford case. But she still hadn't been able to settle, just as she'd known she wouldn't, and she'd cursed the fact that it was November. The house was thick with cold, outside it was dark, and there was nothing to do except wait for the day to start.

'How dare she!' Judith had grumbled to her cat, Daniel, for the hundredth time, as she stabbed the dying embers of the fire with an iron and felt a kinship with the sparks that flew up. She was burning just as furiously. But what could she actually do with all of this energy? She could have phoned Becks and Suzie and asked for their advice, but that would have involved telling them about Eleni, and Judith had known that would prompt questions she didn't want to answer. So she'd taken a copy of *Puzzler* magazine over to her favourite wingback and turned to a logic puzzle. She'd normally have written the answers into the grid as fast as she could read the questions, but she'd found that she couldn't concentrate or even make sense of them.

When the doorbell rang, Judith woke with a start and looked

at the clock on the mantelpiece. It was nearly 10 a.m. For a few seconds she couldn't work out what she was doing in an armchair wearing her nightie and dressing gown, a copy of *Puzzler* magazine spilled on the floor by her feet. And then, with a stab of horror, she remembered Eleni's visit the night before.

The doorbell rang again and Judith's panic sharpened into fury. If Eleni thought she could intimidate her by coming back to her house, then she had another thing coming.

Judith lifted herself out of her chair and, ignoring the sharp stab of pain in her left knee, strode to her front door, unlocked it and threw it open.

'Now what?' she asked.

Detective Inspector Tanika Malik was standing outside in a dark blue puffer jacket that came down to her knees, her breath misting in the morning air. Seeing Judith's dressing gown and wild hair, she realised she'd caught her friend at a bad time.

'I'm sorry,' she said. 'I should have rung ahead.'

'Yes, you should,' Judith said as she turned and walked back into her house, leaving the door open. *Why had Tanika turned up now? Had Eleni already handed all of her evidence in to the police? Was Tanika here to arrest her?*

'I would have called first,' Tanika said, following her friend into the sitting room, 'but I needed to see you as soon as possible.'

'I suppose you're here about the Oliver Beresford case?' Judith asked, hoping she didn't sound on edge.

'I'm sorry to say that I'm not.'

Judith grabbed hold of the mantelpiece to steady herself.

'Are you all right?' Tanika asked.

'Of course.'

'You don't look it.'

'But if you're not here about him, then why are you here?'

'I've caught you at a bad time, haven't I?'

Seeing the concern on Tanika's face, Judith realised that she needed to pull herself together. Whatever was about to happen, she couldn't do anything about it now.

'No, it's me who should apologise,' she said. 'I didn't get a wink of sleep.'

'I can imagine,' Tanika said. 'Your performance last night was spectacular. And such a privilege for me to see you solve the case in front of my eyes. Not that it hasn't caused a few problems . . . but that's not why I'm here. You see, there's been a murder.'

Judith's eyes widened.

'Not Eleni Paphides?'

'Eleni who?' Tanika asked, confused. 'Who are you talking about?'

'Eleni's not involved?'

'I've not heard that name before. Who is she?'

'It doesn't matter, tell me about the murder.'

'Do you know the footballer Gary Wise?'

'No, I can't say I've heard of him.'

'Well, you're going to be hearing quite a lot more of him. Last night, he went into the woods behind his house and was shot dead – a single bullet through the heart.'

Chapter 2

Tanika saw that her news didn't seem to register with Judith.

'Which is pretty extraordinary if you ask me,' she continued. 'Considering you caught a killer just last night. And now there's been another murder. I know you'll want to hear all of the gruesome details.'

'Actually,' Judith said, 'I'm not sure that I do.'

'I'm sorry?'

'Can it wait?'

'Are you ill?'

'Not ill. Just tired. Do you mind if we take a rain check on this Gary chap?'

'No, there's something else, there has to be. Is it that Eleni woman you mentioned? Who is she?'

'Really, Tanika,' Judith said, letting her irritation bubble over. 'You can't expect me to help you solve every murder that comes along.'

'But you can't help yourself!' Tanika said, refusing to believe what her friend was telling her. 'All puzzles have to be solved – that's what you always tell me. And your interest has to be piqued by Gary Wise. He's such a famous person.'

'Honestly, I've never heard of him.'

'You must have done. He played for Arsenal and England.'

'It will perhaps come as no surprise to you that I don't really follow the football. Now, thank you for coming round, but I need to get on with my day. As I'm sure you do.'

'No, no, no, I'm not having this. I refuse to believe you're turning your back on a murder.'

'But that's exactly what I'm doing. Turning my back on it.'

Judith went over to her card table, picked up an unplaced piece of her jigsaw puzzle and made a great play of trying to find where it should go.

'OK,' Tanika said, ignoring her friend's dumbshow. 'Then how about if I tell you that Mr Wise was shot just after eleven o'clock last night? Would that interest you?'

'All I'm interested in is finding the other wheel of this sea tractor,' Judith said without looking up.

'And that the only other person in the house at the time of his death was his wife, Bethany. She's badly shaken up. Which is hardly surprising, when you think about it. Someone killing your husband in the woods behind your house? It makes you shudder. No?' Tanika asked to see if she'd caught Judith's attention.

She hadn't.

'What else?' she mused. 'Whoever killed him very possibly took his mobile phone as well. We've not been able to find it. And then, when we were attending the scene this morning, his house phone rang.'

Judith continued to make a show of checking over her jigsaw pieces instead of listening to Tanika.

'Aren't you at least going to ask me who called?' Tanika asked.

'No.'

'You're really making this hard for me. You're not the only one who's been up all night. I've only just left the scene and wanted to brief you myself.'

Hearing the frustration in Tanika's voice, Judith realised that she wasn't being fair. She put her jigsaw piece down and looked at her friend properly.

'No, of course,' she said. 'I'm sorry. I'm just crabby because I'm tired.'

'Don't worry, I'll finish saying my bit and then I'll get off to the station. The call came in from a journalist at the *Daily Mirror*. She explained that she covered her paper's crime beat. Yesterday, Mr Wise rang her out of the blue. Said there was something he needed to tell her. Something "important" – that was the word she used. It was "important" that he tell her something. The journalist – her name is Mary Pert – tried to get him to tell her what it was, but Mr Wise refused to explain, only saying that he'd speak to her tomorrow. Which would have been today, but he was shot last night. Although, I suppose the whole thing could just be a coincidence.'

Judith couldn't help but smile at her friend's final, desperate attempt to snag her attention. As they both knew, when it came to murder, Judith didn't believe in coincidences.

'Nice try,' she said.

There was the sound of footsteps in the hallway and Becks Starling and Suzie Harris bustled in. Or rather, Becks bustled in, Suzie galumphed.

'Is it true, there's been a murder?' Suzie asked.

'It's like Piccadilly Circus in here,' Judith grumbled.

'Oh good,' Tanika said. 'You got my texts.'

'Is it connected to Oliver Beresford?' Becks asked.

'I don't think so, seeing as Mr Beresford's killer made a full confession last night.'

'Oh, that's brilliant!' Becks said.

'You see, Judith?' Tanika said. 'This is what I was expecting. A bit of excitement.'

'What's up with Judith?' Suzie asked.

'She's tired.'

'I can understand,' Becks said, going to stand by her friend's side. 'Last night would have taken it out of anyone.'

'That's not why I'm tired,' Judith said.

'Oh?' Suzie asked. 'Then why?'

Judith realised she'd said too much.

'I need to get dressed,' she said, and then headed for the oak staircase.

As she went upstairs, she heard Tanika tell her friends that the footballer Gary Wise had been shot, and then Suzie and Becks deluged her with a series of follow-up questions. Judith was glad to leave them all behind as she entered her bedroom and closed the door behind her. This room had always been her refuge; the place she felt safe. She went over to the mantelpiece and picked up an old letter opener. Turning it over in her hands, she looked back at her four-poster bed and considered what the little knife meant to her. She hoped she wouldn't be forced to use it. But if she was, she knew she'd need some kind of way of communicating with Becks and Suzie. They'd need to know what she was doing. She'd have to have a good think about how she could best do that. She put the knife back down on the mantel.

While she had her shower and got dressed, Judith tried to formulate a plan for dealing with Eleni. Surely, after forty-nine years, it was impossible that there could be any actual proof that anything untoward had happened to Philippos on the day he'd died. Eleni hadn't even been alive at the time for heaven's sake. No, she concluded, for some reason or other, Eleni was trying to stir up trouble. In which case, Judith decided, the best thing would be to ignore her.

Having made her decision, Judith felt ready to face the day. She left the bedroom and headed downstairs. Becks and Suzie were still in the sitting room. Judith paused before entering and couldn't help but smile. Becks was twittering about, picking up old plates and glasses and tidying them into a stack, while Suzie was sitting solidly by the fire, in the eye of Becks's storm, reading an old copy of the *Marlow Free Press*.

'You could help a bit,' Becks said to Suzie.

'I am helping,' Suzie said.

'No, you're not, you're just sitting there.'

'This is me helping – I'm staying out of your way because you'll tell me I'm tidying up all wrong.'

'You make me sound like a monster.'

'You have views on stacking.'

'I wouldn't go that far. You can't stack one glass inside another – that's all.'

'And . . .?' Suzie asked, raising an eyebrow.

'Well, plates have to go together at the bottom of the pile, and you can only put something on top if it's smaller than what's below. That's it.'

'And . . .?'

'And you have to make sure you always use two hands when you – oh God, I *am* a monster, aren't I?'

'No – not a bit of it. You're just you, which is why you're tidying up. And I'm me. Which is why I'm sitting here.'

'Where's Tanika?' Judith asked to announce her presence.

'She's gone back to the station,' Suzie said. 'But she's left instructions. We're to go to Gary Wise's house in Hurley village. We're to see if we can talk to his wife as soon as possible.'

'"As soon as possible"?' Judith asked.

'Those were her words,' Becks said. 'Which I don't need to tell you isn't like her at all. In fact, it's borderline suspicious if you ask me. I wonder what's changed?'

'What does it matter?' Suzie said, heaving herself out of the armchair. 'She said we should go and talk to the victim's wife, so let's go and talk to her. What do you say, Judith?'

'I think that's a splendid idea,' Judith said, trying to access an enthusiasm for the case she wasn't feeling. 'Although, can I ask you both a question first? How are you getting on with your crosswords?'

'What's that?' Becks asked as she took her perfect tower of neat plates and mugs through to the kitchen.

'Are either of you doing cryptic crosswords at the moment?'

'Hang on,' Suzie said. 'We've got a dead body to investigate and you're asking about crosswords?'

'It's a simple question. Have either of you been doing any cryptic crosswords? For example, the one I set in the *Marlow Free Press*?'

'What are you like?' Suzie said as Becks came out of the kitchen.

'I'm so sorry,' Becks said. 'I know they're important to you, but they're just gobbledygook to me.'

'Judith, can we focus on what matters here?' Suzie said. 'Someone's been murdered. We've got a killer to catch.'

Chapter 3

Suzie drove her battered van through the jumble of brick and flint buildings in Hurley village, past the ancient Olde Bell Inn, and parked up by a crumbling brick wall. Once she and her friends got out, they headed towards a little path that led in between a clutch of houses. To their left was an old wooden lychgate, a faded brass plaque screwed to the side announcing that this was the entrance to Hurley Manor House.

'OK, so this is it,' Judith said as she pushed through the gate and then stopped to take in the view.

In front of her there was a wide lawn that was mown into regimental stripes. A white gravel driveway led from the gate, with olive trees in terracotta pots standing to attention on either side. Then, at the end of the drive, two enormous SUVs with blacked-out windows were parked outside one of the finest Elizabethan manor houses Judith had ever seen. It had diamond-shaped leaded windows, an ancient wisteria growing across its frontage and a riot of chimneys on top that twisted high into the sky.

'A footballer lives here?' Becks asked, amazed.

'It's the address Tanika gave us,' Suzie said, before heading towards the house. As she got nearer, she looked about herself, at the manicured grandeur, and made her decision.

'Nah, it's not for me,' she pronounced.

'Are you serious?' Becks said with a laugh.

'Look at those windows! Imagine the draughts! And I reckon fifteen chimneys is about fifteen chimneys too many. You give me my modern house with double glazing and a nice combi boiler any day.'

'I know what you mean,' Becks said, thinking of her draughty vicarage. 'There's nothing like a home with all mod cons. But I'd still move to a house like this in a heartbeat.'

'But would you bring Colin and the kids with you?'

'Suzie!' Becks exclaimed as they arrived at the oak front door.

Suzie pulled on a metal chain that was hanging to its side and a bell rang distantly from within the house.

As they waited, Suzie said, 'So what do the pair of you know about Gary Wise?'

'I know he was a footballer,' Becks said.

'He was a central defender. But he was one of those guys who was always in the tabloids. You know, he'd be pictured falling out of nightclubs, And he kept getting into fights on the pitch.'

'He was violent?'

'He was the kind of player who went into tackles studs up.'

'And that's a bad thing?'

'You really don't know anything about football, do you?' Suzie said, before noticing that Judith looked distracted. 'You all right there, Judith?'

It took Judith a short while to register that Suzie was talking to her.

'Me?' she said. 'I'm fine, don't you worry about me.'

The door creaked open to reveal a man in his fifties wearing a tweed jacket and brown corduroy trousers. His face was angular, his skin was sallow and his thinning hair was combed over his head to hide his balding pate. He looked, Judith decided, like any of the very many disappointed headteachers who'd had to deal with her as a teenager.

'Can I help you?' the man asked with a condescending tone.

Suzie pulled her civilian adviser warrant card and lanyard from her bum bag and held it up, making sure that her finger casually rested across the expiry date.

'Detective Inspector Tanika Malik sent us,' she said.

'Are you the family liaison officers?'

'Something like that,' Suzie said. 'Is Mrs Wise in?'

'You'd better follow me,' the man said, and then turned and led the three friends down a dark, oak-panelled hallway that had oil paintings in gilt frames on either side. He then pushed open a door that led into a modern extension.

'Wow,' Becks said as she took in the vast room.

Every surface seemed to be made of white marble. There was a chandelier hanging over a glass table that could easily have seated twenty people. And, behind a huge kitchen island, there was a wall of appliances that included, as far as Becks could tell, four ovens.

The air was thick with the scent of flowers and Judith counted three different vases that were full of beautiful bouquets. The owners of the house liked the finer things in life, she noted.

A woman was sitting at the dining table wearing a white fluffy dressing gown over a pink velour tracksuit. She looked over as the women entered, her eyes red-rimmed.

'What is it now?' she asked.

'These women have been sent by the police,' the man said.

'We're sorry to intrude,' Becks said, going to the woman. 'I'm the wife of the vicar of Marlow,' she added, knowing the information would further burnish their credentials.

'Bethany,' the woman said. 'Bethany Wise.' As she said her surname, a sob caught in her throat and Becks put her hand on Bethany's in support.

From the doorway, Judith and Suzie could see that Becks had 'done her thing' and went over and introduced themselves. Once they'd done so, the man, who was still hovering in the doorway, coughed discreetly.

'Do you want me to stay any longer?' he asked.

Bethany looked over as though she'd completely forgotten he was standing there.

'Oh,' she said. 'No,' she added. 'I'll be fine. I mean, it's hardly gonna get any worse, is it?'

'No, I suppose not,' the man said. 'I promise I'll keep my phone by my side this time. You ring me any time. Anything I can do to help, just let me know.'

With a bob of his head, he turned and left.

'He seems nice,' Becks said.

'He's all right,' Bethany conceded.

'Is he a relative?' Suzie asked with a smile that she hoped hid the fact that she was getting down to business.

'God no, there's no one with a silver spoon up their arse in my family. That guy's Harry Asquith. He's been writing Gary's autobiography. You know, coming to the house every day.'

'He came today?' Suzie asked, surprised. 'Even after what happened?'

'He didn't know what had happened,' Bethany said, and then the women saw the moment that her thoughts once again swamped her.

'Yes, we're so very sorry for your loss,' Becks said.

'I still can't believe it,' Bethany said. 'I'm just numb. You know? Like they've injected me with something.'

'What happened?' Suzie asked.

'That's the thing – nothing. That's what I can't get my head around. We were here on our own. Watching the telly. I went to bed about ten o'clock, maybe a bit after. Gary said he wanted to look at his socials, so I left him downstairs. And that's the last time I saw him . . .'

The women gave Bethany time to gather herself.

'How was he last night?' Becks asked.

'That's what the Detective Inspector wanted to know. But he was normal. You know? And I keep going over what I could have missed, but I can't think of anything.'

'Are you sure? Did he get any phone calls or texts?'

'Not that I saw, and we were sitting together on the sofa. I reckon I would have seen.'

'It really didn't feel any different to any other evening?'

'It was just a normal Tuesday night.'

'So what happened after you went upstairs?' Suzie asked.

'I got ready for bed. And I was in my dressing room when I heard this bang. It came from outside and I sort of knew it was a gunshot straightaway. I went to the window and saw a light in the woods. We own the woodland at the back of the property. It looked like a torch. Maybe on a phone. Whatever it was, the person who was holding it was moving fast. And the thing is, I knew something bad had happened, I just knew it. It was like a sixth sense. So I went downstairs to tell Gary about it, but I couldn't find him. It was freaking me out. Gary's family are all in Leeds, so I rang Harry to ask him to come over.'

'The man who was here just now?' Suzie asked.

'He lives in Marlow. It's one of the reasons we chose him to write Gary's autobiography. He's local.'

'What time did he get here?' Judith asked.

'He didn't answer his phone, it went straight to voicemail. Not that it's a surprise he didn't pick up. It was late.'

'If the wife of my boss rang me at 11 p.m., I'd answer,' Suzie said.

'The point is, I was on my own, so I rang the police. Said I thought I'd heard a gunshot and that there was an intruder in the woods at the back of the house. Gary's what the police call a "High Profile Individual". They take security more seriously.'

'They do?' Suzie asked, impressed.

'He's had his fair share of stalkers and loonies over the years, sending him stuff through the post and hanging around the training ground. Anyway, a police constable arrived about twenty minutes later and she didn't hang about. She went and looked in the woods for herself. And that's when . . . she found him. I'll never forget that moment. When she told me.'

'I can't imagine how tough that must have been for you,' Becks said.

Bethany looked at Becks, entirely lost.

'There's no point asking me what happened next,' she said. 'The rest of the evening's a blur.'

'Then can I ask something?' Suzie asked. 'Who do you think did it?'

'I've no idea. Everyone liked Gary.'

'You said he had stalkers?'

'Gary used to joke that you're not really famous unless you've got a stalker. But he's not had anyone crazy go after him for years. Our lives turned around when he left Arsenal and he came back to Wycombe Wanderers. He's stopped drinking. He doesn't go to clubs or hang out with any of the bad lads. He's a changed man now.'

'He is?' Suzie asked, raising an eyebrow. 'That's not the impression the papers give.'

'Vermin! That's all the papers are. Gutter rats. Always looking for an angle to paint Gary in a bad light. Following him around. Trying to catch him out. Just because he used to be a bit wild back in the day. But that was before he met me.'

Bethany stared defiantly at the women, daring them to disagree with her. Even Suzie got the message and kept quiet.

'Then can I ask something else?' Becks asked. 'Did you or your husband have anything to do with Oliver Beresford or the Marlow Amateur Dramatic Society?'

'Who?' Bethany said, surprised by the question, until she realised why Becks had asked it. 'That's the guy who died on that *Marlow Belle* boat, isn't it? The Detective Inspector asked me that as well. The answer's no. I'll be honest, when you're a professional footballer, you train twenty-four-seven during the season, and the weeks Gary gets off every year, we go somewhere far away and very hot. We don't really know anyone in town. That's partly why we hired Harry Asquith. We thought he'd be able to add local colour to Gary's story.'

'And how well did he get on with Gary?' Suzie asked.

'You reckon Harry could be involved?' Bethany asked, unable to take the question seriously. 'You saw what he was like with me.

And he was the same with Gary. He's one of those guys who'll do whatever you say because you're paying him.'

'Are you really sure you have no idea who did this to your husband?' Becks asked.

'I said, didn't I?' Bethany replied, and the women could see that her patience was wearing thin. 'All I can think is that it was some crazed football fan who got past all of the security cameras around the wood. And then, for some reason, Gary went out to see them. And then . . .'

'And then,' Becks said, finishing the sentence for Bethany. 'Look, we've taken up enough of your time—'

'I want whoever did this strung up,' Bethany cut in.

'I'm sorry?'

'I want them in prison – the key thrown away. Because they don't deserve to live. And you'd better work out who it is before I do, because I'm telling you, if I get to him first, I'm going to tear him limb from limb.'

'An eye for an eye,' Suzie said, appreciatively.

'Thank you so much for helping us,' Becks said.

'Although, before we go,' Suzie said. 'Do you have any questions, Judith?'

'What's that?' Judith said, the question catching her by surprise.

'I've never known you so quiet, you haven't asked anything.'

'That's because you were doing such a good job,' Judith said with a smile, before she turned to face Bethany.

'And I do have a question, actually,' she said. 'I understand your husband rang a journalist yesterday?'

'Yeah, that's what the Detective Inspector told me,' Bethany said. 'The journalist called the house this morning.'

'Do you know why?'

'No idea.'

'Gary didn't mention anything to you?'

Bethany shrugged by way of answer.

'But it wasn't just any journalist, was it? It was someone who writes about crime. And your husband told her he had something "important" he needed to tell her.'

'Yeah, I didn't understand that bit, either,' Bethany said. 'But Gary wasn't mixed up in anything dodgy, I can promise you that. I'm his wife. I'd know.'

'I'm sure you're right,' Suzie said as a phone on the kitchen counter started ringing.

Bethany went over to see who was calling and Becks said, 'Don't worry, we'll let ourselves out.'

'It's my mum,' Bethany said and then picked up the phone.

As the three friends left the kitchen, they heard Bethany greet her mum and then burst into tears. Her sobs accompanied them all the way to the front door.

Chapter 4

As soon as they were outside, Judith, Becks and Suzie took a moment to gather themselves.

'OK, what was that about?' Suzie asked.

'Bethany?' Becks replied. 'I think she behaved exactly how I'd expect a grieving widow to.'

'No, I mean you, Judith,' Suzie said. 'You didn't say a thing.'

'You just heard me ask a question,' Judith said.

'But only when I told you to. There's something up, isn't there?'

'There really isn't. Don't worry, I'll ask as many questions as you like when I have to. But I tend to agree with Becks. I think Bethany came across very plausibly.'

'Seriously?' Suzie snorted. 'All that "my husband is perfect" malarkey? Show me a wife who thinks her husband's perfect and I'll show you a liar. Never mind her saying that whoever killed Gary must have been some passing random person. If that was the case, why did Gary ring a crime journalist on the day he died? What are the chances?'

'And I suppose we only have Bethany's word that what she says happened last night is actually what happened,' Becks said. 'It was only her and Gary in the house.'

'My point exactly!' Suzie said. 'What's stopping her from going into the woods with her husband, shooting him dead and then making up the story of seeing someone when the police arrived?'

As the women approached Suzie's van, they saw that Harry Asquith was smoking a cigarette by an old blue estate car that was parked around the side of the house. As he saw them, he threw his cigarette into a flower bed and came over.

'Hope you don't mind me waiting for you,' he said in a way that suggested he wasn't remotely interested in their answer.

'Not at all,' Judith said. 'In fact, you can perhaps help us. Bethany says that Gary was a reformed character. Not at all how the papers painted him.'

'Of course,' Harry said as he realised what was behind the question. 'You want to know what I thought of him.'

'If it's not too much to ask,' Suzie said as sarcastically as possible.

Harry was too superior to even notice.

'Where to begin? Well, I suppose the point is, I've ghostwritten any number of autobiographies and top sports people are often very similar. They're driven – and selfish with it. They have to be. They're only one ACL injury away from the end of their career. And their greatest fear is that their talent will one day just leave them. You see, no one really knows where talent comes from. Least of all the person who's got it. So you look into their childhood. Into their schooling and upbringing. Because everything in their past helps to explain the present day.'

'And what was there in Gary's past?' Becks asked.

'He's basically a classic of his type. His mum worked on a supermarket checkout and his dad was a bouncer for a chain of nightclubs. But he was raised in a home of love and support. And he was prepared to work. So, all was smooth sailing at first. As a local lad, he joined the Leeds United academy. He was on the fast-track to the top. And then, when he was sixteen, they let him go. Just like that. It nearly crushed him. That's how he told it to me. That feeling of betrayal at such a young age. And that's when he started going off the rails.

'After being dumped by Leeds, he signed with Wycombe Wanderers, moved down here and became a bit of a folk hero. He was a central defender, but don't think Rio Ferdinand, he was more of an "enforcer" like Terry Butcher. It was no surprise when a big club like Arsenal came knocking, and he was with them for the next ten years. But that's also when he started to cut loose in London. He got into the papers more and more. And once the tabloids have got you pegged as a wild boy, they'll paint everything you do in that light. So Gary started to play up to it. I've seen it in other famous people.'

'I see,' Judith said as she wondered if there was a way to speed up Harry's story.

'But messing around like that has consequences,' Harry said, mistaking Judith's mild impatience for strong interest. 'As I'm sure we can all agree. You see, he always had the talent to play for England, but when the chance came along, he was so into his "bad boy of football" persona that he'd turn up late for training sessions – would oversleep and miss the team bus, that sort of thing. In the end, he only got three caps before he was dropped. His talent deserved so much more. The way he told it to me, that rejection – this time at the highest level – put him into a real spiral. And each year, he was getting older. And drinking more. By the time he was in his early thirties, he wasn't even a guaranteed pick in the Arsenal first team. They had a novice centre-back they were developing who was edging him out of the side. Which is when his old club, Wycombe, asked for him back on loan. Because everyone around here wanted their star player back. Not that Gary was interested. Not until he met Bethany. He told me she was the one who turned his life around. She was his rock – that's what he called her. He changed his ways. He stopped drinking. And he's been a big success for Wycombe Wanderers ever since he came home.'

'What can you tell us about Bethany?' Suzie asked.

'Only that there's no way she could have had anything to do with her husband's death. Those two loved each other. I mean, I was only with them a short while, but it was obvious for anyone to see. He'd ask her how she was the whole time. And was constantly making her cups of tea. Attentive – that's the word I'd use. He was attentive around her.'

'And how did you get on with him?' Suzie asked.

'Me? You think I killed him? That's preposterous. But since you're asking, I got on with him just fine. You ask Bethany. And it doesn't matter how we got on, I was home alone last night.'

'Can you prove that?'

'I doubt it. It's like I said, I live on my own.'

'And yet you didn't answer your phone when she called you.'

'I didn't hear it.'

'Even though you were in an otherwise empty house?'

'I leave my phone downstairs on silent when I go to bed so I'm not distracted. Do try and be sensible. I've only known the man a few weeks. Do you really think I could have built up a reason to want him dead in that time? What's more, with his death, I've lost a rather significant amount of money. You see, I get royalties if we manage to shift enough copies. And his book could have netted me quite a few tens of thousands of pounds. Maybe even more if it had really taken off. So please don't even think of pinning this on me.

'Anyway, I want to help – that's why I've been waiting out here. There's something you need to know. Gary asked me yesterday if I had a contact in the press he could get in touch with. Someone who handled crime. It really threw me. There was a look in his eyes as he asked me that I'd only seen in him once before. I gave him the number of an old colleague of mine, a woman called Mary Pert.'

'Did he tell you why he needed to talk to her?'

'I didn't ask.'

'Seriously? You're his autobiographer and you didn't ask any follow-up questions?'

'You learn in my line of work when you can push and when you have to wait. And I could tell that this was something deeply private to him. I was planning on biding my time before I got whatever it was out of him.'

'You said you'd seen the same look in his eyes once before?' Judith asked.

'That's right. When Gary and I started getting to know each other, we spent a few days chatting about his life. Just so I could get a sense of him. Then, as we wound up those first talks, he asked me if I was going to have enough material for the book. I told him that as long as he told me the truth about everything, I'd always have enough. And he said he could be one hundred per cent truthful about just about everything. I picked him up on that. What did he mean he could only be truthful about "just about" everything? All he'd say was that there was only one thing in his life he couldn't tell me about because he'd never told anyone. And if Bethany ever found out about it, she'd kill him.'

'Those were his words?' Suzie asked, stunned.

'His precise words. She'd kill him.'

'Do you have any idea what he was referring to?' Becks asked.

'He didn't want to tell me, and I pushed him hard. I told him that if the book was going to work, he had to be completely honest. So he said he'd tell me some of it as long I didn't ask any follow-up questions. At that stage, I just wanted to find out what it was, so I agreed. And that's when he told me that after the final match last season, he went out drinking with his teammates. Even though he'd promised Bethany he wouldn't touch alcohol again. But the "last game of the season" bender is a strong tradition in football. And then . . .'

'And then what?' Suzie asked.

'He clammed up. Wouldn't tell me what happened next. No matter how hard I tried to find out what went on that night. He just point-blank refused to say. But that's not what sticks in my mind. It's how he looked when he said he couldn't ever tell me what happened that night.'

'Why?' Becks asked. 'How did he look?'

'He looked haunted,' Harry said. 'Like he'd just seen a ghost.'

Chapter 5

'Told you Gary was up to no good,' Suzie said as she drove her van down Marlow High Street. In the summer months, the street always had an air of leisure about it as people stopped to chat to friends or sat out drinking coffee, but now it was winter and everyone had their heads turned down against the wind and their hands thrust deep into their coat pockets as they strode towards wherever they could next get warm.

'Assuming he was telling the truth,' Becks said.

'You think he lied to us?' Judith asked.

'I've no idea,' Becks said. 'But we only have his word that Gary got up to something on the last day of the football season.'

'I wonder if we can find out what it was?' Judith said.

'Maybe whatever happened made it into the newspapers the next day,' Suzie said.

'Then how about we stop in at the vicarage?' Becks said. 'I've a homemade Victoria sponge and we could have it with a nice cup of tea while we see what we can find out about him online.'

'Good idea,' Suzie said as she drove across the mini roundabout at the end of the High Street, turned onto the little road that led to the church and pulled up outside the vicarage.

As the women got out, Judith saw a figure standing on the pavement across from them. It was Eleni Paphides. She was looking directly at her.

Judith stepped back behind the body of the van.

'OK, what was that?' Suzie asked.

'What was what?'

'You're hiding behind the van.'

'I am not.'

'You are.'

'Really, Suzie, you do talk drivel sometimes.'

'It's how it looks to me as well,' Becks said apologetically.

'But why would I do that?' Judith said. 'I'm a grown woman. Why would I be hiding behind a van?'

'Hello, Judith,' a voice said, and Judith spun around to see Eleni standing nearby.

'Oh,' Becks said. 'Hello?'

'Go inside,' Judith said to her friends.

'Aren't you going to introduce me to Mrs Starling?' Eleni asked. 'And the famous Suzie Harris?'

'You think I'm famous?' Suzie said, delighted.

'*Please*,' Judith pleaded. 'Go inside.'

Becks and Suzie could see how much the other woman's arrival was upsetting their friend.

'You'll come straight in when you're done?' Becks asked.

'I promise,' Judith said. 'I'll be with you in a few minutes.'

'We'll be inside if you need us,' Becks said, taking Suzie by the arm and leading her into the vicarage.

Suzie kept looking over her shoulder at Eleni the whole way

inside, somehow managing to keep her eyes on her up until the moment Becks closed the front door behind them both.

'What on earth was that about?' Becks asked as soon as they were on their own.

'I told you she was being weird,' Suzie said, going into the sitting room so she could look through the window at Judith. 'I bet it's because of that woman.'

'We shouldn't spy on her!' Becks said.

'I'm not spying on her! I'm just looking through the window.'

'Come on, let's go into the kitchen. We need to give her space.'

'No, I'm staying here,' Suzie said. 'But you're right – I don't want to be caught. Hold on . . .'

Suzie moved to the side of the window. She then, very slowly, leaned over so that only her head could be seen from the street.

'I don't think that's any better,' Becks said.

'Shh, I'm concentrating!'

Out on the pavement, Judith was still struggling to cope with Eleni's sudden reappearance.

'What are you doing here?' she asked.

'I want to find out everything I can about you. And the company you keep.'

'You keep my friends out of this. Whatever problem you have with me, my friends have nothing to do with it.'

'I've upset you,' Eleni said, pretending to be saddened by the realisation.

'You haven't upset me. And if you think you can intimidate me, then you've got another thing coming.'

'Oh, I'm not sure I agree. I think I'm intimidating you quite well.'

'You haven't answered my question. What are you doing here?'

'I wanted to see where your friend Mrs Starling lived.'

'How do you even know she's my friend?'

'You'd be surprised how much I know about you.'

'Is that why you're staying in the Tollgate Hotel?' Judith asked, nodding at the old coaching inn a few doors further down the High Street.

'I couldn't get a hotel that was near you, so I did the next best thing – I got one near her.'

'You can't spy on her.'

'But I can learn so much. For example, I've already worked out why you solve murders with your two friends.'

'You haven't the first idea.'

'It's because of the guilt you feel. You're trying to right the wrongs of the present because of the wrong you did to my father in the past.'

'That's not remotely true,' Judith said and went on to explain that what Eleni didn't know was that she set crossword puzzles for a hobby, and she'd been a puzzle-solver her whole life. She helped the police solve murders because, as far as she was concerned, all puzzles had to be solved. But even as the well-worn words came out of her mouth, she suspected that on some deep level, Eleni was right. And she'd never known this about herself. Part of the reason why she'd started investigating her first murder case must have been because of her feelings of guilt.

As she finished talking, Judith tried to look at Eleni properly. To try and imagine what it must have been like growing up without a father, the daughter of an unwed mother.

'Did your mother ever marry?' she asked.

'No,' Eleni said. 'She had offers, but there was only one man for her.'

Judith realised that there was nothing she could say or do that would change Eleni's mind about her. By dying before she was born, Philippos had taken up an almost mythic status in his daughter's mind. His absence had thrown a shadow over her whole life.

'You look like him,' Judith found herself saying. Her words surprised her almost as much as they surprised Eleni.

'That's what everyone says,' the younger woman admitted.

'It's not just that. It's your spirit.'

'You were married to him,' Eleni said. It was almost as if she was looking properly at Judith for the first time. 'What was he like?'

Judith considered how she could even begin to answer the question.

'He was joyous. On the right day. Spontaneous. Handsome.'

'You loved him,' Eleni said, her brow creasing.

'That's what I thought. Sadly, while I loved him, I wasn't the only woman he loved. Not that I knew that at first. Even though my mother tried to warn me off. She knew the type, she said. We had the most terrible rows when I told her I'd become engaged to him.'

'My father was a good man.'

'I'm sorry, Eleni. He wasn't.'

'Everyone on the island says he was.'

'He was popular. He was exciting. But he was not a good man. I know it's hard for you to hear, but it's the truth – speaking as one woman to another. I'm sorry that I married him. And I'm sorry you grew up without a father. Even before he died, I suspected he was seeing your mother. But please believe me, when I left the island for good after Philippos's tragic accident, I had no idea he'd got your mother pregnant.'

'My father's death was no accident.'

'We went through this last night.'

'Do you really deny being involved?'

'Fervently,' Judith said. 'Passionately.'

'Then come to my hotel room. I can show you proof that you're lying.'

Chapter 6

Judith followed Eleni into her small hotel room and took in the double bed, the suitcase open on the only table and the grimy window that overlooked the hotel car park. The whole room smelled of dust and ancient cigarette smoke.

'You wait there,' Eleni said as she went over to a safe that was hidden within the built-in wardrobe and tapped numbers into the keypad. The mechanism whirred and the door popped open. Grabbing a yellowing document, she brought it over and gave it to Judith.

Judith saw that she was holding an old report from the Corfu Police Directorate. Looking down at the handwriting, she felt a depth charge explode inside her. She was holding a copy of the witness statement that she'd given following Philippos's death.

'Where did you get this?' she asked, her voice barely a whisper.

'I have a friend in the police. He gave it to me.'

Time collapsed and Judith was back in the furnace of the interrogation room. The bare lightbulb. The flies buzzing. The smell of the detective's body odour. The memories were buried deep, and their sudden resurfacing made her gasp.

Eleni smiled, happy to see the older woman's pain.

'But this says I was nowhere near when he set off,' Judith said, confused that Eleni considered her statement so damning.

'That's right,' Eleni agreed. 'It says you told my father that a storm was coming in, but he wouldn't listen to you. It says you both left your house together just before midday. But he went down to the bay on his own and, instead, you went to the church in the village to pray for him.'

'That's what happened.'

'Before then, you argued.'

'Of course we argued, he wouldn't listen to me! All he'd say was that he was the sailor. The islander. He knew whether it was safe to sail better than me.'

'It also says he hit you, which is a lie. Why would you say such a thing?'

Judith could see that Eleni had no interest in hearing about the rage Philippos directed against her when it was just the two of them. His temper when he felt he wasn't as clever as her. Or when she dared accuse him of infidelity. If he'd been drinking ouzo with his friends in the square, it took even less to trigger him. And he'd been drinking on the morning he'd died.

'You see?' Eleni said in triumph. 'You don't deny it! You can lie to the police, but you can't lie to me.'

'My statement was true,' Judith said. 'I was in the village church over a mile away when your father set sail.'

'A witness saw you on his boat.'

'He was discredited at the inquiry.'

'He went to his grave believing he saw you and my father together on his boat.'

'He was a local farmer. He never liked me. But he never even said it was me he saw. He just said he saw Philippos's boat as it passed the headland and he thought he saw two people on it.'

'And that second person was you – which fits with the statement from the village priest. He said you didn't go to the church that day.'

As she spoke, Eleni went to the safe, returned with another piece of age-yellowed paper and handed it over.

'Here's his statement,' she said.

'The priest, like the farmer, was mistaken. I was in the Lady Chapel when he came through the church. I was praying that your father would be spared in whatever storm was coming. That's why he didn't see me.'

'The priest said you never went to church.'

'I went every week.'

'But never through choice. Only because you had to.'

'And I felt I had to that day. Praying was all that was left to me.'

'You're lying. You were on the boat with him.'

Judith barely heard the younger woman's accusation. She was in Philippos's house. On the rocky bluff that overlooked the Ionian Sea, with steps cut into the rocks that led down to an old, concrete jetty where he'd moor his little fishing boat. With a blue-painted hull and steps down to a cabin that barely had room for a double bed, it had been his pride and joy. When times were good, he and Judith had gone out for days at a time, cooking the fish they caught during the day and sleeping out under the stars on the deck at night. As Philippos had told Judith at the time, his boat was him and he was his boat.

'You knew bad weather was coming, so you went out with my father on his boat and drugged him,' Eleni said. 'Or hit him over the head. But you made sure he drowned somehow.'

'You have to believe me, I never went near his boat on the day he died.'

'And there's the lie!' Eleni said as she returned to the safe. She pulled out another document and strode back, forcing it into Judith's hands. 'Then how do you explain this?'

Judith saw that she was holding an old photograph. It showed the cove beneath Philippos's house. The boat was moored at the end of the wooden jetty and he was standing on it.

'This was taken on the day he died,' Eleni said.

'You can't know that,' Judith said.

'That's the T-shirt and shorts he was wearing when his body was found.'

'He wore those clothes most days.'

'How come you're on the jetty with him?'

It was true. It was the first thing Judith had noticed. She was also in the picture. And although Philippos often wore the clothes he had on, she'd never forget that the day he'd died was the first time that she'd worn the dress she was wearing in the photograph. If the photo was real, it could only have been taken on the last day of his life.

'You told the police you never went near my father's boat that day,' Eleni said.

'Someone's tampered with this photograph.'

'It's not been tampered with.'

'Where did you get it?'

'Grandmother Sofia.'

'She's still alive?'

'Women like her don't die. She's old now, but her mind is still sharp.'

Judith remembered Philippos's mother well. And not with affection. Sofia had always known that her son was violent, but she'd told Judith that any Greek woman would have been able to tame him. As far as she was concerned, if Judith couldn't control her husband, then she should leave the island.

'I go and see her every year,' Eleni said. 'On the day of my father's birthday. She's always been kind to me. And this year, she said she'd been given a photo of my father and she wanted to show it to me. It's the photo in your hand.'

'Who gave the photo to Sofia?'

'Does it matter? It proves you lied in your statement.'

'I didn't.'

'Yes, you did. We both know it. The police will have to re-open the case.'

'There's no way this photo could result in a conviction.'

'Are you willing to bet your life on it? And you should know, I've got even more evidence than this photo. So I'm giving you a choice. You go to the police and confess the truth of what happened that day, or I'll give them all the evidence I've got. Not just this photo.'

'Are you trying to blackmail me?'

'I'm giving you the chance to confess. The jail sentence from the judge will be less if you do.'

Judith wanted to protest – to fight Eleni's accusations with a firestorm of denials – but she couldn't help but be drawn back to the photo in her hand. She didn't doubt for one second that it had been taken on the day that Philippos had died. And, just like Eleni said, it seemed to prove that her witness statement to the police had been a lie.

But then, as only Judith had known for the last forty-nine years, it *had* been a lie.

Chapter 7

The following morning, Suzie arrived at the vicarage bright and early to find Becks clearing away her family's breakfast things. Becks rinsed the used cups, saucers and plates in the sink before putting them in the dishwasher.

'Why do you do that?' Suzie asked.

'If you don't rinse them off, they don't clean properly in the machine.'

'Then get a new machine. I don't see the point of having a dishwasher if you're going to wash the dishes beforehand. Next you'll tell me you clean the house before your cleaner gets here.'

'Of course I clean the house before Patricia gets here!'

'Seriously, Becks, you've got your priorities all wrong.'

'I'd rather we talked about Judith,' Becks said.

'Tell me about it! It's all I've been able to think about. I mean, she said she'd come to us the moment she finished talking to that woman, but where did she go?'

'You were the one watching her.'

'But it's like I told you. They went off down the street and

I lost sight of them. Who do you think she was? That woman? I keep wracking my brain and I just keep coming up blank. And we both know what Judith's like. She won't tell us what's going on unless she has to. Oh, hold on, it's the news,' Suzie said as an alarm went off on her phone. She turned on Becks's radio, pleased to see that it was already tuned to the BBC's local station. 'I reckon they'll lead with the Gary Wise murder, but then they'll have to cover how we caught Oliver Beresford's killer.'

Suzie was gratified to hear that the news anchor started her bulletin with the murder of Gary Wise. She and Becks listened to Tanika give a statement outside Maidenhead police station, asking for any witnesses to come forward.

'She's good,' Becks said.

'She's *very* good,' Suzie agreed.

Then, once a football pundit had explained what a loss to the game Gary was, the news anchor went on to the next story.

'I don't know what's wrong with this country!' Suzie said, as the anchor revealed that there'd been further developments in the corruption scandal against Lord Harleyford. 'You catch the killer in a local am dram society and it's not worth mentioning, but you have one lord up to some kind of shenanigans and it's all the press want to talk about.'

Becks couldn't help but smile as her friend slapped the off button on the radio. She loved how melodramatic Suzie was, if only because it reminded her how grateful she was that she wasn't like that at all.

Becks's phone rang and she grabbed it when she saw who was calling.

'It's Tanika,' she said, as she answered the call on speaker phone. 'Good morning, Tanika.'

'Is Judith with you?' Tanika asked. 'I've been ringing her since yesterday and she's not picking up.'

'She's not answering our calls either,' Suzie said.

'Is she OK?' Tanika asked.

Suzie frowned, not sure how they should respond.

'Yes . . .?' Becks eventually offered.

'Because she was definitely a bit off with me yesterday,' Tanika said.

'Then maybe we can help you?' Becks said.

'It's not help I need. I just wanted to update you on where we're at with the Wise case.'

Becks looked in surprise at Suzie. They both knew that Tanika had never voluntarily told them how a police investigation was going before. In fact, she normally tried to keep the information from them.

'But don't get your hopes up,' Tanika said. 'We've not developed any significant leads.'

'Then what have you got?' Suzie asked.

'Well, we've run Mr and Mrs Wise's names through the police computer and they're both clean.'

'Are you sure?' Suzie said. 'Doesn't Gary have a whole heap of police cautions?'

'Not really. He's had plenty of run-ins with the police in the past, but they get wiped from the system after a number of years. So there are only a few left. There's a bit of a push and shove with some paparazzi for one of them. A drunk and disorderly coming out of a pub for another. But there's nothing from the last three years – not since he met Bethany.'

'Was there a police report from earlier this year?' Becks asked.

'What makes you ask?'

'His ghostwriter told us that Gary got drunk on the last day of the football season and something happened that later haunted him.'

'Yes, we spoke to Mr Asquith yesterday. He told us the same thing. But whatever happened that day, it didn't result in a police report being filed.'

'Have you been able to dig anything up on Harry?' Suzie asked.

'In his statement he said he was at home at the time of Mr Wise's death. Although he's not been able to provide a definitive alibi.'

'Could he be the killer?'

'There's no suggestion from anyone, Mrs Wise included, that Gary had any problems with Mr Asquith. Or vice versa. Although we did find out one thing about him that's possibly of interest. Mr Asquith is up to his ears in debt. In fact, he's in a real mess, with credit cards that he takes cash out of so he can pay off what he owes on other credit cards.'

'He told us he could earn tens of thousands of pounds from Gary's book,' Suzie said. 'Which kind of suggests he's the last person who'd have wanted him dead. That sort of money could have really helped clear his debts.

'What have you got on Bethany?' Becks asked.

'She was quite senior in a public relations firm in London before she met Gary. Her clients included Arsenal football club, which is how they met. At a charity event. They were married three months later. I've read an interview with her in *OK!* magazine where she said it was love at first sight, but she made Gary promise to change his ways before she agreed to marry him.'

'Which he basically did,' Becks said. 'Apart from – perhaps – whatever he did or didn't get up to on the last day of the football season.'

'I'll do some digging at this end,' Tanika said. 'See what I can find out.'

'What did you get from the murder scene?' Becks asked.

'Nothing much. There are CCTV cameras on the side of the house that the killer managed to avoid.'

'So whoever it was knew the layout of the garden?' Suzie asked.

'Or maybe they were just lucky,' Tanika said. 'But we've not been able to pick up any significant leads from the crime scene where Mr Wise's body was found.'

'Are you sure he was definitely killed there?' Becks asked.

'It's our working theory. There are no signs that the body was moved postmortem. But I suppose it's theoretically possible he was killed elsewhere and then his body was dumped in the woods.'

'Then what have you got from Gary's emails and texts?' Suzie asked.

'His emails are pretty innocuous. According to his wife, he ran his life from his mobile phone – which is still missing. We're waiting on his phone provider to send through copies of all of his text and phone messages. Look, are you sure Judith is all right? Only it's not like the three of you not to be together during a case.'

'Don't you worry about her,' Suzie said confidently. 'I'm sure she's on her way to join us right now. And we'll fill her in on everything you've said when we see her.'

She then thanked Tanika for phoning and ended the call.

'This is bad,' Becks said. 'If Judith's not taking Tanika's calls during a murder case, then something's seriously wrong with her.'

'I suggest we go to her house and have it out with her,' Suzie said.

'No, we can't just barrel in there and put her on the spot. You know what she's like. We'll frighten her off.'

'All right, then how about this,' Suzie said, inspiration coming to her. 'We take something to her – a new lead in the case. And she'll be so pleased with what we've done that she'll *have* to tell us what's going on with her.'

'You know what? That's a pretty good idea. But where can we find a new lead?'

'That shouldn't be too hard,' Suzie said as she went over to some cut flowers near the hob and pulled them out of their vase.

'Suzie!' Becks said. 'I've only just arranged those.'

'Fans always pay their respects at the football ground when one of their own die,' Suzie said, ignoring her friend's protest.

Suzie went over to a drawer and pulled out a pair of scissors and a ball of string. 'I suggest we go to his club and see what we can find out about Gary.'

As Suzie started to tie the stems of the flowers together, Becks realised what her friend's plan was.

'Actually, that's a very good idea,' Becks said. 'Do you know where the Wycombe Wanderers stadium is?'

★

Half an hour later, Becks and Suzie arrived at Adams Park, the home of Wycombe Wanderers Football Club. Suzie parked on the road outside the stadium and could see that there were dozens of people milling about. The main gate had club scarves tied to it and the ground was festooned with bunches of flowers, lit candles and pictures of Gary Wise. Suzie held her bunch of flowers in front of her.

'Let's mingle,' she said. 'Meet back here in fifteen minutes?'

'Good plan,' Becks said.

'Bet I can find out more than you,' Suzie said and then disappeared into the crowd.

Becks couldn't help but smile at her friend's self-confidence as she moved off to join the mourners. She soon found herself standing by a middle-aged man who had his arm around the shoulders of his son. The boy looked about ten years old and he was dabbing at his eyes with a Wycombe Wanderers scarf. Becks waited for them to become aware of her presence. When they did, it was easy for her to ask them for their memories of Gary Wise. With a smile of sympathy for everyone she met, she then moved among the other people, asking leading questions about Gary and listening to the answers.

After fifteen minutes, she slipped back to Suzie's van where her friend was already waiting for her.

'Well, that was a waste of time,' Suzie said.

'No one would talk to you?' Becks asked, surprised.

'The opposite! Everyone just said how great he was.'

'It was the same for me,' Becks said.

'He looked after the kids who were mascots before each game. He was always the last person to leave the training ground when people were asking for autographs. I'll tell you what the problem is. Everyone here's a fan, aren't they? They only saw Gary when he was out and about in public. We need to speak to someone who knew him when he let his guard down.'

'You're right,' Becks said, realising the wisdom of her friend's words.

'Hold on,' Suzie said as she saw a young man in a Wycombe Wanderers tracksuit getting out of a car that had parked nearby. 'Who's our friend over there?'

The women saw the man go to the boot of his car and get

out a large kit bag. He then headed towards the main gates of the club. Unfortunately for him, this put him on a direct line towards Becks and Suzie.

'Excuse me?' Suzie said as he passed.

'Yes?' the man said, and it was only as he stopped that the women saw how very toned and tanned he was. And square-jawed. With the clearest blue eyes.

'It's such terrible news,' Becks said, and the man exhaled in agreement.

'He was such a good man, wasn't he?' Becks continued.

'The best.'

'Although that's not quite true, is it?' Suzie said. 'No one's actually that perfect.'

'Of course not, but he was pretty damned close.'

'Are you one of his colleagues?' Becks asked.

'I'm one of the physios here,' the man said. 'I just wanted to mingle with the fans. Pay my respects before going in to work.'

'What was he like?' Becks asked.

'Well, he wasn't anything like the image the press print of him. He always had time for everyone. And he looked after his body, ate the right food, didn't drink, didn't stay out late – he did everything to be the best footballer he could be.'

'Although he got drunk on the final day of the last season,' Suzie said.

'You know about that?' the physio said, surprised.

'Why don't you tell us all about it?' Suzie said as she fished out her police lanyard, held it for a split second in front of the man's eyes, and then put it away just as quickly again. 'We're with the police.'

Becks almost felt sorry for the man. He might have been

young, tanned and toned, but he was never going to be a match for a Suzie Harris in full spate.

'OK,' the man said, 'but don't say this came from me. The day after the last match of the season, Gary came to see me. He said he'd had a skinful the night before and he'd hurt himself. When I checked him over, I saw that he had contusions across the lateral aspect of his thigh. And a fair bit of subcutaneous haemorrhaging and swelling.'

'In English?' Suzie asked.

'He had bruises and cuts all down his leg. I patched him up as best as I could and sent him on his way.'

'Did he say how he got injured?'

'He didn't want to, but I made him. You can't really mend someone if you don't know how they injured themselves. He told me he'd been in a car crash.'

'A car crash?' Becks asked.

'That's what he said. The point being, the injuries weren't too bad. I was able to get him mended in time for pre-season training.'

'What was the date of the last match of the season?' Suzie asked.

The man thought for a few seconds before replying, 'April the seventh.'

'And he said he'd definitely been in a car crash?'

'That's what he told me,' the physio said, and then he looked at the women more carefully. 'He also told me that the police attended the scene of the crash. So how come you don't know that? Can I see that card you showed me again?'

'I'm sorry?' Suzie said, pretending she hadn't heard the question.

'If you're from the police, how come you don't know about his car accident?'

'Who's saying we don't know about it?'

'You are. You just said. And you could be anyone – the press, even. It wouldn't be the first time one of the tabloids tricked information out of us. Can you show me your card again?' he asked, and this time he held out his hand to Suzie.

Suzie pulled her police lanyard out of her bum bag as slowly as it was physically possible for her to do, and she made sure that her thumb covered the written information on it. As soon as it was close enough to the man for him to read it, she whipped it back, but his reactions were faster than hers and he was able to whisk it out of her bag before she could zip it up again.

'This expired last year,' he said as he looked at it.

'It did?' Suzie said, in what she hoped sounded like surprise. 'Well, I never. I'll have to speak to HR. Get a new one issued.'

'You're from the tabloids, aren't you?'

'No, I promise you,' Becks said in a panic. 'We really are civilian advisers. Or we were at least.'

'I can't believe you'd do this,' the man said. 'I'm taking this card straight to the police and reporting you.'

'Don't do that!' Becks said.

'And there it is!' the man said as he shoved the pass into a pocket of his tracksuit. 'All the proof I need that you aren't who you say you are.'

With one last glare at the women, he turned and headed for the main gates.

'Bugger,' Suzie said.

'Yes,' Becks agreed. 'I don't normally swear, but this feels like an exception. Bugger.'

Chapter 8

When Suzie and Becks arrived at Judith's house, they found their friend in front of the fire wearing a dressing gown, her hair damp.

'Have you been for a swim?' Becks asked, surprised.

Judith smiled by way of an answer, but her friends could see how tired she looked.

'It must be zero degrees out there!' Suzie exclaimed. 'And before you say the Thames can't be zero degrees because it would be frozen over, you know what I mean.'

'I imagine you've got news or you wouldn't be here,' Judith said.

'As it happens, we do,' Suzie said proudly. She then explained that they'd found out what had happened to Gary on the last day of the football season.

'But it makes no sense that he was in a drink–driving accident,' Becks said. 'Because, according to the man we spoke to, Gary said the police attended the scene. But Tanika told us the police hadn't had any interactions with Gary in the last three years.'

'So that's your plan,' Judith said.

'What plan?' Suzie said in mock outrage. 'We don't have a plan. Do we, Becks?'

'You knew I'd have started putting the case together,' Judith said, nodding at the wood-panelled wall behind her desk. The evidence from the Oliver Beresford case had been removed and replaced with photos of Gary Wise, his wife Bethany, and his ghostwriter, Harry Asquith. There were also index cards with hand-written notes pinned next to the photos. 'And you thought that if you offered me a nice juicy lead, you'd get into my good books and be able to ask me about what happened yesterday.'

'Was it really that obvious?' Suzie asked, surprised that her plan had been exposed so easily.

'We're worried about you,' Becks said. 'That's the truth of it. I've never seen you as rattled as you were when that woman appeared. Whatever it is you're going through, we want to share it with you.'

As much as Judith knew that she wasn't going to do what her friends asked, Becks's demeanour was so sympathetic that she felt a sudden yearning to unburden herself. *Bloody hell*, she thought, *this is how she gets suspects to confess, isn't it?*

'Don't you practise your dark arts on me, Becks Starling,' she said.

'No dark arts,' Becks said. 'But we're here to help in whatever way we can.'

Judith knew that while she didn't want to share her predicament with anyone – in fact, she knew she could never reveal the full truth of what had happened on the day her husband had died – her visit to Eleni's room had put her into a tailspin, and she suddenly realised that she needed her friends now more than ever.

'Very well,' she said, turning to look back into the depths of the fire. 'Two nights ago, after I got back from the theatre, I was visited by a woman who claimed to be my stepdaughter.'

Suzie's mouth fell open, but the flash of warning in Becks's eyes kept her quiet. Into the silence that followed, Judith haltingly told her friends about how Eleni had accused her of killing her father; how Judith had next encountered her outside the vicarage and how she'd ended up going to the Tollgate Hotel, where she'd been shown the apparent proof that Judith had lied to the police about her movements on the day her husband had died.

'She has proof?' Becks asked, still trying to come to terms with Judith's extraordinary story.

'You have a *stepdaughter*?' Suzie asked, just as stunned as her friend.

Judith went over to a bookshelf and pulled down her cloth-bound copy of Brewer's *Phrase and Fable*. From its pages, she plucked the photo Eleni had shown her and handed it over to her friends.

'She gave it to you?' Becks said.

'This is a copy. She's kept the original. It was taken on the day Philippos died. Even though I told the police in my statement that I never went anywhere near his boat that day.'

'I remember the first time I went on your punt,' Becks said, realising how carefully she'd have to tread. 'It was after we'd solved our first murder. We were all in high spirits and Suzie asked whether you'd been involved in your husband's death. I remember your answer so well. You said, 'No comment'. It was all a bit of a joke. But if you're saying you didn't tell the truth to the police, it does rather beg the question: were you, in fact, involved?'

'You can't ask Judith that!' Suzie said, appreciating the danger Becks was putting them all in. 'If Judith says anything incriminating, you'll just go and tell the police. We know what you're like.'

'It's not a character flaw,' Becks said, hurt by her friend's accusation.

'As far as I'm concerned,' Suzie said expansively, 'any of my friends want to commit murder? I'll cover up for them, no questions asked.'

'You can't possibly mean that,' Becks said.

'Blood is thicker than water, and friendship is thicker than blood,' Suzie added, turning to Judith. 'So you messed up in your witness statement when you said you didn't go down to your husband's boat? He'd just died. We all know how confused people get when they've lost a loved one. Where was this photo taken?'

'On Philippos's jetty, just below our house,' Judith said.

'Then that makes it even more understandable that you'd get your story muddled. Were you in your house? Were you at the jetty? They're so close to each other, it's no wonder you got confused.'

'But did you go out on his boat like Eleni said?' Becks asked.

'DON'T ASK HER THAT!'

'No, it's all right,' Judith said, turning to Becks. 'My witness statement was incorrect. And it wasn't because I was confused after he died. It was because I didn't dare tell the police the truth. You've no idea what it was like as an outsider joining that community. Especially when everyone in the village had expected Philippos to marry someone else. Eleni's mother, as it happened. And it's true . . . I went on his boat that day. But I was back on the jetty by the time he left. I promise you. And before you ask, Philippos was alive and well when he set sail. As the autopsy said when his body washed up on a beach, he drowned at sea when his boat sank in the storm. There were no toxins or poisons in his body, and no evidence of foul play.'

'Then why does this photo even matter?' Suzie asked. 'And how do we even know it's real? I reckon it's possible someone's digitally inserted you into the image. Your shadows are all wrong.'

'The shadows were the first thing I looked at,' Judith said. 'But they're correct for both Philippos and me for the time of day that he set off. The sun is right above us in the sky. I don't think anyone's doctored it.'

'Then who took it?' Becks asked.

'That's what I can't work out,' Judith said. 'There was no one about that morning. Or rather, there was someone – a shepherd up on the cliffs who thought he saw me on the boat after Philippos left. But his testimony was rubbished later on. He had cataracts. There's no way he could have seen more than the dimmest shape of a boat out at sea. And anyway, he couldn't have both been in the cove taking photos of us and up on the cliffs so soon after. There must have been someone else hiding nearby who took the photo.'

'How did Eleni come into possession of it?' Becks asked.

'It was given to Philippos's mother – Eleni's grandmother – who then gave it to her.'

'So the photo was taken by someone who knows Philippos's family?'

'Is there really no chance it's a fake?' Suzie asked. 'You know how clever computers are these days at manipulating images.'

'It certainly looks like the real deal,' Becks said. 'I know you're much younger in the photo, but there's a way Judith stands that's very distinctive. And look – you can see the wedding ring on your hand,' Becks added, pointing to Judith's left hand in the photograph. 'There's a flash of light where it's caught the sun.

'My wedding ring?' Judith asked as she took the photo from her friend to look at it again.

'But I agree with Suzie,' Becks said, wanting to conclude the conversation as positively as possible. 'If your husband left the island on his own in his boat, then none of this matters. Maybe you should pop along to the police to correct your witness statement, but that's all you'll have to do. You couldn't have conjured up the storm that ended his life, could you?'

'Not unless you're a witch,' Suzie said with a chuckle. 'And while the two of us know that could be true – and a mighty fine witch you'd be – the rest of the world doesn't.'

Judith's phone started ringing and when she looked to see who was calling, she saw that it was Tanika.

'Oh, you're picking up now, are you?' Tanika said by way of an opening when Judith answered.

'Have you got something for us?' Judith said, ignoring the barb.

'We've found a lead in the Wise case. And it's significant. Mr Wise's phone company has just sent through copies of all of his voicemails and texts. They're all pretty vanilla – or so we thought until we found a text conversation that he'd archived. I've got a screengrab of it. Let me send it to you so you can see for yourself. I'll stay on the line while you look at it. Hold on.'

Judith's phone chimed and she saw that Tanika had sent an image file. She tapped on it so it filled the screen. It showed a sequence of text messages that Gary Wise's phone had received throughout the year.

14 April 25, 13:01

£1k Thursday, woods behind your house, 11pm

03 June 25, 09:37

£1k Underpass by Gossmore park, 10.30pm

22 August 25, 16:23

£1k Thursday, bin by the Higginson park skatepark, 11pm

16 November 25, 10:07

£5k Tuesday, woods behind your house, 11pm

16 November 25, 11:01

That's too much.

16 November 25, 11:33

£5K Tuesday, woods behind your house

16 November 25, 11:01

No.

16 November 25, 10:07

You have no choice

16 November 25, 11:01

I'll go to the press.

16 November 25, 17:00

You want to end your career? £5k Tuesday, woods behind your house, 11pm

'Someone was extorting money out of him!' Suzie said.

'And that last exchange was just before he died, wasn't it?' Becks said. 'The guy who was demanding money from him said they had to meet behind his house at 11pm on Tuesday the eighteenth. And he died at 11pm, behind his house, on Tuesday the eighteenth.'

'And it all fits with him contacting the press the day that he died, doesn't it?' Suzie said in excitement. 'In these text messages, Gary threatens to reveal the name of his blackmailer.'

'If only Gary had told the *Daily Mirror* journalist the name of who was behind this,' Judith said. 'Rather than losing his nerve. Maybe he'd still be alive.'

'But this is the person who killed him, isn't it?' Becks said. 'Whoever this blackmailer is, they knew that Gary was about to reveal their identity. So, when they met up on the eighteenth, they killed him to make sure that he never would.'

'We need to speak to Bethany Wise at once,' Judith said. 'We need to know what she has to say about this.'

'No need,' Tanika said. 'Brendan's already talking to her.'

'*Brendan*?' Suzie asked.

'He's a Detective Sergeant and perfectly capable of running an interview.'

'He's not capable of running a bath,' Suzie said.

'But why's he interviewing a key witness instead of you?' Judith asked.

'The point is,' Tanika said, ignoring Judith's question, 'he's busy with her, so how can I help you?'

'You want to help us?' Becks asked.

'Don't question it,' Suzie said. 'Just accept it. Because I can't help noticing that these text messages start on the fourteenth of April, don't they?'

'Why's that important?' Tanika asked.

'We've heard Gary Wise was injured in a car crash on the night of the seventh of April.'

'I don't think that's possible,' Tanika said. 'He can't have been involved in any kind of road traffic accident or we'd have picked that up in background checks.'

'That's what we thought,' Becks said.

'Is it possible someone deleted the file from the system later on?' Judith asked.

'I suppose that's a possibility. Although, even if the digital record was deleted, we keep hard copies of all of our files in a warehouse just outside Reading. Do you want access to it? If an accident was the cause of him being blackmailed, it sounds important that we find out what happened that night.'

'You can get us in there?' Becks asked.

'Let me text you the address and make sure your names are cleared with the security guards at the gate.'

With that, Tanika hung up.

The women were stunned.

'OK, you're right, Becks,' Suzie said. 'There's something going on with Tanika, isn't there?'

Chapter 9

When Suzie parked her van in the courtyard of the police depository, she peered through the windscreen at the imposing building in front of her. It was huge – a modern warehouse of aluminium and brick – and the parking area was surrounded by high walls that were topped with vicious-looking razor wire. At each corner there were security cameras on high poles. It all felt more like a prison than a warehouse.

The three friends were buzzed into a reception area where a smartly dressed receptionist checked their credentials and asked them to fill in a form listing the records they were requesting. They didn't have the exact reference, but they knew that it would have been logged on the evening of seventh April, or early on the morning of the eighth, so they asked to see everything that was created on those two days. The receptionist sucked air in through his teeth, but agreed to the request, explaining where in the stacks they'd need to look. Then he asked if they needed help locating the records.

'What are you talking about?' Suzie said, offended by the

question. 'If I can find a Billy bookcase in IKEA, I can find a police record here.'

Thanking the receptionist for his help, the women approached a locked door and were buzzed through into a huge room that was filled wall to wall with metal stacks, all of them full of hanging files.

'And you thought *you* had an archive?' Becks said with a smile to Judith.

Judith didn't respond, but Becks was already heading towards a group of stacks near the right-hand side of the room. Suzie followed, checking the numbers on her piece of paper against each stack she passed. As she caught up with her friend, Becks told her that she'd found the start of the files from 2025.

'All of these records begin with the number twenty-five.'

'OK,' Suzie said, consulting her piece of paper again. 'So we need to find section oh-four, which I suppose refers to April. And then it's the number seven to represent the seventh.'

'So we're looking for twenty-five dot zero four dot seven,' Becks said, vanishing behind a stack.

'And dot eight for the eighth as well,' Suzie called after her friend, before turning to see where Judith had got to. She couldn't see her. With a shrug, she followed after Becks. As she rounded the corner, Suzie saw that she was already moving down a different row.

'Right, I think I'm getting there,' Becks said.

'See?' Suzie said as she caught up with her friend. 'Told you it would be easier than IKEA.'

'Easier than IKEA, but harder than finding trifle sponges in Waitrose.'

'Trifle sponges? What are you talking about?'

'You see? No one knows what they are anymore. But you can't make a trifle with those sponge fingers, it's not the same.'

'You *make* trifles?' Suzie asked. 'You don't just buy them and eat them from the tub before you've even got them into the fridge?'

Becks couldn't help but smile at the image as she inspected the files in front of her.

'OK,' she said. 'Here's the first file from the seventh of April. How about you start with this one, and I'll go to the last file on the eighth? We can then work towards each other and meet in the middle?'

'Good plan,' Suzie said as she pulled the first hanging file from the rack and opened it up. 'So, what have we here? A chap called Stephen Thatcher, drunk and disorderly in charge of a bicycle. So that's not it . . .'

Suzie clunked the file back onto its hanger and pulled the next one down. It wasn't what she was looking for either, so she carried on working through the files that were created on seventh April as Becks went and found the last records that had been created on the eighth.

'Where's Judith?' Suzie asked after a few minutes of silent work. 'We could do with her here.'

'I don't know,' Becks said, 'but we're nearly there. Let's keep at it.'

The two women worked on until they were pulling files down from the racks that were only separated from each other by a few numbers.

'Bloody typical that his file would be slap bang in the middle,' Suzie said as she pulled down another hanging file. 'Oh dear. Mister Christopher Davies here got into a fist fight with a Mister

Graham Pulsford on the eighteenth hole of the Gerrards Cross golf club. But sill no Gary Wise. Hold on, what's this?'

'Have you got something?'

'It's the numbering on the files. This record – of the fight at the golf club – is file thirty-eight. But the one next to it is numbered forty. Where's the file that's supposed to be at thirty-nine? It's missing.'

'But this is good!' Becks said. 'Was number thirty-nine the hard copy of the report on Gary's car crash that night?'

'I don't know, but what would that mean? Someone deleted all mention of the crash from the police computer and then, later on, came down here and removed the physical file as well? We need to speak to Judith. Where is she? Judith!' Suzie bellowed.

'She hasn't got lost, has she?' Becks asked, once she'd recovered from the sonic boom.

'Sorry,' Judith said in a fluster as she appeared at the end of the stack. 'The two of you disappeared and I couldn't find you.'

'But you knew the date we were looking for,' Becks said. 'We were always going to be somewhere around here.'

'What have you found?' Judith asked Suzie, ignoring Becks.

Suzie explained that they'd just discovered that a file from seventh April was missing.

'Then we need to talk to Tanika,' Judith said. 'She'll be able to tell us how a police report could end up being removed like this.'

'She can also tell us why she's being so helpful all of a sudden,' Becks said.

'Good thinking,' Judith replied. '*And* she can tell us how Brendan's interview with Bethany went. In fact, there are really quite a lot of reasons why we need to see her, aren't there?'

The women left the depository and together they drove up

Winter Hill and through Cookham village towards Maidenhead. They didn't need to go into the main body of the town, as the police station was located on the ring road in between two multi-storey car parks. Suzie parked by a row of three police cars and then locked her car as she and her friends walked towards the red brick building.

'Ah, there she is!' Judith said as she saw Tanika walking out of the entrance holding a large cardboard box.

'Ladies?' Tanika said, heading over to a white Peugeot car and balancing the box on her knee while she opened the boot.

'If we handled evidence like that, you'd give us a right ticking off,' Suzie said with a twinkle.

'This isn't evidence,' Tanika said, dumping the box into her boot where it landed with a thud.

'What is it then?' Suzie said as she reached in and opened the lid.

'My personal possessions.'

Suzie could see that the box contained a couple of police manuals, a small pot plant, some framed photos of Tanika's daughter Shanti and husband Shamil, and loose papers and stationery.

'Why are you putting all this in your boot?' Suzie asked.

'As of about ten minutes ago, I've been suspended.'

'What?' Suzie said, horrified. 'No!'

'But you just caught Oliver Beresford's killer!' Becks said, outraged on Tanika's behalf.

'In what was quite an unorthodox manner. And I was already on probation, so obtaining a confession from a suspect in a public setting without a lawyer present was seen as the last straw.'

'It was a sell-out audience in Marlow,' Suzie said. 'I bet there were dozens of lawyers present.'

'You know what I mean.'

'Brendan's behind this, isn't he?' Judith said. 'He was behind the last complaint against you.'

'It doesn't matter who lodged the complaint.'

'Of course it matters!' Suzie said. 'He's never forgiven you for getting promoted to DI when he couldn't even pass the exam. He's been gunning for your job ever since.'

'Not every day,' Tanika said in a weary attempt at a joke. 'There was a time a month or so ago when he went to the Med on holiday. I had a break from him then.'

'So, is that really it?' Judith asked. 'You're booted out?'

'I've had to hand in my warrant card.'

'Which is why you were trying to get us to investigate this case as fast as we could!' Suzie said. 'You knew this was going to happen.'

'I had an inkling.'

'But what happens now?' Becks asked.

'I'm no longer a police officer until the tribunal meets to consider my case. So I go home and wait. At least I'll be able to spend more time with Shanti.'

'But if it's not you who's leading the Gary Wise case, then who is?'

As Suzie asked the question, the door to the police station opened and Detective Sergeant Brendan Perry strode out.

As he approached the four women, he looked like thunder.

Chapter 10

Brendan was a heavy man who, to Judith's eyes, always looked as though he'd just finished a large meal and was now suffering from indigestion.

'I've just received a complaint from a colleague of Gary Wise's at Wycombe Wanderers Football Club,' he said to the women.

'Hello, Brendan,' Judith said, refusing to be intimidated.

'Ladies,' Tanika said, 'while I'm suspended, Brendan's been asked to act up as Senior Investigating Officer on the Wise case.'

'Is it true you've been investigating using your civilian adviser cards, even though they're out of date?' he asked.

'It's as true a statement as saying that you're threatened by a female boss,' Judith said.

'What did I tell you?' Brendan said, turning with venom towards Tanika. 'If you continue to get this lot involved, it will look even worse for you.'

'Tanika caught Oliver Beresford's killer!' Suzie said.

'And Tanika didn't get us involved in the Gary Wise case,' Becks said. 'We've done all that off our own bat.'

'Becks is right,' Judith said. 'In fact, Tanika warned us off.'

'That's not true,' Tanika said. 'I encouraged them to get involved.'

'Why would you tell him that?' Suzie said, before turning back to face Brendan. 'We've uncovered important information.'

'You're not police officers,' Brendan snapped. 'You have no authority to be talking to anyone.'

'You're right,' Becks said, realising how much danger they were in. 'It's always been a stretch, hasn't it?'

'Thanks for the support,' Suzie muttered.

'You'll be wanting our civilian adviser cards back, won't you?' Becks said.

'Damned right I do,' Brendan said, holding out his hand.

Becks handed over her lanyard while Suzie shrugged.

'You'll have to get mine from that physio guy at the football club,' she said.

'He's sending it to us in the post,' Brendan said before turning to face Judith.

She smiled sweetly at him.

'Your lanyard please, Mrs Potts.'

'I'm sorry, Brendan, but I've lost it.'

'I beg your pardon?'

'I normally keep it in my handbag, but when I went to get it this morning, I discovered it wasn't there. If I find it again I'll be sure to bring it into the police station for you.'

Brendan pulled a face that made it clear he hadn't, in fact, been born yesterday.

'Open your bag,' he said.

'Oh, I don't think I'll be doing that,' Judith said.

'I said, open it.'

'Do you have a warrant?'

'Of course I don't have a bloody warrant!'

'Then my handbag is private property, and if you want to see what I keep in it you'll have to apply for a warrant. Seeing as you're such a stickler for the rules.'

Before Brendan could reply, the door to the police station banged open and Detective Sergeant Alice Hackett bombed out, followed by a clutch of uniformed police officers.

'Boss!' she called as she headed over.

Both Tanika and Brendan turned to face Alice as she arrived.

'No – of course,' Tanika said, as she saw the confusion on Alice's face. 'Sorry,' she added and went back to closing the boot of her car.

'What is it?' Brendan asked.

'There's been another murder in Marlow,' Alice said. 'We need to get to the scene, sir.'

Brendan barely had time to sneer at Tanika before he was following Alice and the other police officers to the squad cars. And then, blue lights flashing, they raced onto the gyratory and the sound of their sirens disappeared into the distance.

'*Another* murder?' Becks said, horrified. 'Do you think it's connected?'

'Two murders in three days,' Suzie said darkly. 'They're connected.'

'What should we do?' Becks asked Tanika.

'Nothing,' Tanika said.

'But there's been a murder!'

'And it's got nothing to do with you. Or me for that matter. Brendan's in charge now. It's over for the four of us.'

'It can't be,' Suzie said. 'This is how we solve crimes. We

investigate, you try and stop us, and then together we catch the killer.'

'Not anymore,' Tanika said. 'And if you don't mind, I don't much enjoy hanging around here knowing people can see me. I'm going home.'

Tanika got into her car with her three friends telling her how brilliant she was, and how wrong it was that she'd been suspended. But she just closed the door and drove off, leaving the women on their own.

'That man,' Suzie said, summing up the feelings of them all.

'He's not keeping us from this murder,' Judith said as she pulled her mobile out of her handbag and headed towards the police station.

'Judith!' Becks called out after her friend. 'What are you doing?'

'I'm not having him sideline us,' she called back as she pushed through the door and strode up to the young police constable who was behind the reception desk. His name was Paul Merchant and Judith had learned over the years that he'd gone to Borlase's School, loved amateur photography, was engaged to a local girl called Veronica and, when he left the force, he wanted to travel and open a bar somewhere tropical.

'Good morning, Paul!' Judith said.

'Mrs Potts!' PC Merchant said, his face lighting up.

'A terrible thing's happened – Brendan's just dropped his phone,' Judith said, wafting her iPhone vaguely in the air.

'He did?' PC Merchant said, concern etched on his face. 'Then you'd better hand it in, I'll give it to him the next time I see him.'

'There's no time for that, there's been a murder!'

'I know, but correct procedure means—'

'Correct procedure? You'd hide behind weasel words at this critical time?'

'It's important—'

'That Brendan gets his phone. He'll need it, seeing as he's attending a murder scene.'

The enormity of the situation hit PC Merchant.

'I'll take it to him,' he said.

PC Merchant started to slide shut the glass screen that separated him from the public.

'But you can't leave your post,' Judith said. 'You've got to stay here.'

'Oh God, you're right, I can't. What shall I do?'

'I know!' Judith said, inspiration apparently coming to her only in that moment. 'How about you tell me where he is and I'll take the phone to him.'

'You'd do that for me, Mrs Potts?'

'I'm here to do whatever I can to help. Where has he gone?'

'Gossmore Recreation Ground,' PC Merchant said. 'A body's just been found under the A404 flyover.'

'I'll take his phone to him at once. Thank you very much, Paul.'

'No, thank you, Mrs Potts – you've been a great help.'

Judith smiled broadly as she strode back outside to where Suzie and Becks were waiting.

'The murder happened on Gossmore Recreation Ground. But before we go there, I think we should swing by Suzie's house and collect Emma. Gossmore is where everyone walks their dogs, isn't it?'

Once the three friends had picked Emma up and driven to the other side of Marlow, they were able to park Suzie's van just around the corner from Gossmore Recreation Ground. After getting Emma out of the boot, Suzie put her on her lead and together they approached the park's smaller side entrance. As had been the case ever since they'd left the police station, their conversation was focused on what Brendan had done to Tanika.

'He's never been able to cope with a female boss,' Judith said.

'Especially one who's more brilliant than him,' Suzie agreed.

'Although he had a bit of a point,' Becks said.

'I wish you'd stop saying that!'

'I know, I know,' Becks said, holding up her hands to stop her friends from attacking her. 'But we shouldn't have been using our civilian adviser cards once they'd gone out of date. And Brendan was right when he said Tanika didn't follow correct procedure.'

'Poppycock!' Judith snorted. 'She spends her whole time following correct procedure. It's us who don't follow it. But we're not police officers – there's no correct procedure for us to follow. It's why we get results.'

'Amen to that,' Suzie said as she unclipped the lead from Emma's collar and let her tear off across the grass of the nearby football pitch. Just beyond it there was a line of trees that had lost their leaves, their jagged branches standing starkly against the grey sky. But the women's eyes were drawn to the far side of the park, to the concrete road bridge that crossed the river Thames. Underneath one of the arches, they could see police officers working by a clutch of police cars and an ambulance.

'So, what's the plan?' Becks asked. 'I'm sure we can all agree we *really* don't want Brendan to see us. We do agree on that, don't we?'

'Don't worry,' Judith said. 'You're right, we don't want him knowing how near we are. So how about we keep our distance and see what we can find out from over here?'

The women found a nearby bench and Suzie threw a ball for Emma to chase. Then, every time a member of the public headed in their direction from the other side of the park, the three friends got up as casually as they could and headed across the grass to home in on their quarry. Then, a few exclamations of surprise from one or other of them at the presence of the police cars would provoke the person they were stalking into revealing what they'd seen as they'd passed the crime scene.

After half an hour, Judith and her friends had learned that there was a single body, that the dead person appeared to be a man and that there was a large trilby hat on the ground by his head.

In a lull in the conversation while they were waiting for their next informant, Judith turned to her friends.

'So, what did you think of the crossword in the *Marlow Free Press* this morning?' she asked.

'What's that?' Suzie said.

'Did either of you do the cryptic crossword this morning?'

'Why would we do that?'

'Because it's fun!'

'That's a pretty strange definition of fun.'

'But they're so simple! The key is to realise you shouldn't treat the clues like a real sentence.'

'The key is to realise you shouldn't read them at all.'

'It's just a code that needs breaking,' Judith said. 'Each clue is always made up of two halves. One of those halves will give you the synonym for the word you're looking for. And the other half is the puzzle that also gives you the same answer. It's why cryptic crosswords are so superior to concise ones. You always know when you've solved a cryptic clue because both halves of the question give the same answer.'

'I remember you giving us a masterclass about all of this when we were catching Stefan Dunwoody's killer,' Becks said.

'I put special messages to you both in the *Marlow Free Press* crossword today.'

'You did?' Becks said.

'"This bird initially hit a Rolls Royce in Scotland" – six letters.'

'What are you talking about?' Suzie asked.

'It's a clue I wrote specially for you, Suzie.'

'How can it be for me?'

'You'll see. You're looking for a type of bird.'

'A Scottish bird?' Becks asked.

'No – that's the surface meaning and you need to ignore that. Remember, it's a puzzle – that's all. You need to split the clue in two, with one half of it being the literal definition. In this instance I can tell you that the word you're looking for is a type of bird.'

'Then what's all that stuff about a Rolls Royce in Scotland?' Suzie asked.

'That's the other half of the clue. The puzzle. So what do you think the answer is to "initially hit a Rolls Royce in Scotland"?'

'I've no idea,' Becks said.

'It's easy. "Initially" just means that you should take the initials of the words that follow. So, if you take the first letters of "hit", "a", "Rolls", "Royce", "in" and "Scotland", you spell "Harris", which is your surname.'

'I know it's my surname,' Suzie said.

'But it's also a type of bird – the Harris hawk. Both halves of the clue give the same answer,' Judith said, now struggling not to sound irritated.

'What was your message to me?' Becks said, acting, as ever, as peacemaker.

'As it happens, I was rather pleased with yours,' Judith said. '"It's thrilling when a confused bear takes Essex County Council hostage". Seven letters.'

'Sorry, what?' Suzie said. 'What is it with posh cars in Scotland and now bears in Essex?'

'It just sounds harder than it is,' Judith said. 'Let me help by saying that we're looking for something that's thrilling.'

'So am I,' Suzie said, 'because I can tell you that this isn't it.'

'But that's the first half of the clue – what we're looking for. Meaning that the second half is the cryptic part. And I know it seems like it's a nonsense, but you just have to break it down. What do you think Essex County Council stands for?'

'Probably Botox and lip fillers,' Suzie grumbled.

'Suzie!' Becks yelped.

'It stands for the letters ECC,' Judith said, realising that she was at risk of entirely losing control of the conversation. 'So, the finished word is "a confused bear" that takes ECC hostage. In other words, it has ECC within it.'

'Is it an anagram?' Becks asked.

'Exactly!' Judith said, delighted.

'Because "confused" in crosswords means you need to do an anagram?' Becks said, finishing her thought.

'Meaning what?' Judith prompted.

'Meaning what – my point exactly,' Suzie said, but her friends could see that she was being so curmudgeonly that she was at risk of cheering herself up.

'Meaning we're looking for an anagram of bear,' Becks said.

'So, if you create an anagram of "bear" and put the letters ECC somewhere within it, what answer do you get?'

'And the answer's a synonym for "thrilling"? Oh, I get it, it's my name, isn't it?' Becks said, suddenly excited. 'An anagram of bear is R, E, B and A, and if you put ECC in there you get *Rebecca*, which is a book by Daphne du Maurier.'

'And not just any type of book,' Judith said, delighted with her student.

'It's a thriller,' Becks agreed. 'Which makes it thrilling. You know what? I actually quite liked that.'

As Becks spoke, they saw a dark red Bentley drive down the track towards the police cars and stop. A woman with auburn hair got out and Brendan approached her.

'Hold on,' Judith said. 'Who's that?'

'The next of kin?' Becks offered. 'If I were guessing.'

'You know what, I think I recognise that car!' Suzie said. 'Oh, bloody hell, is that Serena? Oh God – of course – the trilby! I think the dead guy's Mike Saxon.'

'You mean the novelist?' Becks asked, amazed.

'The very same.'

'Who's he?' Judith asked.

'You're not serious, are you?' Suzie asked. 'Always wears a dark trilby hat. He's sold about a bazillion copies of his books around the world. His main character is an ex-soldier called Fraser Steele. You must have heard of him.'

'I'm sorry, I haven't. So who's that woman?'

'His wife. I used to dog-sit for her every Thursday morning when she went to yoga classes. If I was still there when she got back, we'd sometimes have a cup of tea together.'

'This is the most brilliant news!' Judith said, rubbing her hands together. 'I mean, obviously it's bad news that he's dead, but how lucky that you know the family. What was he like?'

'I only ever met him a few times. He works in an office at the bottom of the garden. But I didn't like him. He's full of himself and treats Serena like staff. Which is crazy. They've got so much money from his writing that they actually have staff.'

'But if you know his wife . . .?'

'You're right, we could go and see her. And don't tell me we can't, Becks Starling.'

'Don't worry, I'm not going to do that,' Becks said. 'Now that Tanika's off the case, we can't get her into any trouble. As long as we stay out of Brendan's way, we can do what we like.'

'Are you being daring?' Suzie asked, impressed.

'Maybe a little,' Becks admitted. 'Solving crossword clues one minute and murders the next.'

'I like it,' Suzie said in appreciation.

The women looked over and saw a female police officer accompany the woman to a police car as a second police officer went over to the Bentley.

'But this is another celebrity, isn't it?' Judith said in realisation. 'First a famous footballer is murdered, and now it's a famous novelist.'

'I suppose it could just be a coincidence,' Becks said.

'It's not a coincidence,' Judith pronounced. 'Two celebrities have been killed within days of each other, there's going to be a link between them. We just have to find it.'

Chapter 11

Serena Saxon was in a haze as the family liaison officer drove her back to her house. She didn't notice the people on the High Street going about their day. Or the children starting to pour out of Sir William Borlase's Grammar School. Even after the car had pulled up at her house, she just carried on sitting there.

'Mrs Saxon?' the family liaison officer said, and Serena woke from her reverie.

'I can take it from here,' she replied, pushing at the door handle.

'Are you sure you don't want me to come in with you?'

'No, I'll be fine,' she said as she felt the crunch of gravel under her feet.

Looking at her house, she noticed – as she always did – how very ugly it was. It was a modern brick recreation of a Georgian mansion, even including scalloped pillars to the side of the entrance that looked like they were made from stone but were in fact painted plywood.

She could sell it now.

She could get rid of everything that was horrible about her life. She was free.

Serena watched her husband's monstrous Bentley pull into the driveway. The officer who had driven it came over and handed her the keys, asked if she'd be OK, and then, when she said she'd be fine, got in the police car with the family liaison officer and drove off. Serena watched it all happen as though in a dream. Then she let herself into her house and put her keys on the side table, vaguely wondering why her dog, Cosmo, hadn't come to greet her.

She hated the vast hallway, with its marble staircase that split halfway up so it served both wings of the house. Her heels clicked on the black and white tiles as she headed through into the kitchen. Once there, she was surprised to see that her dog-walker, Suzie Harris, was fussing Cosmo.

'I hope you don't mind,' Suzie said. 'I let myself in.'

Serena saw that there were two women with Suzie. One of them looked like the sort of busybody who got too involved in her local community, and the other she recognised as the vicar of Marlow's wife.

'Dear God, Suzie Harris,' she said, realising why Suzie was there. 'You don't hang about, do you?'

Suzie shrugged by way of apology.

'Sorry,' she said.

'We're friends of Suzie's,' Becks said. 'And we're so sorry for your loss. But when we heard the news, Suzie said she should offer to look after Cosmo for you. If it helps at all.'

Serena went to the fridge and pulled the door open.

'Is that really the best you can do? White wine? Or something stronger?' she asked, with a sly smile.

'I'm sorry?' Judith asked.

'The three of you are here because you want to catch my husband's killer. Your reputation precedes you.'

'Honestly,' Suzie said, 'we were only concerned about Cosmo.'

'You don't have to lie to me. And you really don't need to worry, I think this is a loss I'm going to survive. In fact, I think it calls for champagne.'

Serena pulled a bottle of Bollinger out of the fridge, went over to one of the kitchen cabinets and pulled out four champagne flutes.

'You're celebrating?' Becks asked.

'If I'm honest, I don't know what I'm doing. I've just had one of the biggest shocks of my life. Identifying Mike is something I'll never get over. But I'm not going to pretend this doesn't make things easier for me. At the very least, Mike would be offended if we drank to his life with anything less than champagne.'

With a gentle hiss, Serena twisted the cork from the bottle and poured four glasses of champagne. Once she'd handed them out, she raised her glass.

'To Mike Saxon,' she said. 'Wherever he may now be.'

'It's a bit too early to have a drink,' Becks said disapprovingly.

'I don't think you can break into my house and then get on your high horse,' Serena said, raising her glass. 'To Mike Saxon, wherever he may now be.'

The women noticed that Serena's glance to the floor seemed to suggest the possibility that her husband wasn't necessarily spending his afterlife in heaven.

'To Mike,' the three friends said and then took a sip from their glasses.

'So, what do you want to know?' Serena asked.

'Are you sure you don't mind us asking questions?' Becks asked.

'Not at all. Shoot – although that's in rather bad taste considering how he died.'

'He was shot?' Judith said, catching her friends' eyes.

'The police officer I spoke to said it was one shot – directly to the heart. Mercifully, death would have been instantaneous.'

'Do you know when it happened?'

'They couldn't say, but they're thinking sometime last night.'

Judith noticed that there was a laptop on the kitchen table with various pieces of paper and opened books by it. She went over to look as she asked, 'When did you last see him?'

'Last night,' Serena said.

Judith looked down at the pages of handwritten notes and couldn't help noticing that the books were various travel guides to Sierra Leone.

'I'd rather you didn't look at that,' Serena said. 'It's Mike's latest novel. Or his notes for it,' she added.

'No – of course,' Judith said in a rare moment of tact.

Serena downed the rest of her glass and topped it up with more champagne.

'So, you'll want to know what happened last night,' she said.

'No, you don't need to tell us,' Becks said, politeness as ever being her first reflex.

Her friends glared at her.

'Sorry,' Becks said, correcting herself. 'Actually, we *do* want to know.'

'Well, I'll tell you. We had supper here last night and then sat down to watch some godawful show about commandos or special forces or something. What we watch at night is Mike's choice. As he used to say to me, he'd paid for the TV, he could choose what we watched on it.'

'Seriously?' Suzie asked.

'He was full of homely aphorisms like that. "My house, my rules" was another one. So we watched the TV and finished the bottle of Chablis we'd had at dinner. Although, if I'm being honest,' Serena said, casting her mind back to the night before, 'it was me who drank most of it. It's how I anaesthetise myself when it's just him and me. Then, at about ten or so, we went to bed.'

'You saw him go to sleep?' Becks asked.

'No. We don't sleep in the same room. It's about the only upside of living in a house like this; there are always rooms to spare. But we share a bathroom. The last time I saw him, he was in his pyjamas and had just brushed his teeth. I wished him good night, and do you know what he did? He grunted. That's the last interaction he and I had. He grunted at me like a walrus. It seems apt somehow that that's how it ended.'

'You didn't see him again?' Suzie said.

'No, I went to bed and was soon asleep.'

'So you have no idea what he did after then?'

'None whatsoever.'

'Is it possible he came down here and went back to work?' Judith said, indicating the laptop on the table.

'I very much doubt it. But I didn't hear him clattering about, which is generally what happens when he stays up. I sleep very lightly – it's my bloody age. But the next thing I knew, I was woken by what I'm pretty sure was a door slamming. I remember looking at my bedside clock, seeing it was midnight and wondering if I'd get back to sleep. Luckily for me, I did.'

'You think that's when your husband left?' Becks asked.

'I don't know, but it could have been.'

'You didn't think of following him?'

'I didn't know he'd left the house.'

'Did you hear his car start up?'

'I didn't hear anything. Not wheels on the gravel – nothing. It was just that one door slamming. And then I didn't see him again until just now.'

'Then do you have any idea who might have done this to him?'

'Ha! It might be quicker to list the people who wouldn't. Mike was . . . difficult.'

'You're prepared to admit you had a motive?'

'God, yes!' Serena said with a manic laugh and then downed the rest of her drink. 'Or at least, that's how it would look to an outsider. He was demanding, selfish, full of himself and a self-important bore. Which is not to say I killed him. I made my peace with my lot years ago. I mean, look at this place! It's not to my taste, but I get to live like a queen. Our staff means I don't have to lift a finger. Mike's feted at literary festivals and I get to travel with him to some of the most beautiful spots in the world. Last year we were the guests of the Maharaja of Baroda for two weeks. I've always considered life with Mike to be more than worth it.'

'So if you didn't kill him, then who did?' Becks said, increasingly frustrated by Serena's breezy cynicism.

'Anyone who's served him in a restaurant. Anyone who's ever worked with him – with the exception of his editor. He's put up with Mike all of these years for the same reason that I have. He brings in a lot of money.'

'Can we ask if you or Mike knew the footballer Gary Wise?' Judith asked.

'You think there's a link between the two deaths?'

'It's too soon to say. But he was also shot.'

For the first time, Judith's words seemed to land with Serena.

'Bloody hell,' she said.

'You knew Gary?' Becks asked.

'I didn't. And, as far as I know, nor did Mike.'

'Then what about his wife, Bethany?'

'I'm sorry, but we didn't know either of them.'

'What about the local writer Harry Asquith?'

'No,' Serena said, 'I can't say I've heard his name before. But seriously, are you saying that both that footballer and Mike were killed by the same person?'

'We don't know that yet, but we'll find out,' Becks said.

'Then how has Mike been recently?' Judith asked. 'Has he seemed worried at all?'

'No way, he doesn't do introspection. Although there was one thing that happened yesterday that was out of the ordinary.' Serena picked up the bottle of champagne and returned it to the fridge. 'Mike had a stand-up row with his personal assistant. A woman called Jamilah. He ended up sacking her – God knows why – and he all but physically bundled her out of here.'

'He manhandled her?'

'I saw him grab her by the shoulders and march her off the premises. This was down by his office. You can see it from the downstairs windows. Later on, when he was back in the house, I asked him what had happened, but he refused to talk about it. He just said Jamilah wouldn't be working for him any longer. As it had nothing to do with me, I left him to stew. If he's going to sack his assistant, that's his business.'

'Do you have his assistant's address?' Becks asked.

'She lives in Marlow. I'm sure I've got her address somewhere.'

Judith's phone started ringing. She got it out and saw that the number had a +30 dialling code.

'It's a Greek number,' she said.

'It will be Eleni,' Suzie said, a warning tone to her voice.

'But how has she got hold of your number?' Becks asked.

'You're right,' Suzie said, 'that's spooky. Did you give it to her?'

'Of course not,' Judith said, her finger hovering over the green icon to answer the call. 'I have no idea how she knows it.'

Judith pressed the red icon to cancel the call and then looked at Serena with a smile that she hoped didn't look too forced. 'If you could get Jamilah's address for us, that would be lovely.'

Chapter 12

Jamilah Khalil lived on the first floor of a red-brick terraced house near Marlow train station. There was only the smallest of gaps between the garden gate and the front door, and Judith and her friends had to push some wheelie bins to the side so they could get to the buzzer for Flat B. After Judith pressed it and a voice said 'Hello?' out of a speaker, Judith explained who they were and that they wanted to talk to her. After only the shortest of pauses, Jamilah said they should come straight up to the first floor and the door clicked open.

The three friends entered a narrow corridor and headed up the stairs, where a door was opened by a fresh-faced woman in her mid-twenties. She had straight dark hair, was wearing jeans and a T-shirt, and she gave off an air of distraction as she showed the women into her front room.

Judith smiled as she saw a futon on the floor, a spider plant on a windowsill and floor-to-ceiling shelves either side of the fireplace that were stuffed full of books. The first bed she'd bought for herself after university had also been a futon. She remembered how much she'd loved it. But now, looking at one again after many decades, she marvelled at how she'd ever managed to get in and out of the thing.

'I hope you don't mind us calling unannounced like this,' Becks said.

'I'll be honest,' Jamilah said, 'I could do with the company. It's all been quite a shock.'

'You've heard?'

'It's all over my socials. I can't believe it. He was alive only yesterday and now . . .?' Jamilah shuddered. 'Can I get you ladies a drink? A cup of tea? Or a coffee?'

'No, we're fine,' Becks said, 'and we don't want to take up any more of your time than we have to. It's just, we've come from talking to Serena Saxon.'

'Huh,' Jamilah said.

'You don't like her?'

'It's not for me to like or dislike her, but I didn't warm to her. I suppose I'd put it like that. Don't get me wrong, Mike was a tricky customer, but he had a lust for life and was always full of ideas for his next book. Or for characters or plot moments. He was an enthusiast. But Serena is a cynic. Nothing is worth doing, nothing is good enough. If I'm honest, I don't know how Mike put up with her.'

'She suggested to us that her husband was more of the problem.'

'He could be spiky, I'd agree with that. But she has a wonderful life and nothing makes her happy. And don't even think about trying to get any sense out of her after 6 p.m. She's always drunk. And she has a temper on her. So yes, give me Mike over Serena any day.'

'Even though he sacked you yesterday,' Suzie said.

'That was something I wasn't expecting,' Jamilah admitted.

'What happened?' Becks asked.

The younger woman didn't immediately reply, and Judith realised she was weighing up what she should say.

'Sure, I can tell you what happened,' Jamilah eventually said. 'You see, the two of us generally rubbed along just fine. I'd get to the house for about 9.30 each morning and Mike would tell me what emails and letters had come in from fans. Or media requests and so on. And then I'd set about replying on his behalf. Or that's what I was supposed to do. He really wasn't very good at boundaries. So I'd also be sent out on errands for the house or act as his driver. I sort of ended up doing a bit of everything.'

'What do you mean he wasn't very good at boundaries?' Suzie asked, her eyes narrowing. 'He made a move on you?'

'No – nothing of the sort. All I meant was that he was happy to use me as his general dogsbody.'

'That must have been irritating,' Becks said.

'It could be a bit irritating,' Jamilah agreed.

'And how did he work?' Suzie asked.

'Mostly in the mornings. Although I'll be honest, there was a lot of procrastination in there as well. Whenever I took him a cup of tea, he always seemed to be playing some kind of shooting game on his computer.'

'You took him cups of tea?'

'I'm his personal assistant,' Jamilah said. 'It's my job to look after him. Or rather, it was my job.'

'Yes, what happened yesterday?' Judith asked.

'That's what I'm trying to make sense of. I got to work a bit early – maybe quarter past nine – and I saw Mike talking to some guy outside his office. It's a log cabin at the bottom of the garden. Anyway, Mike and the other guy looked like they were arguing or having a disagreement of some sort. And then I saw the person he was talking to look over at me as I approached. He turned tail and strode off into the woods, which was unexpected. It's a massive wood at the bottom of the garden. No roads and no paths to speak of, either. But the man disappeared into it and was long gone by the time I arrived.'

'Can you describe him?'

'Not really, not at that distance. But I'm pretty sure it was a man. In a green raincoat and flat cap. And his face seemed ruddy when he looked over at me. You know – he had red cheeks. Although I could be wrong about that. I only had the briefest glimpse of him.'

'What did Mike say when you reached him?' Becks asked.

'He laughed it off. Said the guy had just been some fan and he'd sent him away with a flea in his ear. But I could tell he was on edge about it. Something about the encounter had upset him.'

Jamilah sighed and crossed the room to sit at a little dining table that had a milk bottle at the centre of it, containing a single plastic sunflower.

'He didn't try to hide his bad mood from me from that moment on,' she said. 'Everything I did was wrong. And to make matters worse, yesterday was when I was supposed to give him feedback on his latest Fraser Steele book. It's something I've been asking to do for months. It's partly why I took this job. Mike told me I could talk to him about his work.

'But yesterday was not the right day to start giving him notes – that much was obvious. I tried to get out of it, but Mike wouldn't let me off the hook. So we went ahead with the notes session and it went wrong from the start. Apparently, I wasn't positive enough before I got into what I felt needed mending. And when I tried to pull out of giving any sort of criticism at all, he insisted I had to tell him everything I thought was wrong.'

'Like what?' Becks asked.

'Like the fact that his hero is a misogynist and I wasn't sure how that would play to a modern readership. And how his representation of the terrorists in the story is basically racist. He doesn't try to explain their motivations. Or show where they're from. They're just these faceless fanatics. That's when he really lost it and started shouting at me.'

Jamilah drifted off into her memory and her eyes filled with tears. Becks went and sat down on the chair opposite her.

'You don't have to do this if you don't want to,' she said.

'No, I need to say this,' Jamilah said.

Suzie went and got a tissue from a box on the windowsill and offered it to Jamilah. She took it and blew her nose.

'The truth is that he scared me,' she said. 'I had no idea where all of his anger was coming from. And then, he announced that if I thought I knew better than him, I should try and make it as a writer on my own. He grabbed me and marched me out of his office and back towards my car. Even though I tried to apologise. He just shoved me into my car and slammed the door shut on me. When I got home, I found bruises on my arms. From where he'd held me.'

'He assaulted you,' Suzie said.

'I was shaking when I got back here,' Jamilah said, not denying it. 'When I saw on Insta just now that he'd died, it hit me like a brick. I couldn't believe it. But I think it maybe explains what happened to me yesterday. Why he was so angry.'

'Sorry,' Becks said, 'I don't follow that.'

'His death is something to do with the guy who visited him in the morning. The man he argued with.'

'Do you really have no idea who he was?'

'I've been trying to think, but I didn't recognise him. I'm sorry. And I'd got to know most of Mike's male friends. It wasn't one of his regular crowd.'

'Then who could have wanted Mike dead?' Becks asked.

'No one.'

'His wife Serena suggested otherwise.'

'That's so like her – seeing the worst in people. I mean, it's true that he didn't mind who he upset. He sort of liked it when he made other people angry. Especially if they were involved in the publishing industry. But it was all pantomime stuff. No one really took him too seriously. He was a cartoon character.'

'Did he know the footballer Gary Wise or his wife Bethany?' Becks asked.

'You think the two deaths are connected?' Jamilah asked. 'He never mentioned either of them to me. And I don't think I remember seeing those names in his emails or contacts, either. Mike hated football and would tell anyone who asked that he thought it was for "proletarians". That was his word, not mine.

'Then what about Harry Asquith?' Becks asked.

'That name doesn't mean anything to me, either. Honestly, I've no idea who could have done this to Mike. No idea at all.'

'Except for you,' Suzie said. 'Because I can't help noticing, yesterday morning he sacked you in a fury and, by the next day, he was dead. Where were you last night?'

'I was here,' Jamilah said in a small voice.

'On your own?'

'No, my boyfriend Viv stayed over. We went to bed at about

midnight and then we didn't get up until the alarm went off at 6.30 a.m. Viv works in Canary Wharf, so he left at about seven.'

Remembering what Serena Saxon had said about hearing a door slam in her house. Judith asked, 'Were you both in the house at about midnight?'

'Of course we were. We were asleep.'

'So your boyfriend can't actually alibi you for that time,' Suzie said.

'You can't possibly be suggesting I had anything to do with this?'

'We're only asking what the police—'

'I liked Mike – believe it or not. That's why it was so upsetting him sacking me yesterday. But I couldn't have ever hurt him, I couldn't hurt anyone.'

'No, of course,' Becks said. 'We understand. And we're so sorry to intrude at this difficult time, you've been a great help.'

Suzie and Judith didn't feel as though the interview had finished, but Becks ushered her friends out before they could disagree with her.

'We were only warming up,' Suzie whispered as they emerged from the house onto the pavement.

'We can't push it,' Becks said. 'We can't risk her complaining to Brendan.'

'This is crackers! We need access to the case and Tanika's no longer able to help us.'

'Well, maybe we can do something about that,' Judith said.

'I don't see how,' Becks said. 'She's been suspended.'

'But that means she's got a lot of free time on her hands.'

'Oh, I see what you mean,' Suzie said in appreciation. 'You think we should recruit her?'

'I think that's exactly what we should do,' Judith said. 'After all, four heads are always going to be better than three. I think it's time Tanika joined our gang.'

Chapter 13

Judith and her friends strode up to Tanika's house and knocked loudly on the door. It was answered by an old man in a cardigan, with tufty white hair and a face lined by a lifetime well lived. He beamed at the sight of them.

'Hello, ladies!' he called out.

'Oh, hello,' Judith said. 'Is Tanika in?'

'You mean my daughter?'

'Yes, we do,' Becks said with a smile. 'How lovely to meet you, Mr Malik.'

'Please – it's Sajid. And who are you?'

Judith introduced herself and her friends and Sajid once again said how happy he was to meet them, but didn't move from the doorway or invite them inside. It began to dawn on Becks what the issue was.

'We're coming in now if that's OK?'

'OK?' Sajid asked. 'Of course it's OK!'

'Dad?' Tanika called from inside the house. 'What are you doing?'

Sajid turned as Tanika joined him.

'Ah, there you are!' he said, delighted to see her.

'Come on, let's get you back inside,' Tanika said, taking her father by his arm and leading him back into the house. 'I told you not to answer the door. Come in!' Tanika called back to her friends as she went through to the kitchen. The women followed her and saw Tanika sit her father down at the head of the pine dining table. In front of him was a wicker basket full of socks, with plenty of others laid out on the table.

'You're matching socks,' Suzie said.

'Here we go,' Tanika said, picking up a black-and-white-striped children's sock and finding its pair in front of her father. As she picked up the two socks, her father took one of them from her.

'Let me find this one,' he said, scanning the table.

'I've already got its pair,' Tanika said, holding up the other sock in her hand.

'Not now,' her father said, his brow furrowing. 'I'm concentrating.'

'It's here,' Tanika said with a smile, although her friends could see the tiredness behind her eyes.

Sajid Malik looked at his daughter and his eyes lit up as he saw the sock in her hand.

'You've got it!' he said, thrilled. 'You always were my best daughter,' he added with a chuckle, taking the sock and matching it to the one in his hand.

'I'm his only daughter,' Tanika said with a smile. 'That's not his dementia, he's always done that joke.'

Judith and her friends had known that Tanika's father had been struggling with his memory for a few years now, but they hadn't known the extent of his decline.

'How's it going?' Becks said.

'We have good days and we have . . . less good days,' Tanika said. 'One of the benefits of being suspended is that I can have him over from his care home more often.'

'Can we ask you a question about the case?' Judith asked.

'The answer's no,' Tanika said.

'You don't know what I'm going to ask you.'

'I do, and the answer's no.'

'But it could be anything!' Suzie said.

'You're going to ask me for help.'

'Actually we weren't,' Suzie said. 'We were going to ask you to join us.'

'I'm sorry?'

'We could really do with an extra person on the team,' Becks said. 'And imagine what you'd be able to bring!'

'I'd love to,' Tanika said. 'In particular, I really want to know whether or not the two murders are linked.'

'So pick up the phone to the station and ask them,' Suzie said.

'And that's what I can never do. Ever. Don't get me wrong, my career's not the most important thing in my life,' Tanika said with a nod at her father. 'But it's one of the most important things. Along with Shanti and Shamil. I'm the main breadwinner, and I can't jeopardise that by doing some freelance investigating on the side. You have to understand.'

'You're slamming the door in our face?' Suzie said, hurt.

'I'm not slamming any door, Suzie. I'm just politely pointing out that it's closed and locked, and I'm not going to try and open it.'

There was such a weariness to Tanika's answer that Suzie, Becks and Judith were briefly at a loss for words.

'There's no match for this sock,' Sajid said as he picked up the black-and-white sock again and started looking for its pair in the basket.

'OK,' Suzie said. 'I know what it's like to be the only bread-winner. I get it. But if you can't help us, then we'll have to catch the killer by ourselves.'

'I'm happy for you,' Tanika said. 'Really, I am. And I'll be honest, I want you out there hunting down whoever did this. It's driving me crazy being sidelined from the investigation. So you go out there and do what you do because you aren't police officers. I've got to stay here and keep my nose clean because I want to remain one.'

'We understand,' Becks said.

'Here,' Tanika said as she got up, 'let me show you out.'

Tanika went to the front door and opened it for the three women.

'If there's anything I can do that doesn't involve breaking any rules – or laws – just let me know. I'll be here and I'll be ready,' she added before closing the door.

'Well, that's no good at all,' Judith said, as they returned to Suzie's van.

'I suppose it was always going to be a bit of a long shot,' Becks said. 'But she was right about finding out if the two murders are linked. Until we know that for sure, I don't know how we can possibly proceed.'

'They're definitely linked,' Suzie pronounced. 'They were both shot dead through the heart.'

'I know that's the most likely explanation, but it would be good to have it confirmed. For example, was the same gun used both times?'

'Let's have a think about how we can best find that out,' Judith said. 'Until then, how about we all go to my house? There's so much we need to learn about Mike Saxon. And what links – if any – he had with Gary Wise.'

As the women got into Suzie's van and Suzie started to drive to Judith's house, Judith and Becks pulled out their phones and started researching Mike Saxon.

'Have either of you read any of his books?' Suzie asked.

Judith and Becks said that they hadn't.

'Well, you're not missing much,' Suzie continued. 'I had a boyfriend who was really into him, but as far as I could tell, they were all the same. It was always about some ex-soldier who'd go somewhere on the other side of the world and sign up to be a mercenary for a corrupt regime or drug lord or whatever. He'd then get drunk a lot, sleep with women a lot and kill a lot.'

'Sounds ghastly,' Judith said.

'They were books for men. And Mike was a man's man, you know? I think there are photos of him hunting lions in Africa.'

'Seriously?' Becks said, typing a search request into her phone.

'Tell us about the times you dog-sat for him,' Judith said to Suzie.

'There's not much to say. I tried to avoid him as much as I could. He was one of those guys you just knew you didn't want to spend any time with. But there was this one time – I remember I was getting Cosmo into the back of my van. He came out to talk to me. And he started banging on about how he could trace Cosmo's family tree back seven generations.'

'He was into pedigree dogs?' Judith asked.

'I got the impression his interest in purity was about more than just dogs.'

'Got it!' Becks said as she held her phone up and showed Judith a photo of Mike Saxon kneeling by a dead lion, dressed in hunting khakis, a rifle over his shoulder. He was grinning broadly.

'That's disgusting,' Judith said. 'And you should know, according to his Wikipedia page, he doesn't limit his violence to defenceless animals. There's a "controversies" section which says he got into a punch-up at the Henley Literary Festival last year.'

'He got into a fight at a literary festival?' Suzie asked, sounding impressed.

'It's what it says here. With an author who he was on a panel with. Mike had apparently been drinking quite heavily, he told the other writer that his books were so bad that he should employ a ghostwriter to write his next one, and it all kicked off. An off-duty police officer was nearby and had to intervene to break up the fight. It says here that Mike was lucky the other author didn't press charges.'

'So why did Jamilah try to tell us that he was just a lovable old rogue?' Suzie asked as she drove her van onto Judith's drive and parked. 'He shoots endangered animals for sport and gets into fist fights at literary festivals.'

'That's a good point,' Becks said. 'At the very least, she was softening his image for us, wasn't she? I wonder why.'

The women got out of the van, approached Judith's front door and went inside. As they entered the sitting room, Judith crossed the room to the window. She'd forgotten to open the curtains that morning. As she swished them open and light flooded the room, Becks let out a scream.

'Oh God, I'm so sorry, Judith!' she said.

'What is it?' Judith said, spinning around to see what was up.

Becks and Suzie were staring at the large gilt mirror that hung on the wall above the fireplace.

Across it, there was a smeared scrawl written in what looked like blood.

ομολογισε

A chill ran down Judith's spine.

'What is it?' Becks asked.

'It's a message.'

'What does it say?' Suzie asked.

'It's Greek,' Judith said. 'It says, "Confess".'

'It's her again, isn't it?' Suzie said, going to stand in between the message and Judith, hoping to block her view of it. 'It wasn't enough to stalk you – she's now broken into your house and is committing criminal damage.'

'How did she even get in here?' Becks asked, to keep them focused on practical issues.

Judith indicated one of the ground-floor windows. It was ajar.

'I left that window open while I was out,' she said.

'In the middle of winter?' Suzie asked, surprised.

'So I don't get a cold.'

'Because that's how colds work?'

'It is, actually.'

'So how do we get this off?' Suzie said, going up to the mirror and looking more closely at the angry mess of red. 'It looks like lipstick to me.'

Judith explained that if it was lipstick then white vinegar mixed with water should be all they needed, and the women were soon using pieces of kitchen towel to wipe the message off. When they were finished and Judith had gone to the kitchen to pour the dirty vinegar mixture away, Suzie pulled Becks to one side.

'She's got to stop this,' she said in what, for once, was a genuine whisper.

'Who? Eleni?' Becks asked.

'Yes, Eleni,' Suzie said darkly. 'No one treats Judith like this. Cold calling her, and now breaking into her house. How dare she?'

'I agree.'

'So, this is what we're going to do. At the first opportunity, you and me, we're going to find her and we're going to warn her off. It's a deal?'

'It's a deal,' Becks said. 'This has to stop.'

Judith's phone rang on the coffee table and Judith returned to the room, announcing to her friends, 'If it's her again, I think I might answer this time. Give her a piece of my mind.'

'You do that,' Suzie said.

'Oh,' Judith said, surprised as she saw the caller display on her phone's screen. 'It's Maidenhead police station.'

She answered the call and put it on speakerphone.

'Hello?' she said.

'Is that you, Mrs Potts? This is DS Perry.'

'Oh, Brendan!' Judith said, pretending to be pleased. 'How can we help you?'

'One of my officers just told me he saw you and your two friends at Gossmore Recreation Ground today while we were processing a crime scene. Would you care to comment?'

Chapter 14

'Gossmore Recreation Ground?' Judith said, pretending to be surprised by the accusation. 'No, I've not been there for weeks.'

'Nor have I,' said Becks, before realising she maybe should have kept quiet.

'Oh, you're all together, are you?' Brendan asked.

'Not a bit of it,' Suzie said, before clapping her hands over her mouth and grimacing.

'Because you need to know, I won't tolerate the three of you getting in the way of the investigation like DI Malik did.'

'How interesting,' Judith said. 'You're saying it's "investigation" singular, rather than "investigations" plural.'

'What are you talking about?'

'The same gun was used for both murders, wasn't it?'

'How do you know that?'

'So it *was* the same gun!'

'I didn't say that.'

'I think that's very much what you just said. I told you we'd find out the truth soon enough,' Judith said to her friends.

'You're putting words into my mouth.'

'And you're so new in your detecting career, I'm sure you wouldn't want it getting out that you've just revealed such a key piece of information to mere civilians.'

'Are you trying to blackmail me?'

'Absolutely not. But just to confirm, to stop us talking to other people – like the *Marlow Free Press* for example – the same gun was used for both murders?'

A pause developed in which the women could imagine how Brendan's fury was chasing his desire not to get into trouble.

'It was the same gun,' he eventually huffed. 'But you can't tell anyone I told you that.'

With that, he ended the call.

'Oh dear,' Judith said, unable to keep the laugh out of her voice. 'He's not exactly the sharpest knife in the drawer, is he?'

'But you know what this means?' Becks said, as she went over to the wall of photographs and picked up some drawing pins. She put a pin in the middle of the photo of Gary Wise, and a second pin in the middle of the photo of Mike Saxon. Then she picked up the ball of red wool that sat on Judith's desk, wrapped the loose end around the pin in the centre of Gary's photo and then ran the wool over to the pin that she'd just placed in the centre of the photo of Mike.

'If it was the same gun, then it's like you said, Judith. The two deaths are linked.'

With that, Becks snipped the wool with some scissors to release the ball.

'Although it doesn't necessarily mean it was the same person behind each shooting,' Suzie said, remembering the first murder case they'd solved together.

'But it seems like a good place to start,' Becks said.

'Agreed,' Judith said.

'So what links a footballer with a famous novelist?' Suzie asked. 'Why did they both have to die?'

'I've got a theory about that,' Judith said. 'After all, it seems that Gary Wise was killed in connection with whatever it was he was being blackmailed over.'

'His text messages suggest it's the most likely explanation,' Suzie agreed.

'So, if we're trying to be logical, now we know that Mike was killed by the same gun, then perhaps he was also killed by the same person.'

'You think the person who was blackmailing Gary was also blackmailing Mike?' Becks asked.

'I don't know. But it might explain the link between the two men.'

There was a sharp rat-a-tat-tat at the door and the women looked as one in the direction of the hallway.

'Not again,' Becks said.

'This is harassment!' Suzie said.

'But that's very much her game,' Judith said, as she went over to a bookcase and started to look through her books.

The knocking started up again from the front door.

'Aren't you going to answer?' Becks asked.

'Oh, I'm going to answer all right, but I'm going to do this first,' Judith replied, pulling down two paperbacks. 'I'd like to give you a couple of books.'

'What?' Suzie asked.

'I'd like you to read them,' Judith said, handing a book to each of her friends.

Suzie's was called *How to Solve Cryptic Crosswords* and Becks's was called *Breaking the Cryptic Code.*

'Why are you doing this?' Becks asked.

'The pair of you need to learn how to do crosswords properly.'

'Why?' Becks asked.

'Just promise me you'll keep these books to hand,' Judith said.

The knocking at door started up again.

'I don't see this replacing my bedtime reading,' Suzie said as Judith left the room. Suzie and Becks followed, still holding their books. At the front door, Judith put her hand on the doorknob and then paused.

'Good luck,' Becks said quietly.

Judith looked at her friend.

'I'm not the one who's going to need good luck.'

Judith threw the door open, but was surprised to see that it wasn't Eleni standing outside. Instead, it was a woman in her sixties with a wild mane of frizzy grey hair that was barely contained by a maroon velvet cap. She was wearing bright red lipstick, heavy fake eyelashes, blue eyeshadow, bright orange dungarees, black DM boots and had finished the whole ensemble off with a purple woollen cape with gold brocade woven into it. She looked as though she'd got dressed in a hurry from a theatrical costume store, having first blindfolded herself, Judith thought.

The woman grabbed Judith by the shoulders.

'Hello, Judith!' she said in a breathy rush.

'Who are you?' Suzie asked.

'You don't know who I am?' the woman said, amused rather than offended.

'You're Angela Gulliver, aren't you?' Becks said. 'The TV presenter.'

'I am,' she replied. 'I'm glad at least one of you recognises me.'

'Not that I watch daytime TV,' Becks said. 'Or rather, I try not to. Sorry, that's not very polite, is it?'

'What on earth are the pair of you banging on about?' Suzie asked.

'My name's Angela Gulliver,' the woman said. 'Many moons ago, I was an agony aunt, but I now have a mid-morning chat show on Channel 5. It's a mixture of therapy and conflict resolution, with a twist of devilish humour.'

'Well, that's lovely,' Judith said, 'but what on earth are you doing at my house?'

'I happen to know that you're the people who catch killers,' Angela said. 'And you're helping the police with the Gary Wise and Mike Saxon murders.'

'It's actually a bit more complicated—' Becks said before Suzie talked over her.

'Yes, we are,' she said. 'But why does it matter? What's your connection to the case?'

'That's the thing,' Angela said, her hand going to her throat as she considered the horror of her situation. 'You see, I think I'm going to be the next victim.'

Chapter 15

Angela looked at Judith and her friends, knowing the impact of her words.

'What on earth makes you say that?' Judith asked.

'May I come in?' Angela replied, ignoring Judith's question.

The very last thing Judith wanted to do was let a complete stranger into her house.

'Of course,' Suzie said, stepping to one side.

Judith glared at her friend as she was forced to follow Angela inside.

'Wow!' Angela exclaimed, walking into Judith's sitting room and taking in the grand piano, antiques, oil paintings and view of the river Thames beyond.

'And why do you think the killer could be after you next?' Becks asked, picking up on Judith's irritation.

'Oh, this is wonderful!' Angela said, as she went over to the wall where Judith and her friends had pinned up the photos of the various witnesses and victims.

'You're just like the police!' she exclaimed, twanging the red wool that connected the two victims.

'Could you leave that alone?' Judith said.

'You see, I was right!' Angela turned back to face the women.

'Right about what?' Suzie asked.

'I can see you've got red wool that goes between the two victims. They're linked, aren't they? This is simply terrible news!'

'You're not wrong there – especially if you're Gary Wise or Mike Saxon. But what's it got to do with you?'

'Don't you see? Whoever this killer is – this sick and deranged individual – he's going around killing the celebrities of Marlow one by one. Isn't he?'

'Which is why you think he's coming for you,' Becks said, understanding coming to her.

'How many celebrities do you think there are in Marlow?'

'I've never really counted,' Suzie said.

Judith tried to make sense of Angela. On the one hand, she was speaking and behaving as though she was terrified by the threat to her life, and yet she was also clearly having a wonderful time being the centre of attention.

'As far as I can see, Gary Wise was the most famous person here. An ex-England footballer – you don't get much bigger than that. And then I think it's fair to say that Mike Saxon was next. His name is known the world over – he's an international bestseller.'

'You really think the killer's working through a list?' Judith asked.

'I do! So I'm here to tell you that I'll do whatever I can to help you. I can explain to you what life is like as a celebrity in Marlow.'

'You think you lead a different life to the rest of us?' Suzie said.

'We don't want to, but it can't be helped. I mean, I can hardly get on a bus to go to the shops, can I? I'd be mobbed.'

'That's very interesting,' Becks said, recognising that her two friends were on the verge of losing their tempers, 'but we really don't need any help.'

'Is that honestly why you're here?' Judith asked.

'I'm worried for my life!' Angela said, putting her hand to her chest once more. Judith thought that if she'd been wearing pearls, she'd have clutched them.

'Did you know Gary Wise?' she asked.

'Why are you talking to me like I'm a suspect?'

'Did you know him?' Judith repeated.

'As it happens, I didn't. Although I met him a few times at social events. At the Marlow Regatta a few years ago, we were both guests of the vice chair, Sarah Campbell. And we've attended a couple of charity events as well.'

'So you did know him, in fact?' Becks asked.

'Hardly! And he was a nice enough man I suppose, but we didn't have anything in common. I don't know the first thing about football. If anything, I knew his wife better. When Gary was out and about at these events, he was surrounded by fans. Bethany and I would end up downing the white wine off to one side.'

'You were friends with his wife?' Judith said, picking up a notebook and pen and jotting down a few notes.

'I'd say more friendly than friends.'

'And what can you tell us about Mike Saxon?'

'Are you really doing this?'

'Could you answer my question?'

'Well, I think I met him only once, and he was a pig.'

'I see you don't mind speaking ill of the dead,' Suzie said in appreciation.

'I wouldn't have got anywhere in my career if I wasn't direct,' Angela said with a smile. 'And he was a nasty piece of work.'

'How did you come to that conclusion?'

'We met at an author event in London. We share the same publisher.'

'You write books?'

'Perhaps you've read my autobiography?' Angela asked. When the women didn't respond, she barrelled on to list the numerous self-help books she'd written and then explained exactly how long each one had spent on the *Sunday Times* bestseller lists.

'What happened when you met Mike?' Becks asked to stop the litany of self-congratulation.

'If you must know, he made a move on me. It was our publisher's summer party last year. They hire out the Natural History Museum and it's a massive shindig. Lots of lovely authors to talk to. Lots of champagne to drink. I was admiring the skeleton of the blue whale in the main hall when I felt a hand brush my bottom and found Mike Saxon standing next to me. I think his opening line to me was, "What are you doing later?". I was so surprised that I didn't immediately do anything, when what I should have done was throw my champagne straight in his face. Instead, I asked him what on earth he meant and that's when he came out with it. He was staying in a suite at the Ritz that night, he thought I looked "game" and did I want "a tumble" with him? I was still on the back foot – it's how men like that operate, isn't it? – so I don't quite remember what I said, but it was something along the lines of asking what on earth made him think I'd want to sleep with him. And he just laughed. Can you believe it? He laughed and said I wasn't to take offence, he was just working on the ten per cent rule.'

'What's that?' Becks asked.

'I asked the same question and I wish I hadn't. He said that if he asked ten women to sleep with him, then one would say yes – the ten per cent rule.'

'He honestly said that to you?' Suzie asked.

'He did! And he really wasn't bothered in the slightest when I told him I wasn't going to be one of his ten per cent. In fact, he looked so smug that I'm sorry to say I laid into him a bit. I said I was sure that being made love to by him would be like being jumped on by an old and very ugly toad.'

'Good for you,' Becks said.

'That finally got under his skin – which was the effect I was going for. And he said something like, if he was so ugly, how come he always had "a woman on the go". And he really leaned in to me to tell me this. I could smell his terrible breath. It was repulsive. So I just turned and walked away from him. He ruined my evening, if you must know, and I left soon after.'

'He said he always had a woman on the go?' Judith asked.

'Can you believe it? The arrogance!'

'It is horrible,' Becks agreed. 'But if he was having affairs, that could give his wife a motive to kill him.'

'Or maybe he was killed by one of the girlfriends he'd discarded,' Suzie offered.

'But I don't think his death has got anything to do with his girlfriends,' Angela said. 'Mike was killed because he was famous. Plain and simple. There's someone out there who's got a grudge against famous people. And I'd like to join your team and help you catch whoever that person is.'

'I'll have to stop you there,' Judith said. 'Before we go any further, are you being blackmailed?'

'Me?' Angela said in surprise, but the women could see that the question had rattled her. 'What on earth makes you ask that?'

'It's simple enough,' Suzie said, not wanting to let Angela off the hook. 'Is someone blackmailing you?'

'It's really very horrible that you're treating me like a suspect,' she said in a rush. 'I'm just here because I want to help you stop the killer before he strikes again. His next victim could be me!'

'No, we're good,' Suzie said. 'We don't need help. We're like the musketeers. There are only three of us.'

'There were four musketeers,' Becks said.

'*What*?'

'D'Artagnan was the fourth musketeer.'

'You mention that now?'

'No – you're right. Sorry.'

'Either way,' Judith said. 'We've got a job to do. Would you mind leaving?'

Despite her protests, Judith and her friends managed to bundle Angela out of the house.

'"There were four musketeers"?' Suzie said to Becks once they were on their own again.

'I'm sorry,' Becks said. 'It came out before I could stop myself.'

'None of that matters now,' Judith said, 'because we've got a bigger question. Why did Angela Gulliver just turn up at my house?'

'You don't think she could be the killer, do you?' Becks asked.

'I don't know. It doesn't feel very likely, does it? But she definitely got flustered when we mentioned blackmail to her.

I think we need to find a photo of her online and pin her picture to the incident board, don't you?'

'Do we have to?' Suzie said. 'It's been quite a long day already.'

Judith looked at the clock on the mantelpiece and saw that it had just gone 7 p.m.

'But Angela arriving like that has thrown the cat among the pigeons as far as I can see,' Judith said. 'We've got research to do.'

'Actually, I could do with getting back to the vicarage,' Becks said. 'Chloe's got a Zoom call with her tutor in half an hour. It would be good if I could be there for it.'

Only a few weeks before, Becks's daughter had dropped out of university to go travelling with her boyfriend, but had then discovered, when he skipped the country with all of their money, that he'd had very different – and borderline criminal – plans.

'Then let me give you a lift back into Marlow,' Suzie said.

'You're really both going?' Judith asked.

'We do have lives to lead.'

'Then at least don't forget your crossword books,' Judith said, picking up the two books and giving them to her friends.

'Right,' Suzie said, taking her book from Judith as though it might explode. 'Thanks.'

Once her friends had left, Judith threw herself into investigating the case. She printed out a photo of Angela Gulliver that she found online and pinned it to the incident board on the wall. She then tried to find connections between Angela and the two victims. But the truth was, she knew that she was only play-acting someone who was investigating a murder. Put simply, her heart wasn't in it. And that was because her heart was upstairs, and had been ever since she'd shown the photograph of herself and

Philippos to her two friends. When she realised she'd drifted off into her memories again, Judith knew she couldn't put it off any longer.

She was going to have to open the suitcase in the box room.

Chapter 16

Judith poured herself a glass of scotch, drank it down in one, put her glass down and then went upstairs, gripping tightly to the banister for support. Crossing the galleried landing, she approached a white-painted door and opened it. Stepping through, she found herself in the old servants' quarters – an area of the house that she didn't go into from one year to the next. There was a tiny bedroom to one side that had dusty floorboards and peeling wallpaper, and a bathroom on the other side with a yellow-stained porcelain sink and small hip bath. Judith passed the narrow back staircase that led down to the room where she'd previously kept her secret archive of newspapers and stopped in front of a little door. The door wasn't much more than a hinged hatch in the wall and it only reached up to her chest.

There was a little clasp that should have had a padlock on it. She was puzzled to see that the hasp had been broken off and the padlock was lying on the floor, still locked. But she remembered that the last time she'd been up here, she'd been very drunk. In fact, she wasn't sure she'd ever gone into the room in daylight hours before, let alone sober.

She took a deep breath, bent over, pushed the door open and entered the room. The smell of dust filled Judith's nostrils as she reached for the Bakelite light switch to the side of the hatch and clicked it on. A single lightbulb on a twisted brown cord lit up with obscene brightness. There were shelves down each side and bare bricks at the end. The shelves contained a few used paint pots and rolls of unused wallpaper, but were otherwise empty. A small, leather suitcase sat on the floorboards by the far wall. Judith went over to it, picked it up and returned to the door. Ducking her head, she left the box room, closed the door behind herself and then returned to the warmth of the landing, trying to resist the feeling that spiders had got down the neck of her top and were now crawling over her skin.

She'd never brought the suitcase out of the box room before. Where should she take it?

She went into her bedroom, pulled the satin eiderdown up from where it had piled on the floor and smoothed it down over the duvet. Yes, she thought, that would do for a table very well. She put the suitcase down and clicked the two brass hasps open. She then lifted the lid and looked inside.

It was stuffed full of old photos — all loose, or in faded envelopes, and mixed among them were strips of orange negatives.

It was Judith's past. Her whole life.

From her childhood on the Isle of Wight through to Oxford University. Judith with her family and friends. Judith with her Great-aunt Betty. But the bulk of the photos were of her and Philippos. First in Marlow, where they'd met at the Bourne End Sailing Club. And then the many hundreds of photos from the eighteen months she'd spent as a married woman on Corfu. And it was those photos that were the reason why the suitcase had to be hidden away. She couldn't bear seeing how beautiful she'd been – how her tanned skin glowed in the sunshine – and yet remember the pain she was hiding in every single shot. Her desperation, that she could now see with the distance and wisdom of time, to appear happy. To show her great-aunt and the wider world that she'd made the right choice.

Just looking at the photos made her feel sick with grief.

But she knew she had a job to do. There was one particular photo she was looking for. Or, if her theory was correct, there'd actually be two photographs that she needed to find. In among the hundreds – maybe thousands – of others.

Judith picked up the nearest photo. It showed a group of perhaps two dozen people sitting under an awning in the vil- lage square where Philippos's family lived. She could see that Philippos's mother was offering a plate of sardines to a young boy who was sitting to her side, but nearly everyone else in the photo was looking at the camera. Philippos was at the far end of the table. His head was turned to look at a beautiful woman to his side. Even from the distance of decades, Judith recognised the woman instantly. She was Eleni's mother, Michaela.

It had always been obvious what was going on, if only she'd known to look.

Judith put the photograph to one side. She still had all the others to work through, and she settled herself on the bed. She wouldn't stop until she'd found what she was looking for.

The only problem was, she couldn't find it. Even though she made sure she inspected every single photograph in the case. She was careful. Methodical, even. All of the things she hated being when it came to completing mundane tasks. But she knew she was involved in an endeavour that was life and death to her, and she couldn't risk cutting any corners.

As the minutes turned into hours, it was with an increasing sense of dread that she came to realise that she wasn't going to be able to find the two photos she was looking for. The irony was, she didn't even know if she'd ever seen them before. But she knew she'd recognise them if she found them now.

Once she'd removed every single photograph from the case, she took a few moments to try to control her anxiety. It had been ratcheting up as the hours had passed. If she were being logical, the fact that she couldn't find two photos she didn't even know existed didn't necessarily mean what she feared it meant. But there was possibly a way of proving it. As she'd sorted through all of the photos, she'd also been making a pile of all of the loose negatives for the photos: little slips of dark orange plastic, their perforated edges showing how much they belonged in a bygone age.

Judith picked up her bedside lamp, placed it on the flat surface of the suitcase and removed the frilly green shade. The bare bulb was an assault on her eyes, but she knew she'd need a strong light source for her next task.

She picked up the first strip. Holding it up to the light and peering carefully, she was just able to see that all of the six negatives were of her and her friends in a formal hall at Somerville College. She put the strip down, reached back into the pile, picked up the next piece of celluloid and, as she did so, made herself a promise. She wouldn't stop until she'd found what she was looking for. Or not found it. Which was what worried her far more.

★

The following morning, as soon as it was light enough to see, Judith strode through the wet grass of her garden wearing only a floppy hat, a silk dressing gown and an old pair of wellington boots. She entered her boathouse, kicked off her wellies, slipped out of her dressing gown and put it and her hat on a hook. She then walked down the slipway and entered the freezing water of the Thames until it was up to her shoulders. She grabbed her nose with her finger and thumb and plunged herself down into the water, completely submerging herself.

As the current tugged at her hair, Judith told herself that she was no longer the fox who knew many things from the ancient poem by Archilochus. From now on, she was going to be the hedgehog, who knew only one big thing. And, as she kept her eyes scrunched shut against the ice-cold water, she knew that the one big thing she'd learned the previous night was that she was now in mortal danger.

Judith's head burst through the surface and she let out a roar of freezing breath as she shook the river out of her hair.

Whatever Eleni threw at her, she'd be equal to it.

No one got the better of Judith Potts.

Chapter 17

While Judith was having her baptism in the Thames, Becks was busy in the vicarage. Following her Zoom call with her tutor the night before, Chloe had decided to head back to Exeter Uni and was upstairs packing a bag. Becks could hear her daughter singing, which was always a sign that she was happy. As for her husband, the Reverend Colin Starling, he was away on the last day of a retreat, but he'd just emailed to say that he had some dry cleaning that he needed picking up from the High Street. Becks decided that it would wait. First, she and Suzie had a job to do.

As the grandfather clock in the hallway chimed for nine o'clock, Becks removed her apron and hung it up.

It was time to go into battle.

Suzie was already waiting outside the Tollgate Hotel as Becks crossed the little green opposite the vicarage to join her.

'You look as though you're ready to commit murder,' Becks said, arriving at her friend's side.

'Uh-huh,' Suzie said in a way that suggested that murder was very much one of the options on the table.

'So, what's the plan?'

'We march into the hotel, demand to see Eleni and then we put the fear of God into her. What do you reckon?'

'Good idea, but can I ask you about those crossword books Judith gave us yesterday? It felt like she had some kind of ulterior motive, but I can't even begin to work out what it was.'

'There's no time for that now,' Suzie said, nodding at the entrance of the hotel as Eleni Paphides stepped out of it.

Together, the women watched as Eleni started to walk along the pavement. Suzie and Becks followed the younger woman, but were surprised when they saw her heading towards All Saints' church. They were even more surprised when she went inside. They followed after her and, once they'd entered, took a few seconds to work out where she'd got to.

Eleni was standing to the side of the altar, lighting a candle.

Becks and Suzie walked down the central aisle, their footsteps echoing in the silence. As they approached the altar, Becks struggled to shake the feeling that she was in the last scene of a gangster movie, and that she was one of the baddies.

Eleni's head was bowed as they arrived.

Suzie looked at her friend and shrugged. *What are we supposed to do now?*

Becks stepped forward, picked up a candle, lit it from a spill and put it on the rack.

'For my grandma,' she said to Eleni.

'My father,' Eleni said without looking up.

'You're Judith's stepdaughter,' Suzie said, deciding that she couldn't rely on Becks to stamp her authority on the conversation.

Eleni took a step back to look at Suzie and Becks properly.

'I'm her husband's daughter, yes,' she said. 'What do you want with me?'

'We just want a quiet word,' Becks said.

'If she wants a quiet word,' Suzie said, not letting Eleni reply, 'I want a louder one. You're to stop tormenting Judith.'

'You don't get to speak to me like that,' Eleni said.

'And you don't get to break into someone's house and write threats on their mirror. That's criminal damage.'

'How do you know that was me?'

'How many people do you think would write warnings to Judith in Greek?'

'I don't know,' Eleni said, unconcerned. 'I've met the woman. Possibly many.'

'We could report you to the police.'

'You wouldn't dare. Because the moment you do . . .?'

'Yes, this is very much why we wanted to speak to you,' Becks said. 'You see, you've claimed that you have evidence against Judith.'

'She killed my father.'

'You don't know that.'

'Have you any idea what that's like? Growing up without a father in my life? Seeing my friends with theirs, seeing what they meant to them. I've not had any of that. None of it!'

'I'm sorry—'

'I don't want your pity!' Eleni spat at the women. 'I want my father back! But I can't have him, because of her!'

'She didn't kill him,' Becks said.

'Can she prove that?'

'How can you prove you *haven't* done something?'

'And talking about proof,' Suzie said, 'I don't think you have any. Not *real* proof.'

'I'm sorry?'

'That's why you're phoning Judith and then breaking into her house and threatening her. Because you don't have anything concrete.'

'You dare question me?'

'If you've got any real evidence, then go to the police.'

'Suzie!' Becks yelped.

'No, I'm fed up with it. We've got Cruella de Vil here stalking about the place causing *so* much aggro. If she has evidence, she should take it to the police.'

'Very well, I will!' Eleni said.

'Then get on with it!'

'Don't you worry about that. The next time you see me, it will be too late for her.'

'Yeah – whatever,' Suzie said. 'I'll believe it when I see it.'

Eleni turned on her heels and strode out of the church, her head held high. As she went, the sun came out and she was suddenly bathed in light. It looked to Becks as though the young woman's exit was receiving the seal of approval from a higher authority.

'"Get on with it"?' she asked Suzie, once the large wooden doors to the church had closed. 'We were supposed to warn her off, not spur her on!'

'I know!' Suzie said by way of apology. 'And that was my plan, I promise you. But she irritated me with her attitude. How can she be all high and mighty when she's the one going around breaking into houses and smearing lipstick all over the place? And think about it. If she's prepared to break into Judith's house, what could she do next? No, I say it's time to cut to the chase. Whatever evidence she's got, she needs to take it to the police. We need to move this onto the next stage.'

Becks considered her friend's words and realised that there was a warped logic to what she was saying. But the strategy relied on Judith being innocent – meaning Eleni couldn't have any significant evidence against her – and that was a gamble that Becks wasn't sure they should be making.

'OK,' she said carefully, 'I think you're right. But considering how you've just lit the touchpaper on what could turn out to be a very large keg of gunpowder, I think we need to get back to Judith.'

When they arrived at Judith's house, they heard her call out 'Good morning!' to them as they entered her sitting room, and then they stopped in shock on the threshold.

Judith had a Hoover in her hand.

'You own a Hoover?' Becks asked.

'Just having a bit of a tidy-up,' Judith announced, as though it were the most natural thing in the world. 'I've also found a bit of time to look into Angela Gulliver's life, and I couldn't find any suggestion that she was up to anything criminal. Or had any links to either of our victims. About the only thing I discovered was a small diary piece in the London *Evening Standard*. It said that the viewing figures for her TV show have recently fallen off a cliff. Apparently the whole show's at risk of being cancelled.'

'Forget that,' Becks said, interrupting her friend. 'You're tidying up?'

'I am,' Judith said proudly.

'Then can we join in?' Becks said as she moved towards a slew of old *Marlovian* magazines that were in a pile on the windowsill. 'For example, we could start by chucking all of these out.'

'Don't throw them away, they may be useful!' Judith said. 'But you're welcome to tidy them up a bit.'

Becks realised that the deal she was being offered was one she was prepared to accept. She started to re-stack the magazines.

'This is how you're responding to Eleni,' Suzie said in appreciation. 'You're getting your house in order.'

'I thought I'd have a quick tidy-up until the pair of you got here,' Judith said. 'Because I've been thinking about what Angela told us, and there's someone we need to talk to.'

'How about we continue tidying for another half an hour?' Becks said more in hope than expectation. 'And *then* we can go?'

'Stuff that,' Suzie said. 'Let's do it right now. Who do we need to talk to?'

★

As she rushed down the stairs, opened her front door and left her house, Jamilah Khalil knew she only had a few minutes to catch the train to London. But after locking the door behind herself, she saw three women approaching along the pavement. She slipped her keys into her handbag as fast as she could and tried to get to the pavement before them, but the biggest of the women pulled the gate closed and then held it in place so she couldn't open it.

'What are you doing?' Jamilah asked, checking her watch.

Suzie, Becks and Judith could see that Jamilah was dressed smartly, as though she were going to an office job.

'Mike Saxon made a pass at you,' Judith said.

'What are you talking about?'

'We've learned that Mike had wandering hands, and I'm afraid I don't believe for a second that he didn't try it on with someone as pretty as you.'

'Are you really doing this here?'

'Are you needed elsewhere?' Suzie asked.

'As it happens, I've got a job interview. In London. I need to catch the train.'

'Then the quicker you answer our questions, the quicker you can go,' Suzie said with a smile.

'OK, you're right,' Jamilah said. 'When I started working for Mike, he "made a pass at me", as you say.'

'What happened?' Becks asked.

'Nothing. He didn't even try that hard. He said he had a deal with a local hotel, and did I want to go to it with him? I just said that I knew he must be joking because what he was suggesting could land him in court. He wasn't even that bothered when I brushed him off.'

'It's his ten per cent rule,' Suzie said.

'I don't know about that, but he went back to being a normal boss after that – or as normal as he could be. He was still difficult. And a bit of a bully, but at least there were no more sexual overtures.'

'Why didn't you tell us this when we spoke to you last time?' Becks asked.

'It hardly seemed relevant.'

'But we specifically asked you if he'd ever tried it on with you and you said no.'

'Look, I've answered your question, I've got to get to London.'

'We're not done just yet,' Judith said. 'Because even if you rebuffed him, that wasn't true of every woman, was it?'

'I need to catch my train.'

'And we need to know about his other women,' Suzie said.

Jamilah looked to Becks for support, but Becks just shrugged.

'It's true,' she said. 'There were other women, weren't there?'

'All right,' Jamilah said. 'I'll do this as quickly as I can. But I don't know any of their names. Or who they are. I don't know anything about them.'

'But there's more than one?' Suzie asked.

'Mike belonged to a real tennis club in Holyport.'

'A *real* tennis club?' Suzie said. 'What even is that?'

'He explained it to me once,' Jamilah said. 'It's like normal tennis but you play it indoors on a funny-shaped court. Anyway, Mike would get me to book him games every now and again. But there were other times he went and I knew he didn't have a game lined up. He'd get his sports bag, racket and spare phone and tell Serena he was off for a game, and then he'd disappear for a few hours. Once, after he came back, I asked him what was going on and he winked at me and said there was more than one type of sport you could play in Holyport. Which cleared up another mystery for me, because I had to pay various invoices for Mike as well, and he kept getting bills for hundreds of pounds from the Holyport Hotel.'

'Oh, I see!' Suzie said. 'So he'd go to his tennis club, get changed into new clothes, go and see his fancy woman across the road in a hotel room and get her lipstick all over his collar.'

'Before going back to the club, having a shower and getting back into the clothes he'd arrived in,' Jamilah said in agreement.

'That's kind of smart,' Suzie said. 'Not that I approve, of course.'

'Did you say he had a spare phone?' Judith asked.

'It's the one he used for his women,' Jamilah said with a shudder. 'He kept it in his sports bag.'

'He had a *second* phone?' Suzie said, stunned. 'Do the police know about it?'

'I've no idea. I've not told them about it. They didn't ask.'

'Do you know where it is?' Judith asked.

'It's probably in his sports bag. He normally keeps it in his office, but it wasn't there the last time I was there. It must be in his locker at the club.'

'Do you know how to get into his locker?'

'I've no idea. I think he had a key for it on his keyring.'

'Do you know where his keys are?'

'I guess Serena has them. Or the police.'

'Then you've been very helpful, thank you for your time,' Judith said, nodding to Suzie to let go of the gate.

Suzie lifted her hand and Jamilah pulled the gate open and rushed past the women on her way to the train station.

'He had a burner phone,' Becks said as she watched the younger woman go.

'And if he used it for his women,' Judith said. 'I wonder what else he used it for?'

'What do you mean?' Becks asked.

'Gary's blackmailer contacted him by phone.'

'Oh I get it!' Suzie exclaimed. 'What if the proof that Mike was also being blackmailed is on his secret phone?'

'It would make sense,' Judith said. 'Seeing as he's already using it for his secret affairs.'

'We need to tell the police about it,' Becks said. 'At once.'

Judith and Suzie looked at their friend in disappointment.

'I mean, obviously we've got to tell them,' Becks said before she realised the truth of the situation. 'We're not going to tell them, are we?'

'Do you really think Brendan's capable of catching the killer?' Suzie asked.

Becks knew her answer to that question.

'So what do you think we should do?' she asked.

'Simple,' Suzie replied. 'We should break into the real tennis club, get hold of the master key to the lockers, slip into the men's changing room without anyone seeing us, get into Mike's locker and recover his phone for ourselves. And, once we've had a good look at it, *then* we can hand it in to the police.'

Becks's heart sank. The idea was so preposterous – so inherently foolish – that she knew Judith would only have one response.

'I love it!' Judith said with glee.

Chapter 18

It was only a fifteen-minute drive to Holyport village and when the women arrived, Suzie slowed her van to a stop outside the Holyport Hotel. It had originally been a row of white stucco Georgian houses that had since been knocked through and converted into a small hotel. But the three friends could see that the paint on the walls was peeling, and there was a brownish-green stain under the eaves where a gutter had broken.

'So this is where Mike took his women,' Suzie said with a grimace. 'Classy.'

'Where's his real tennis club?' Becks asked.

'It's just behind here,' Suzie said, checking her satnav. 'But can I ask, what even is real tennis?'

'I think it was originally French,' Judith said. 'Which is why it's called "real" – it's the French word for royal. It became popular in medieval times.'

'It's that old?' Suzie said, impressed.

'I'm sure Becks will find out during her lesson.'

'You really think this will work?' Becks asked.

'No idea,' Suzie said breezily. 'But you've got the easiest part, so stop complaining. Come on,' she added as she drove off again.

Her van was soon bouncing down a pot-holed driveway that opened out into a large grassy area leading to the enormous red-brick building of the Holyport Real Tennis Club. With its row of vertical windows and gabled lead roof, it had the look of a nineteenth-century chapel.

'OK, it's impressive,' Suzie conceded as she parked her van next to a brand-new MG car.

As the women got out, Suzie and Judith stopped to admire Becks.

'Wow,' Suzie said in appreciation.

Becks was wearing white trainers and socks, her shortest tennis skirt and tightest white top.

'Is it too much?' Becks asked.

'You know what men are like. Too much never is too much.'

'You look sensational,' Judith said. 'Lead on!'

Becks squared her shoulders and headed as confidently as she could for the club's entrance.

'Still got it, girl,' Suzie said as they fell in behind her. 'Mind you,' she added in a stage whisper, 'she looks like that poster from the seventies of the woman who's not wearing any knickers.'

'I heard that,' Becks said, but Judith and Suzie could only smile at their friend's self-confidence; it was wonderful to see.

As they approached the building, the door opened and a man came out wearing cream flannel trousers and cricket shirt. He was holding a canvas sports bag in his hand.

It was Harry Asquith.

'Oh,' he said, his eyes widening as he saw Becks in her tennis outfit, before he noticed that Judith and Suzie with her.

'Harry!' Becks said in lieu of knowing what else to say. 'How lovely to see you. Are you a member here?'

'As it happens, I am,' he replied.

'So you knew Mike Saxon?' Judith asked sweetly, and Harry went very still.

'What's that?'

'He's also a member here, isn't he? Or rather *was*. I suppose you've heard the terrible news.'

'I saw it in the papers. Why are you asking?'

'No reason at all. But it's interesting, isn't it? We've struggled to find anyone who knew Gary Wise and Mike Saxon, and here you are – you knew both men. What was Mike like?'

'Mike?' Harry said, recovering. 'I hardly knew him, if you must know. But whenever I met him, he seemed nice enough. You know, friendly and up for a bit of a chat. Now if you'll excuse me, I need to get to my car.'

'Hold on,' Judith said, grabbing Harry by the arm.

'What are you doing?' he asked.

'Are you saying that that's your car next to Suzie's van?'

'It is,' Harry said, a note of pride in his voice.

'But the first time we met you, you were driving an old estate car. And now, only a few short days later, you've got a brand-new MG.'

'That's none of your business,' Harry said, yanking his arm out of Judith's hand.

'But it is. You see, DS Malik told us that you're up to your ears in debt. You even have to use the cash you take out on one credit card to pay off debts on others. So where did you get this new car from?'

Harry took a few moments before he answered.

'As it happens,' he said, 'I've just signed a contract to write a new book. There was a significant advance, and I've treated myself to a new car. OK?'

'That's quick work,' Suzie said.

'I had to move fast, because you're right, I've had a few money problems over the years.'

'Why?' Becks asked.

'If you must know, I've always had a weakness for the gee-gees.'

'Me too,' Suzie said. 'Although their teeth always make me laugh.'

Harry was thrown by this comment, but so were Judith and Becks.

'I've always loved their hair,' Suzie continued. 'You just want to stroke it.'

'If you say so,' Harry said.

'And I love their harmonies.'

'I'm sorry?'

'I said, I love their harmonies.'

'Horses don't sing.'

'What are you talking about?'

'Horse racing. What are you talking about?'

'The Bee Gees.'

No one spoke for a few seconds, and then Becks snorted a laugh.

'Harry said gee-gees,' she said.

'Oh, I see!' Suzie said, entirely unconcerned. 'Sorry, I wasn't listening properly.'

'And you want to stroke the Bee Gees's hair?' Becks asked her friend.

'Can we get back to Harry's gambling?' Judith said, in a desperate attempt to get the conversation back on track.

'Gambling's not the right term,' Harry said, correcting Judith. 'Not the way I do it. I do proper research.'

'Well, as far as I can see, whether or not you're doing your research properly, you don't win.'

'I'm just on a bad run. That's all. The weather's been too wet – the going too soft. Next season, I'll turn things around. You watch me. Now, if you don't mind, ladies, I need to get back to work.'

With a nod at the women, Harry strode off to his MG and got in.

'How interesting,' Judith said. 'He's a gambler.'

'A gambler who's massively in debt,' Becks said.

'And knew both victims,' Suzie said as the MG engine roared into life.

Harry drove away at speed, gravel flying from his wheels.

'Could he be our blackmailer?' Becks asked.

'It's a possibility I suppose,' Judith said. 'We know he needs the money. But that only makes finding Mike's second phone all the more important.'

'You're right there,' Suzie said. 'Let's do this. Ready, Becks?'

'About as ready as I'll ever be.'

'Good luck,' Judith said as she and Suzie went over to a large border of shrubs to the side of the door and crouched behind it.

'I still can't believe this is the plan,' Becks said.

'Shh!' Suzie and Judith both said from the bush.

As she was about to knock on the door, she heard the bush say, 'I could have sworn he said Bee Gees.'

'Quiet!' Becks said to the bush.

'Sorry!' it said back.

Becks took a deep breath and then knocked on the glass door. After a few seconds, it was opened by a man in his late twenties with long hair that he'd tied up into a bun on top of his head. His manner was easy-going, and his eyes lit up at the sight of Becks.

'You must be Mrs Starling,' he said, offering his hand, and Becks found herself blushing at the warmth of his smile. Suddenly, she felt a little too undressed for the encounter. 'I'm Josh,' the man continued. 'Welcome to Holyport Real Tennis Club.'

'Thank you so much for agreeing to a lesson at such short notice,' Becks said. 'But can I ask one thing before I come in? What's the code for the keypad?'

'Wow, you're keen,' Josh said with a laugh. 'It's one-eight-eight-nine. If you book yourself in for another session, you can just let yourself in.'

'One double eight nine,' Becks said a little more loudly than Josh was expecting, and then she followed him into the building.

Once the door had closed, Judith and Suzie emerged from behind the bush and checked that there was no one else nearby. Judith then typed the code into the keypad, the lock clicked and she pushed the door open.

Slipping inside, they found themselves in a corridor that led to a brightly lit atrium that had a glass roof, polished wooden floors and Perspex boards on the walls featuring the names of all of the winners of the various club cups going back decades. Peering around the edge of the doorway, they could see a reception desk to their right, and beyond that there were glass windows that revealed a seating area next to a large rectangular opening that was covered in thick rope netting. On the other side of the opening, it was possible to see a large, enclosed tennis court. The walls were painted black, and there was a net across the middle like a normal tennis court, but there was a square window built into the far wall and what looked like a row of galleries that ran down the left-hand side that were also covered in rope netting.

The two women could see that Becks was standing in the centre of the court talking to Josh. It looked as though no one else was around.

Opposite, a steep flight of stairs led to the floor above. A little sign to the side pointed upwards and read 'To the Dressing Rooms'. Suzie nodded at the large window, and Judith quickly realised what the problem was. In order to get to the stairs, they would first have to pass the window where they'd be in full view of Josh and Becks on the court.

'Let's see if there are any master keys first,' Judith whispered to her friend.

She and Suzie got down on their hands and knees and scurried around to get behind the reception desk.

'My back!' Suzie wheezed as she joined Judith and looked at the shelves under the counter. They were filled with files and boxes of old tennis balls.

Together, they started opening drawers and looking in boxes. After only a few seconds of searching, Judith pulled a large bunch of keys out of a drawer.

'You've got them?' Suzie asked. 'Sorry,' she added, when she realised why Judith was looking so witheringly at her. 'I can't help it if my voice is loud.'

Judith checked through the ring and realised it contained every type of key imaginable. There were no tabs with names written on them to indicate what each one did. They'd just have use trial and error.

'One of these keys must get into the lockers,' Judith said. 'People must be forgetting their keys the whole time.'

She crawled out from behind the desk and scuttled across the room to the stairs, Suzie following her.

What they hadn't realised was that they hadn't ducked down low enough as they passed the glass windows between them and the tennis court. Becks, in mounting panic, watched their curved backs move across the bottom of the windows like hippos crossing the Okavango Delta. Luckily, she was able to distract Josh by asking him what the various painted lines on the floor of the court meant.

Once her friends had passed, she tuned back into the conversation and heard Josh say, 'The easiest way to view chases is that, from the hazard end, you're trying to set one as low as possible – ideally, in fact, a chase better than one – but from the server's end you don't want to set any kind of hazard chase at all, although a chase of one is so much better than second gallery or door.'

'Oh well, I'm glad you cleared that up, thank you very much,' Becks said, even though she had absolutely no idea what he was talking about.

As soon as Judith and Suzie arrived upstairs, they rushed along the corridor until they found the men's changing room. Before they could decide on their best strategy, Suzie rapped on the door and called out, 'Cleaning!'

Judith put her ear to the door and didn't hear anyone call back – or any sound of movement at all – so she looked at her friend, shrugged once in admission that they were now in the lap of the gods, and pushed the door open.

Chapter 19

Mercifully, there wasn't anyone in the changing room and the two women quickly closed the door behind themselves. There were floor-to-ceiling wooden lockers built along two of the walls, a window that overlooked the club's car park and a large alcove to the side of the room that contained two showers with flimsy white curtains on a rail.

'OK, let's find Mike Saxon's locker,' Judith said, starting to inspect the slips of paper that had been slotted into little brass holders in the centre of each locker. 'Although, there doesn't seem to be any order to the names,' she said as she moved from locker to locker.

'Bloody hell,' Suzie said, impressed. 'This chap's called Major General Sir Percival Cholmondley-Smythe. That's real tennis keeping it real. Oh, I don't believe it,' she said, looking at the name on the next locker.

'Is it Mike Saxon?'

'No, it's Lord Harleyford!'

'Who?'

'The disgraced peer. It's like he's stalking me,' Suzie said. She saw movement through the window and a Rolls Royce car arrive and park up.

'What on earth are you talking about? We need to find Mike Saxon's name. Ah, here he is!' Judith added as she looked at a locker.

The name on it read 'M. Saxon, Esq.'.

'Uh-oh,' Suzie said as she peered through the window and saw a portly man in his sixties heave a sports bag out of the back of the Rolls and start to walk towards the building. 'There's a man coming this way, and he's got his sports kit with him.'

'Then we'll just have to get into Mike's locker as fast as possible.'

Judith held up the bunch of keys, chose one at random and tried it in the lock. It didn't work. She tried another. It didn't work, either. As she tried key after key, Judith found it almost impossible to keep track of the ones she'd used and the ones she hadn't. And it didn't help that she had no idea what shape of key the lock took.

'He's entered the building!' Suzie said while Judith rotated the bunch of keys and tried another in the lock.

'How about this one?' Judith said. 'I don't think I've tried this one before.'

'You have,' Suzie said as Judith tried and failed to insert the key into the keyhole.

'Oh, OK,' Judith said, holding up a little key with two prongs that made it look like a tiny trident. 'This one's new.'

Judith put the key into the keyhole and was gratified to hear a click as the lock engaged.

'Hold on!' Suzie said. 'Footsteps!'

They both heard the sound of someone approaching outside in the corridor. As Judith twisted the lock and popped the door open, Suzie turned around, desperately trying to see where they could hide. Then, as the door to the changing room began to open, she grabbed Judith by the shoulders and bundled her into one of the two shower cubicles, yanking the plastic curtain across to hide them as the man from the Rolls Royce entered.

Judith stood stock still, trying to control her breathing, her blood pumping so loudly in her ears that she couldn't believe the man wouldn't hear.

As the seconds passed, Judith realised that the man had no idea that she and Suzie were hiding in the shower cubicle. Maybe he'd just leave his sports bag and head straight out again. All wasn't necessarily lost. But then, the man started whistling to himself and Judith heard him sit down heavily on a bench and start to kick his shoes off.

Judith caught Suzie's eye, the pair of them thinking the same thing. They were two women hiding in a changing room as a man took his clothes off. The absurdity of the situation hit them both at the same time and Judith's hand went to her mouth to stifle a giggle. Then, as they heard the man slip out of his clothes, she had to crunch her face up to stop herself from guffawing. To make matters worse, the plastic sheeting they were hiding behind didn't block out all of the light, so while they remained hidden in the gloom of the shower cubicle, the man was getting undressed in the well-lit changing room. They could dimly see his figure as he took off his clothes.

'Right then,' the man said to himself. 'Time for a shower.'

Suzie and Judith froze.

There were only two showers for the man to choose from, and

they were hiding in one of them. There was a fifty-fifty chance that a completely naked man was about to whisk the curtain back and reveal himself to them. They looked at each other as the shadow of the man approached. What could they do?

The man's hand went to the edge of their curtain – *he'd chosen their shower!* – which was when Suzie spun the tap and the shower burst into life, drenching them both in an instant.

'Sorry, old chap,' the man said. 'Didn't know anyone was here.'

Ignoring the fact that Judith was now giving her a look that could have sliced through steel. Suzie cleared her throat and made a few spluttering noises that she felt represented the sort of older Home Counties gentleman who could be in the shower.

'No, of course,' the man said. 'I'll use the other cubicle.'

Judith and Suzie continued to stand under the streaming shower as the shadow of the man moved away. Then, a car alarm pierced the air and they heard the man move over to the window, mumble 'Bloody hell!' and scrabble back into his clothes as fast as he could, before dashing from the room. Throughout, the car alarm kept blaring. The moment the door opened and closed, Suzie hurried to turn the water off.

Judith glowered at her friend.

'Sorry!' Suzie said, swishing the curtain open and hanging back while Judith squelched across the dressing room to Mike's locker. The door was still open, so she looked inside and was relieved to see a leather sports bag. Pulling it out and unzipping it, she saw that it contained some women's lingerie in among a change of men's clothes, a pair of brown brogues and a washbag. But there was also an interior pocket to the bag. She unzipped it and pulled out an old Samsung mobile phone.

'Got you,' she said.

The sound of the car alarm stopped and the women went over to the window. Outside, they could see the plump man remonstrating with Becks, who was standing by his car. *Had Becks set off the car alarm?*

'Let's go to the women's changing room,' Judith said. 'See if we can dry ourselves while that man comes back. When we hear him start his shower, we can slip away.'

Judith picked up Mike's bag and she and Suzie went into the women's changing room next door. There wasn't much they could do about their wet clothes, but there were fresh towels and hair dryers, so they were able to make sure they looked slightly less like drowned rats when they left ten minutes later. As they passed the men's changing room, they could hear the sound of running water. And when they got to the bottom of the stairs, they could see that Becks was back on the real tennis court with Josh. Doubling over, they crossed to the reception desk, opened the drawer, put the keys back and then crouched their way out of the main doors.

Once outside, the women straightened up.

'Now what?' Suzie asked.

'I think we need to get dry before we try and get into Mike's phone,' Judith said. 'I suggest we go back to mine; we can wait for Becks there.'

The women got into Suzie's van and then drove to Judith's house, the fan heaters on full blast, pointed at their damp clothes.

Chapter 20

As Becks finished her coaching session with Josh, she smiled sweetly at the owner of the Rolls Royce when he came to take her place on court. Seeing as he believed that she'd somehow tampered with his precious car, he didn't smile back.

Once outside, Becks saw that Suzie's van was nowhere to be seen, so she checked the messages on her phone and saw that her friends had retrieved Mike's bag and phone and had gone to Judith's house to wait for her.

'Yes!' Becks called out to the skies and couldn't stop smiling to herself as she used her phone to order a taxi. The version of her who'd first moved to Marlow would never have got herself mixed up with such free spirits as Judith and Suzie.

She was still smiling to herself when she arrived at Judith's house and found Suzie standing in front of a roaring fire wearing a thick dressing gown over her clothes as Judith poured cups of tea for them both.

'Ah, there you are!' Judith called out and started to pour tea into a third cup.

'Why are you in a dressing gown?' Becks asked.

'We had to go undercover,' Suzie said.

'More like underwater,' Judith said.

'Very funny,' Suzie said with a laugh. 'But we were going to be discovered until the car alarm went off. You were behind that, Becks, weren't you?'

'I was,' Becks said in pride. 'A short while after you went upstairs, I saw a man in a suit arrive with a sports bag and head up after you. I guessed he was heading to the changing room, and I knew I had to somehow get him out. I'd noticed that his suit looked very expensive, which gave me the idea that he'd probably arrived in a fancy car. And men like that care more about their cars than they do about almost anything else. So I told Josh I needed to go to the loo, left the court and slipped out to the car park. When I got there, I saw that there was only one car there other than your van, Suzie. It was a Rolls Royce, so I pulled the silver lady on the front of it as hard as I could and set off the alarm.'

'You vandalised a Rolls Royce?' Suzie said, amazed.

'Well – maybe a bit. When the man came out, I did my best impression of a vicar's wife and told him that I'd had nothing to do with it. I'll be honest, it was brilliant! I could tell that he wanted to accuse me of lying, but he couldn't believe that someone who looked and talked like me would have tampered with his car for no reason. So I went back to the lesson, hoping it had given you time to extricate yourselves.'

'It did,' Judith said. 'What amazing, quick thinking.'

'And we got everything we needed,' Suzie said, before going to a side table, retrieving Mike's sports bag and pulling out his Samsung phone.

'Have you seen what's on it?' Becks asked.

'We've been getting dry first,' Suzie said. 'And it's locked. We've been wondering how to get past his lockscreen.'

'I wonder if it might be quite easy,' Becks said, taking the phone from her friend.

'We don't want to get locked out,' Judith said.

'Of course. But you know how lazy we all are with passwords and passcodes – we're always using the same ones over and over.'

'That's true,' Suzie said. 'If you ever work out the four-digit code to unlock my phone, you'll get access to my computer, the PIN on every bank card I've ever had and the padlock to the gate at the back of my garden. Actually, now you mention it, that's a really bad way to run your life, isn't it?'

'Do you have Serena's phone number?' Becks asked Suzie.

'Of course,' Suzie said, pulling out her phone and scrolling through her contacts. She dialled a number and put her phone on speaker when the call was answered.

'It's Suzie Harris here.'

'Oh,' Serena said, sounding irritated. 'Why are you ringing?'

'Just a quickie. Can you tell me the code your husband used to lock his phone?'

'I'm sorry?'

'We need the code to his phone.'

'I'm not telling you that.'

'Why not?'

'You're not the police; I don't have to.'

'Here, let me take this,' Judith said. 'You're right, Serena, we aren't the police. But we need to know the code to your husband's phone and you can tell us what it is now, or you can tell the police later on. But if you wait until the police ask, you'll have to explain to them why you refused to help us.'

Serena didn't say anything for a few seconds as she weighed up what she should say.

'Of course I want to help in whatever way I can,' she said. 'You just caught me at a bad time. Mike was terrible at numbers, so he had a bit of software that meant he just had to draw a large "M" and then an "S" on the screen to unlock it. Even he couldn't forget his own initials. So try that.'

With that, Serena ended the call.

'Let's see,' Suzie said as she turned Mike's phone on and, when prompted, drew the letters M and S on the screen.

The phone didn't unlock. Instead, a message appeared, saying, 'Two More Attempts Remaining'.

'Damn,' Suzie said.

'That's a bit of a problem,' Judith said in agreement. 'Although, I wonder if he used the same logic – using initials from a name – for this second phone.'

'How do you mean?' Becks asked.

'I suppose I'm asking, if his main phone belonged to Mike Saxon, who did his burner phone belong to?'

'Oh I see what you mean!' Suzie said. 'Well, we're talking about a guy who shoots lions and thinks it's fun. And beds women whenever he can. I bet he thinks he's his hero, Fraser Steele.'

'Then why don't you try his hero's initials?' Becks asked.

'Good thinking,' Suzie said as she awakened the lock screen again, and this time drew the letters F and S on it.

She turned the phone to her friends in triumph.

'We're in, brilliant idea, Judith! Now we can see what he gets up to when no one's looking.'

Suzie looked at the phone's home page and saw that Mike only had a few apps installed. She pressed the email icon, but it opened to a window that invited her to 'Add an email account'.

'OK, so he's not using the phone for email. And there's no WhatsApp as far as I can see. Or X or Bluesky or Insta or anything else. Let me have a look at his call register.' Suzie pressed the green phone icon and opened the list of all of the calls he'd made and received.

'Well, that's weird,' she said. 'According to this, he's never even made or received a phone call.'

'So why does he have a phone if he doesn't use it?' Becks asked.

'Oh, I've found it,' Suzie said as she pressed the 'Messages' icon and the screen filled with messages. Suzie scrolled down the list of names. They were all female.

'This is all pretty sordid. Women he's meeting, where he's meeting them and . . . everything else in between,' she added.

'Any names you recognise from the case?' Judith asked.

'For example, Jamilah Kamil,' Becks asked. 'I still think it's odd that she didn't tell us about him making a move on her the first time we spoke to her.'

'She's not here,' Suzie said. 'And nor is anyone else from the case. Oh, hang on, is this him? Okay, we've found it.'

Suzie showed the screen of the phone to her friends.

12 May 25 10:47

£1k Thursday, Gossmore Park
flyover, midnight

12 May 25, 11:01

Go hang yourself

12 May 25, 11:03

£1k to keep your secret. Gossmore Park, Thursday at midnight

15 June 25, 15:26

£2k Wednesday, Gossmore Park flyover, midnight

15 June 25, 19:01

I told you last time it was a one-off. It's over

23 August 25, 10:07

It's only just started. £2k Wednesday, Gossmore Park flyover, midnight

15 September 25, 9:11

£2k Saturday, Gossmore Park flyover, midnight

01 October 25, 20:50

£2k Monday, Gossmore Park flyover, midnight

19 November 25, 11:01

We need to meet.

19 November 25, 11:13

I said we need to meet.

19 November 25, 11:27

WE NEED TO MEET

19 November 25, 11:53

Tonight. Gossmore Park flyover. 1am.

'You were right, Judith,' Becks said. 'Mike was also being black-mailed. This is what links the two men!'

Judith went over to her phone and got up the screenshot of the messages that had been sent between Gary Wise and his blackmailer. She checked the phone number that Gary's blackmailer had used.

It was the same.

'The same person who was blackmailing Gary was blackmailing Mike,' she confirmed.

'But what was Mike's secret?' Becks asked. 'The one that this guy mentions in the second message. Is it the same secret as Gary's, or is it a different one?'

'I don't know,' Suzie said, 'but look at how Mike responds. In that second message he's trying to be a hard man, isn't he? "Go hang yourself" he writes.'

'But he must have paid up,' Judith said, indicating the next message on the screen. 'Because our blackmailer's back a month later. No preamble. No explanation. Just a straight-forward demand for money. And, once again, Mike tries to refuse. But the following messages from our blackmailer make it obvious he must have capitulated. Until the nineteenth of November, which I can't help noting is the very same day that Mike died.'

'Which is also the same day he had the argument with the mystery man outside his office,' Becks said.

'And look,' Becks said. 'He was desperate to meet his black-mailer that day, wasn't he? He sent three messages in the morning demanding they get together.'

'It's obvious what that's about,' Suzie said. 'Mike woke up that morning, saw the news that Gary had been killed and realised he had to meet up with his blackmailer – the mystery guy in the flat cap – as soon as possible. But it ended badly, with the blackmailer storming off into the woods.

'So Mike texts him a couple of hours later,' Becks said, continuing the story. 'And begs to meet up again. Which is when the meeting at 1 a.m. is arranged. Which is why Mike left his house at midnight that night. That's when he left to go and meet his blackmailer.'

'Who then shot him dead,' Suzie said.

'But why?' Judith said. '*Why* was he being blackmailed?' As she spoke, Judith went to her incident board and looked at the index card that had 'Gary had car crash on April 7th' written on it. 'Is it possible Mike was involved in Gary's car crash somehow? Is that the link?'

'It's a possibility,' Becks said.

'Or he could have been blackmailed for a completely different reason,' Suzie said. 'After all, you take any two people and it's unlikely you'd be able to blackmail both of them for the same reason.'

'That's also true,' Becks said.

'It's so frustrating!' Suzie said. 'How can we even begin to find out what's going on – we need access to the police files!'

'And talking of the police,' Becks said. 'We need to work out how we're going to get this phone to them.'

'Good point,' Judith said. 'I think it's time to train up Tanika's replacement,' she added as she picked up her phone and dialled a number. When the call connected, Judith asked if she could be put through to Detective Sergeant Brendan Perry.

'*Seriously*?' Suzie said.

'Becks is right, we were always going to have to hand in the phone eventually – ah, Detective Sergeant Perry,' Judith said as Brendan came on the line. 'Judith Potts here. I suggest you drop whatever you're doing and come to my house.'

'I'm sorry? You're telling me to do what?'

'I'm not telling you to do anything, I'm merely suggesting you come to my house as it's a matter of life and death.'

'For who?'

'For you. As far as your career goes at least. You see, we've just found out that Mike Saxon was being blackmailed by the same person who was blackmailing Gary Wise. I'd highly recommend you come to my house to find out more. I live just outside Marlow on Ferry Lane—'

'I know where you live,' Brendan said and the line went dead.

'What a rude man,' Judith said to her friends.

'Do you think he'll come?' Becks asked.

'If his desire to prove that he's better than Tanika is as strong as I think it is, I'd say he's got no choice.'

'Was it wise, goading him like that?'

'I honestly didn't mean to, but he does rather have the manner of a goadee. Now, before he gets here, I suggest that you and I, Suzie, make sure we're presentable.

Judith went upstairs to get into fresh clothes while Suzie announced that the fire and the dressing gown she was wearing had dried her clothes just fine.

It wasn't long after that they all heard a man's voice announce 'Mrs Potts?' from the front hallway.

'Come on in!' Judith called out as she came down the stairs and looked at her two friends. Suzie exhaled and Becks grimaced, both of them knowing how high the stakes were about to get.

Detective Sergeant Brendan Perry walked into the room.

Chapter 21

Brendan stopped in surprise when he saw the evidence photos that were pinned to the wall behind Judith's desk.

'That looks suspiciously like an incident board to me,' he said and crossed the room to inspect it.

'As eagle-eyed as ever,' Judith said as Brendan unpinned the photo of Angela Gulliver from the wall so he could look at it more closely.

'Why have you got a photo of a TV agony aunt here?'

'Don't you have one on yours?' Judith said, trying to make a joke of it as she took the photo from Brendan and pinned it back onto the wall.

'This isn't legal,' Brendan said.

'It's perfectly legal,' Judith said.

'Amateurs,' he scoffed.

'Amateurs with a track record of catching killers,' Judith said, irritated by Brendan's belief in his superiority. 'And you're going to need our help if you want to catch Gary and Mike's killer.'

'That's where you're wrong.'

'There's no shame in admitting how ambitious you are. The way you finally managed to sideline Tanika is testament to that. You're desperate to prove to your superiors they were wrong to choose Tanika over you. It's my bet that your desire to solve this case is a smidgeon greater than your desire to have nothing to do with us.'

'You said the same person who was blackmailing Gary Wise was blackmailing Mike Saxon.'

'That's right,' Suzie said. 'Because he is.'

'How can you possibly know that?'

'We've got Mike's burner phone,' Becks said.

'No way!'

'You don't believe we have it?' Judith asked.

'No – it's not that. It's just, I can't believe Mike Saxon had a burner phone. It's just like in one of his books.'

'You're a fan, are you?' Suzie asked, amused.

'As it happens, I am.'

'Really?' Judith said, surprised. 'I didn't have you down as a reader.'

'Actually, I read quite widely. I even went to a few of his author events.'

'Of course you did!' Suzie said with a laugh. 'All of those stories about macho guys running around the place, bedding women and shooting baddies. That was always going to appeal to a man like you.'

'His books are about more than that,' Brendan said defensively. 'He also writes about the environment; that's a big theme in his work. How we have to protect the planet.'

'That doesn't sound very like him,' Judith said.

'But are you serious? Mike had a burner phone?'

'I can't wait to tell you all about it. But first I'd love it if you updated us on where you've got to with the investigation.'

'Then I'll have to disappoint you, because I'm not doing that.'

'Even though we'll let you take all of the credit for this break-through?'

Brendan didn't reply, but the women could see that he was considering what he should say.

'We're not the enemy,' Becks said. 'I know you think we are, but we're just as keen as you are to catch the killer. We can help you to the best of our ability and you can take all of the credit. It's the advantage of us being unofficial. No one ever needs to know about us.'

'And if it all goes arse over tit,' Suzie said. 'You can throw the book at us. It's kind of the deal we had with Tanika.'

Brendan went and sat down in Judith's favourite armchair. The women exchanged glances. *What on earth was he doing?* He picked up a fire iron and prodded the ash in the grate.

'You don't know how hard it was for me to get here,' he said. 'You know – to make detective sergeant.'

He pushed the ash around while he considered what to do. Quite a few seconds passed.

'OK, I agree,' he eventually said. 'I want this killer caught as much as you. More so. This is my job. What I do.'

'Of course,' Judith agreed.

'But it can't be in any way official. And if I see you anywhere near our investigation, I'll have to report you. Or even arrest you.'

'I'd expect no less.'

'And you'd seriously accept these terms? Even you, Mrs Starling? As a vicar's wife, you've got a lot to lose.'

'Please – it's Becks. And it doesn't matter what I might or

might not lose. All that matters is that we catch the person who killed Gary Wise and Mike Saxon.'

'That much I can agree with.'

Brendan looked at the women as though for the first time. He nodded to himself, seeming to realise that he only had one choice.

'All right, but you won't be happy with what I have to say,' he said. 'We've got just about nowhere with both murders. We've looked through Gary Wise's life and found nothing that could explain why anyone would have wanted him dead. Let alone why he would be being blackmailed. He's not in debt. He's got savings and investments worth millions. He was liked at his club. And by all accounts he doted on his wife and she doted on him.'

'Have you come across any kind of car accident on the seventh of April?' Becks asked.

'What car accident?'

'You see?' Judith said. 'You can't do this without us. Cup of tea?'

'Don't push it. You reckon he was in a car crash?'

'Harry Asquith said it was the only thing Gary wouldn't talk about for his autobiography.'

'So that's why you three went to the depository in Reading. You were looking for the report on the incident?'

'But it's now missing – or so it appears. Which is a bit of a worry, because it suggests that Gary – or someone who knew Gary – was able to put pressure on a police officer to pull the file.'

Brendan frowned.

'Does that happen often?' Becks asked.

'Almost never,' Brendan said. 'But there's always going to be the odd bad apple. Someone who'll let their head be turned if they're offered enough money. Normally it's some dodgy journalist who gets their claws into them.'

'A journalist?' Judith asked.

Brendan snorted.

'They're the worst. With their fingers in every bloody pie. Yes, it could easily have been a journalist who put the pressure on a copper to pull the file. But then, it could just have been an officer who was a football nut. There are lots of those on the force. It's possible the attending officer at the crash was a massive football fan and helped Mr Wise because he didn't want him to get into trouble. It really could be as simple as that.'

Brendan went over to look at Judith's incident board again. The women were thrilled to see how seriously he was considering the case.

'But is that the connection?' he asked. 'Mr Wise told some third party that he'd got his police record expunged, and then that third party is the person who's been blackmailing him?'

'It's certainly a workable theory,' Judith said, joining Brendan at the board.

'So who did Mr Wise tell?'

'We know it wasn't Harry Asquith,' Suzie said, indicating Harry's photo on the board.

'Or that's what Harry says,' Becks said, coming to join the others. 'Have you traced the phone number that was blackmailing him?'

'It's a fake number,' Brendan said. 'It's not linked to any kind of person – so that's a dead end.'

'Then what have you got by way of suspects for Mike's death?' Judith asked.

'That's where things get a bit more complicated,' Brendan said. 'I mean, obviously his wife could have a motive.'

'Seeing as he's a serial adulterer,' Becks said.

'You know about that?' Brendan said, unable to hide that he was impressed. 'You three really get around, don't you?'

'Have you found any signs of blackmail in Mike's life?' Becks asked. 'Like large sums of cash that he took out at odd times? Or unexplained diary appointments?'

'I'll be honest,' Brendan said, 'he had so much money coming in, and he spent a lot of money in cash, that I'm not sure it would be possible to tell. Now, I've played along enough. I want to see his burner phone.'

'Of course,' Judith said.

She went over to the mantelpiece, picked up Mike's phone, returned to Brendan and handed it over.

'To get past the lock screen, you have to draw the letters F and S,' Becks said.

'Where on earth did you get this?' Brendan asked, unable to hide how impressed he was.

'We found it in Mike's locker at the Holyport Real Tennis Club.'

'It's where he got changed before seeing his fancy ladies,' Suzie said, going over to get Mike's sports bag.

'The only thing you need to see are the text messages,' Becks said.

As Brendan started to read the messages on the phone, he scrunched up his nose in concentration.

'You're right,' he said. 'This is the same phone number that was used to extort money out of Mr Wise. How did you find out it existed?'

'Jamilah Khalil told us,' Suzie said.

'Amazing,' Brendan said, without realising that he was paying the women a compliment.

Becks, Suzie and Judith exchanged quick smiles of delight.

'We'll speak to her, make sure her story stacks up,' Brendan continued. 'Not that I can officially approve of the three of you scurrying about the place, sticking your noses into where they're not wanted. But well done on this occasion.'

'That's *exactly* what Tanika used to say to us,' Judith said with a smile. 'I'm sure you won't believe it, but she was just like you at first. It was only when she came to realise that we could get results that she softened her position.'

'Let's see about that,' Brendan said as he put the phone into Mike's sports bag and started to leave the room. 'But you were right about one thing, Mrs Potts. I *am* ambitious. Thanks for getting hold of this phone and handing it over to me.'

Before anyone could reply, Brendan left, and the women were wise enough to wait until they heard the front door open and close again before they spoke.

'Judith, you were amazing!' Becks said.

'Hardly,' Judith said. 'It was the phone that gave us leverage, and that was very much a group effort.'

'That bit where he went and sat by the fire,' Becks said. 'I almost felt sorry for him. It was the first time I realised the case really matters to him.'

'I liked the bit where he scrunched his nose up while he read the messages,' Judith said. 'He looked like Squirrel Nutkin.'

'Hey!' Suzie said. 'This is the guy who got Tanika sidelined. Let's have a bit less of the sympathy.'

'No – quite right,' Becks said. 'So what do we do now?'

'That's obvious,' Judith said. 'We need to speak to Serena Saxon about Mike's women before Brendan does. I want to find out if she knew that her husband was a serial adulterer.'

'Good thinking,' Suzie said and went to get her coat.

As the women left the house, Becks paused to check that the front door was properly closed and locked. As she did so, her eye caught some movement by a buddleia bush that was growing out of a pile of old pallets at the edge of the garden.

She tried to work out what it was that she'd just seen.

'You all right there, Becks?' Suzie called from her van.

Becks went over to her friends and whispered, 'I think I saw something by that bush over there.'

'What sort of something?' Suzie asked.

'I don't know,' Becks said, losing confidence almost immediately. 'Maybe a person. But I saw a flash of green.'

'A flash of green? Against a green background?'

'What was Eleni wearing the last time you saw her?' Becks asked as she got into the van.

'You think it was Eleni?' Suzie said.

'It could be the next stage in her campaign of harassment.'

'Then I suggest we leave her to it,' Judith said. 'We've got a witness to interview. Come on, Suzie, let's go.'

As the women drove off, Becks looked back at the bush. Was it Eleni she'd seen, or was it something – or someone – else?

Chapter 22

Serena Saxon was in the process of showing a man from the local Bentley dealership her husband's car when Suzie's van arrived. Telling the dealer that she wouldn't be a minute, Serena strode over to head the women off.

'What are you doing here?' she said as Judith, Suzie and Becks got out of the van.

'Are you selling your Bentley?' Suzie asked.

'That's really none of your business.'

'Sure,' Suzie agreed easily enough, 'but it must be worth a fair few bob.'

'I bloody hope so. I just want shot of everything that reminds me of that man. I can finally get an electric car. Mike never let us have one when he was alive. Worse, he loved winding me up with how much petrol he used.'

'You care about the environment?' Judith said. Something about this new piece of information was piquing her interest but she couldn't quite put her finger on what it was.

'Of course! Don't you?'

'Absolutely. I don't even own a car.'

'She's not wrong there,' Suzie said. 'She uses me as her taxi service.'

'It's why I'm selling that gas guzzler over there,' Serena said, indicating the Bentley. 'But I'm sure you didn't come here to find out about my green credentials.'

'No,' Becks agreed. 'We're actually here on a bit of a ticklish matter.'

Becks didn't quite know what to say next, so Suzie decided to step into the breach.

'We were wondering how faithful your husband was?'

'I beg your pardon?'

'As I say,' Becks said, 'it's a ticklish question.'

'Is this connected with the password you wanted to access Mike's phone?'

'It is.'

'Then I don't want to know about it – I'm not interested. I decided a long time ago that there are some things it's better a wife doesn't know.'

As Serena was speaking, the man who'd been standing by the Bentley came over with his clipboard and held it out for Serena.

'I've finished my visual inspection, Mrs Saxon,' he said, efficiently. 'I'm happy to take the vehicle into the dealership. Just as you say, it's in top condition. If you could just sign at the bottom of the document?'

'Of course,' Serena said, pretending that everything was fine as he handed the clipboard over.

Judith couldn't stop herself from peering at the form to see what it said, but most of it had been handwritten and she couldn't read it very easily. Not without her reading glasses on.

It was as she was trying to decode the writing that it struck her that she'd seen it before.

'Well, blow me down!' she said – stunned – as the facts slotted into place for her.

'What is it?' Becks asked.

'Not now,' Judith said, testing her new theories and realising she was almost certainly correct.

'Thank you very much,' Serena said to the man as she handed the clipboard back to him. 'In fact,' she continued, 'let me walk you back to the car. These women are just leaving.'

'We're not going anywhere,' Judith said.

'I beg your pardon?'

'Mrs Saxon would like to thank you for your help,' Judith said to the dealer, 'but you can go now.'

The man looked at Serena for confirmation, she nodded that he should do as Judith was suggesting, and he returned to the Bentley.

'What is it?' Serena asked, when he was a safe distance away.

'I think you killed your husband,' Judith said. 'Because it's *you* who writes his books, isn't it?'

'What are you talking about?'

'You write Mike's books – not him.'

Serena's eyes narrowed.

'What makes you say that?' she asked.

'The first time we spoke to you, I saw all of your husband's notes for his new book on the kitchen table. And you ushered me away. I thought it was slightly odd at the time. After all, your husband had just died, why did it matter if I or anyone else saw what he'd been working on? But the handwriting on his notes was the same as the handwriting you've used to fill in that form.'

'You noticed that?' Becks asked, amazed.

'It was such a spiky style, it caught my eye,' Judith said by way of explanation. 'And it also explains why Jamilah said that every time she went in to see Mike, he seemed to be playing shooting games on his computer. He was only pretending to work, wasn't he?'

'That must have been tough for you,' Becks said, picking the baton up from her friend. 'Being married to someone who was lionised the world over. But it was actually you who was doing all of the work.'

'And that's why Brendan told us your husband's books are so pro the environment!' Judith added, realising why Serena's comment about electric cars had registered with her. 'You're the environmentalist in the family, not Mike.'

'It was about the only thing I could slip past him,' Serena said bitterly. 'Every other attempt I made to bring his characters and stories into the twenty-first century, he resisted. In Mike's books the men had to be men and the women had to be things the men looked at.'

'No, this is crazy,' Suzie said. 'You did all of the work?'

'He wrote them originally. When he was younger. But they'd been waning in popularity when I met him. Not that he told me. It was only after we were married that he dropped the bombshell that his publisher had decided to ditch him. Well, I wasn't having that, so I wrote the most Mike Saxon book that I could, took it to his publisher, and they agreed to publish it under his name. The rest is history. And it's rather gratifying, actually. These late career books outsell all the books he wrote before he met me.'

'That must have irritated him,' Becks said.

'It drove him mad, but what could he do? He had to keep the secret if he was going to continue to collect all of his royalties.'

'And you didn't mind that no one knew the truth?' Suzie asked.

'Don't worry. A few people in the publishing world know who was behind the Mike Saxon books. It was just a secret to the wider world.'

'And all you asked in return was for him to stop philandering,' Judith said. 'Which he never did.'

'OK, fine, he had other women. I'll admit it. He's always had other women. But it's my own bloody fault. I was Mike's third wife. We got together when he cheated on his second. And I was stupid enough to think he'd be faithful. I thought I was better than the others. That this time it would be different. And when he went to book festivals and stayed over in a hotel when he could just have easily come home, I told myself it was because he had to press hands and make connections in the industry.'

'He didn't hide his affairs?' Becks asked.

'He did everything in his power to hide them, but I could always see through his lies.'

'And there you are, doing all of the work while he gets all of the acclaim,' Suzie said.

'Using the fame that you were creating for him to sleep with any number of women,' Becks added.

'Until the day that you snapped,' Suzie said, 'and decided enough was enough. Judith's right — you killed him.'

'Don't you get it?' Serena said witheringly. 'With him dead, I won't be able to continue writing his books. He can hardly publish them from beyond the grave, can he? And hateful though they are, they earn piles of cash. I don't mind telling you, I loved the money more than I hated my husband.'

'But it wouldn't necessarily have been the end of your lifestyle,' Becks said. 'Whenever someone famous dies, there's always a rush to buy their records or films or whatever it is they made.'

'Are you suggesting I killed my husband to boost sales?'

'I'm saying that maybe there'd have been a financial upside to offset the downside. Especially if you're saying that you want to spend what you earn on greener choices. You can do that now.'

'No, I'm not having this. The three of you can leave right now.'

'You're throwing us off your property?' Suzie asked, offended.

'You just accused me of killing my husband. Yes, I'm throwing you off my property.'

With that, Serena turned and strode back to talk to the man from the Bentley dealership.

'Wow, that escalated fast,' Suzie said. 'And just so you know, I don't buy her story. I reckon he betrayed her one too many times, so it was kaput for him.'

'I'd agree she has a gold-plated motive,' Judith said as the women returned to Suzie's van. 'But it doesn't explain why she'd kill Gary first, does it?'

'And it also doesn't explain who was blackmailing both men,' Becks said.

'You're right,' Suzie said. 'I don't see Serena grubbing around for a few thousand pounds here and there. If we're looking for a blackmailer, my money's on Harry Asquith. He's the one person in all of this who's got money problems.'

'Although we still don't know for sure that both men were killed by their blackmailer,' Becks said. 'I suppose, in theory at least, it's possible that both Gary and Mike were killed for reasons that had nothing to do with them being blackmailed. Hold on, there it is again!'

'What are you talking about?' Suzie asked.

'I think I just saw Eleni again,' she said quietly. 'Over by Mike's office. Although, how does she know how to get to Mike's office?'

'Will that woman never leave us alone?' Suzie said. 'Do you really think it was her?'

'I didn't see for sure, but it was very definitely a person.'

'Then I think it's time we flush her out into the open,' Judith said as she got into Suzie's van and waited for her friends to join her.

'What's the plan?' Suzie asked, putting the van in gear and driving off.

'Whether or not it's Eleni, if they were at my house spying on me, and then managed to get here, then that suggests to me that they must have a mode of transport. In which case, they'll no doubt be following us again when we leave. So how about we let them do just that? But to a location of our choosing.'

As Judith spoke, Suzie turned the van onto the main road that led to Marlow.

'Then it's good news we're in my van,' Suzie said. 'Whoever it is won't have any difficulty following us. But where should we go?'

'We need somewhere where there's a proper dead end,' Judith said. 'So we can trap them.'

'Then how about Gossmore Rec?' Becks suggested. 'There's a small car park, and only the one lane that leads down to it.'

'That's *exactly* what we're looking for,' Suzie said. 'Good thinking.'

As Suzie spoke, she drove over the suspension bridge that crossed the Thames and entered the bustling town of Marlow. People were wrapped up in long coats and thick scarves against the winter chill, and the shop windows were glowing golden from the lights inside. Suzie turned right at the mini roundabout so she could head to the riverside park. Then, as she turned off the road onto the asphalt track that led down to the car park, she stopped so Judith and Becks could get out.

'Quick! You hide in the bushes here,' she said to her friends. 'I'll make sure I park up in a place where the van can be seen from the road.'

Suzie drove down the track until she arrived at the car park and pulled up. Then she got out of the van, pulled out her phone and pretended to be on a call.

Back at the park's entrance, Judith and Becks were hiding in a bush as a red car pulled up in the street. Then it started up again and headed for the track that led down to the car park. As it passed Judith and Becks, they rushed out of the bush, Becks blocking passage of the car while Judith yanked the door open on the driver's side of the car to reveal the person inside.

It wasn't Eleni Paphides.

It was Angela Gulliver.

Chapter 23

Angela's face flushed bright red with embarrassment as she looked at Becks and Judith.

'What on earth are you doing?' she asked.

'I think we could ask you the same question,' Judith said.

'I have no idea what you're talking about.'

'You were spying on us from the bushes when we were at Judith's,' Becks said. 'Then you followed us to Serena Saxon's house and hid behind Mike's office – although I've no idea how you got there, seeing as we didn't see any car parked nearby. But now you've followed us for a third time.'

'You can't possibly believe that.'

'It's not a question of belief – we saw you.'

Angela looked from Becks to Judith, desperately hoping to see a shred of mercy, but found none.

'Oh God,' she said and lowered her head to the steering wheel in dismay. As she did so, Suzie's van arrived. Suzie got out and strode over.

'It was *you*?' she said.

Angela looked up at the women pleadingly.

'I'm innocent, you have to believe me,' she said.

'And why would we believe anything you say?' Suzie asked. 'Seeing as you lied to us when you tried to trick your way into our investigation. And now we've caught you spying on us. You're connected to the murders, aren't you?'

'I'm not, but you're right about one thing, I know what the link between the two murders is. I've always known. I know it sounds bad that I haven't told you—'

'*Sounds* bad?' Suzie said, interrupting Angela's flow. 'Sounds to me like you're the killer.'

'I'm not – you can't say that! But I think I know who it might be.'

'Now this I'd like to hear.'

'Although, could we do this somewhere else?' Angela said, indicating that she was trapped in her car. 'Maybe somewhere indoors? A bit of privacy wouldn't go amiss.'

Becks suggested that they go to the vicarage, which was just a short drive from the park. Judith offered to keep Angela company on the way and climbed into the passenger seat of her car. She and Angela both knew that Judith was really making sure that Angela didn't do a runner, but they arrived at the vicarage without incident and Becks put the kettle on for them all once they were in the kitchen.

'This is so pretty,' Angela said, taking in the room.

'Save it for another time,' Suzie said. 'Just tell us who the killer is.'

'You have to believe me, I don't know anything about what happened. Or why Gary and Mike were killed. But I know who did it.'

'And you think this person could be after you next?' Becks asked.

'That's it exactly!' Angela said.

'I think it's best if we all sit down and you tell us what you know,' Becks said, as she brought over a tray that was piled high with a big pot of tea, cups and saucers and a plate of biscuits.

'Thank you,' Angela said. 'You're too kind, Mrs Starling.'

As Becks poured four cups of tea and added splashes of milk, Judith realised there was something she wanted to ask Angela.

'How's your TV show doing?' she said.

'What sort of question is that?' Angela replied, defensively.

'I read in the newspaper that viewers have stopped watching.'

'Viewing figures in telly are down for everyone. The heady days of millions of people watching the daytime schedule have been over for some time.'

'Do you have any other TV shows on at the moment?'

'Not currently.'

'Or newspaper columns? Or book deals?'

'I want to tell you who killed Gary Wise and Mike Saxon! How well or not my career's going has nothing to do with any of this.'

'Very well,' Suzie said, snapping a bourbon biscuit in half and then popping one of the pieces into her mouth. 'Name the killer.'

'That's why I'm here,' Angela said, and took a sip of tea to steady her nerves. 'Do any of you know Lord Harleyford?'

'*What?*' Suzie said in amazement.

'Have you heard of him?'

'Heard of him? I feel like I'm being stalked by him!'

'How do you mean?' Judith asked.

'Suzie thinks he's been getting too much publicity for his

crimes,' Becks said quickly, not wanting the conversation to get sidetracked.

'Well, you're right about his crimes,' Angela said. 'No one was less surprised than me when he was suddenly all over the papers. You see, it's my belief that he killed Gary Wise and Mike Saxon.'

'I thought he was just in trouble for selling access to government ministers,' Judith said.

'Sell access one day,' Suzie said, as though repeating a well-worn aphorism, 'kill a footballer and a novelist the next.'

'I think there might be something in that,' Angela said. 'Not that I know how you get from the first part to the second.'

'So, what do you know about him?' Judith asked.

'Well, he lives just outside Marlow, on the road up to High Wycombe. In a huge mansion that's on an even larger estate. And he contacted my production company a few months ago. I get approached by lots of individuals – even some rather grand ones – so it didn't seem all that out of the blue. He just said he was a local landowner and, seeing as I also lived in Marlow, did I want to visit his house for afternoon tea. Of course, I said yes. A free cup of tea is a free cup of tea,' Angela acknowledged, as she held up the cup Becks had poured for her. 'Anyway, our assistants found a time that suited us both and I went to visit his house. It's quite something.'

'I think I know it,' Judith said. 'It's not that far from me. Not that I've ever been invited around for tea.'

'Anyway, Lord Harleyford – or William, as he wanted me to call him – was kind of "off" with me right from the start. Don't get me wrong, he was friendly enough, but I could see he was on edge. I'm extremely intuitive like that. In my line of work, you have to be. So we talked about the weather, and how long

I'd lived in Marlow, and my TV show. It turned out William hadn't ever watched it, which made the whole encounter even more peculiar. After a while, I realised he was building up to saying something. You know how it is, you can just tell when someone's delaying what they really want to say.

'But the thing is, he still hadn't said what was on his mind as we finished the tea – so I asked him directly. I just came out with it. "What's the real reason you invited me here?" And that's when he asked me if I knew the author Mike Saxon. It was such a leftfield question. I said I'd met him at a party once, but that hardly constituted knowing him. "Is he a good man?" William asked. "Can he be trusted?"'

'What did you say?'

'I didn't tell him about Mike hitting on me, but I said that I was pretty sure that he couldn't be trusted. To which William asked if I thought Mike would ever break the law? The question flummoxed me. But he kept pressing me. Was Mike "dodgy" in any way? Was it possible someone could use leverage against him?'

'He was trying to find out if Mike could be blackmailed?' Judith asked.

'That's how it sounded to me, but I can't say my memory's all that clear. His questions were so startling, I didn't know what to think.'

'Which is why you got flustered when we mentioned blackmail to you the first time we met,' Becks said.

'It sent me into a bit of a spin, I can tell you.'

'What's he like, Lord Harleyford?' Judith asked.

'He was exactly how I expected him to be. Maybe seventy years old. He looks like he's spent his life eating red meat and drinking red wine. Self-satisfied, that's how he came across.

Someone who's used to getting his own way. Until he started asking about Mike, and then he seemed in a bit of a panic. You know, like he was desperate to hear what I had to say. And then, out of nowhere, he started firing questions at me about Gary Wise. But it's like I told you last time. I don't think I've ever exchanged more than two words with Gary. I didn't have anything to tell him.'

'What did he want to know about Gary?' Suzie asked.

'It was the same sorts of questions that he'd asked about Mike. About whether I thought there was anything that would make Gary susceptible to blackmail. Could he be up to no good? That sort of thing. I was able to deal with his questions easily enough, but things got really strange when I got up to leave. He started asking me if *I* had any skeletons in my closet, and there was this look in his eyes as he asked – it was like I was talking to a madman. I made my excuses and tried to get out of there, but he kept badgering me, telling me that I'd have to be careful in case any of my adoring public found out about my secrets. It could end my career.'

'He was threatening you?' Becks asked.

'That's what it felt like and I fled that place as fast as I could. If I'm honest, I was reeling a bit. But it's why I've been sniffing around the case and trying to find out what you thought was going on. You see, William only mentioned three celebrities to me that day, two of them are now dead, and the third one's me.'

'When did this all happen?' Judith asked.

'At the beginning of the summer.'

'Did you contact Gary Wise or Mike Saxon afterwards?'

'No, it didn't occur to me to. I didn't want to have anything to do with either of them.'

'In which case,' Suzie said, 'we come to the million-dollar question. Why didn't you tell us this the first time we met?'

'It's all my fault, you're right! I thought I could keep the real reason I was interested in the case a secret from you.'

'Why?' Becks asked.

'I didn't want to have to tell you that Lord Harleyford accused me of being up to something or other that was dodgy.'

'Fair enough,' Suzie said. 'But that's because you *are* up to something dodgy, aren't you?'

'I beg your pardon?' Angela asked.

'It's only natural we ask,' Becks said. 'Seeing as this case seems to revolve around blackmail. And you yourself admitted that Lord Harleyford was probing.'

Angela put her cup down firmly on the table. She looked directly at Becks.

'I can tell you that my personal and professional life hasn't ever had even the faintest hint of scandal,' she said. 'I've not so much as had a speeding ticket in the last however-many years. You check the newspapers. Or speak to my friends or my production company. Pull my life apart as much as you want. You won't be able to find anything incriminating.'

'Then why did Lord Harleyford want to see you?' Suzie asked.

'That's what I don't understand. All I can think is that he was shaking me down. You know – like a gangster. He was trying to find out if I had any weaknesses he could exploit. Just like he'd exploited the weaknesses of Gary and Mike. After all, it's like you were saying earlier: the whole world now knows he's corrupt. What if I'm his next victim?'

'You've got nothing to worry about,' Judith said. 'Assuming you really are as innocent as you're saying. But if you are up to anything, your safest course of action would be to turn yourself in to the police.'

'I'm not up to anything, why won't you listen to me?' Angela said in a whining tone that made it clear she thought she was the victim of the story.

'Well,' Suzie said, 'we could start with the fact that you've been hiding in bushes, spying on us.'

'I'm an innocent party in all of this,' Angela said, standing up out of her chair so she could look imperiously down at the women. 'All I've been is helpful to three of you and this is how you thank me? With baseless accusations?'

Angela tossed her head back and stalked out of the room.

'Drama queen,' Suzie mumbled, once she'd gone.

'Can we believe a word she just told us?' Becks asked.

'I don't know,' Judith said. 'A lot of what she said sounded a little too far-fetched to me. Is it really believable that a local landowner – and a lord at that – would be blackmailing local celebrities and then killing them one by one?'

'I'm sure he didn't start out with that as his plan,' Suzie said. 'Just as I didn't start out with the plan of solving murders with you two. It kind of evolved over time.'

'There is, of course, an easy way to find out,' Judith said, a smile at the edge of her mouth. 'We just have to go to Lord Harleyford's house and ask him for ourselves.'

Chapter 24

Suzie's van pulled up at the stone archway that led onto Lord Harleyford's estate. The black and gold ironwork gates were wide open and a wooden board to the side announced that visiting hours for the Harleyford Estate were between 11 a.m. and 3 p.m., and that the tearoom in the orangery was open every day until 4 p.m.

'Do you think he'll mind us turning up unannounced?' Becks asked.

'Let's hope not,' Suzie said as she drove through the arch.

The women found themselves on a gravel driveway that swept down through grass fields dotted with individual oak trees spread across the view at aesthetically pleasing intervals. As they passed a large lake with a fountain that threw water high into the air, they saw a herd of deer standing on the brow of a hill in the distance. And then the driveway rose up again to reveal Lord Harleyford's mansion. It stood starkly grey against the dark winter sky. Like a house in a horror movie, Judith thought.

As they got closer, they could see various trucks, lorries and what looked like a cherry-picker parked up outside the house, while people milled about. Suzie's van reached a wooden barrier that had an arrow pointing to the right and the words 'Car Park' written on it. She turned onto a dirt track that sloped down past a thick wood, following the signs until she parked just beyond an old stable block.

Once the women had climbed out of the van, they saw a sign on a wooden post that pointed to the ornamental gardens in one direction and to the orangery in another.

'What's the plan?' Becks asked.

'I suggest we see if his lordship is receiving,' Judith said.

They headed between two buildings and followed the curve of a track that led back up the slope and through the wood. At this time of year, the leaves had fallen from the branches, so they could still see the imposing house further up the hill.

After a while, the path split in two, with a sign pointing towards the formal gardens. The other path had a little chain strung across it with a sign on it that said 'Private'.

'It's like they're not even trying,' Judith said, stepping over the chain and starting to head through the woods towards the house.

'What if we get caught?' Becks asked, as she and Suzie hopped over the chain and caught up with their friend.

'We can just say we're lost,' Suzie said.

After another couple of minutes of tramping uphill, they emerged onto a large, gravelled area in front of Lord Harleyford's house. Now they were closer, they could see that a dozen or so workmen were gathered around a truck and lifting what looked like a wire-framed sleigh out of the back. There were already two wire-framed reindeer standing nearby. Another worker was in the cherry-picker attaching a vast white bow to an upstairs window. All of the other windows were already similarly festooned. Other people were also buzzing around, some with trolleys of gold-painted chairs, others with swathes of bright fabric. It was all being overseen by a woman who was checking items off on a clipboard.

'I just put up a Christmas tree,' Suzie said huffily.

'Are we really just going to walk in there bold as brass?' Becks asked, as Judith started to crunch across the gravel towards the front door.

'Yes!' Judith said as she reached into her handbag and pulled out her civilian adviser card. 'And this is where you can thank me for not handing over my lanyard to Brendan.'

'I really don't think you should use that,' Becks said. 'What if we get caught?'

'Don't worry, we've got a secret weapon this time.'

'Oh good, what is it?'

'We're going to smile. Good day!' Judith called out to the first worker she passed. Becks and Suzie caught up with her, both grinning as confidently as they could.

The women were soon at the enormous oak front door. It was hundreds of years old and had black iron studs patterned across the wood. It was already open as the workers came and went, so they slipped inside and found themselves in a baronial hall, the walls covered in dark wood panels with crossed swords on them. Two suits of armour stood to attention either side of the main door, and there was a massive stone fireplace at one end surrounded by old sofas and armchairs. Half a dozen people were up ladders stringing fairy lights.

'Bloody hell,' Suzie said. 'That fireplace is bigger than my front room.'

'Excuse me?' a voice called out, and the three friends turned as the woman they'd seen outside with the clipboard entered. She was wearing a cream Arran sweater, tweed skirt and thick woollen tights, and she had an impatient manner about her that suggested she was already irritated with them.

'Are you press?' she barked.

'No – not press,' Judith said, holding up her police lanyard to the side of her head so the woman could see that the photo on it matched her face but lowering it before she could see the expiry date. 'We're working with the Buckinghamshire police. Is his lordship in?'

'Really?' she said, her face souring. 'Haven't you talked to him enough?'

'It's just a few questions,' Becks said as kindly as possible.

'I'm Lady Harleyford,' the woman said. 'You'd better come with me.'

Judith and her friends followed Lady Harleyford out of the grand hall into an old corridor that was lined with Roman busts on plinths. Lady Harleyford didn't give them a glance as she clipped past and turned abruptly through a little door. As the women followed her, they were surprised to find themselves in a domestic kitchen with a black Labrador curled up in a dog bed by an ancient Aga.

A plump man in a checked shirt and dark green cardigan with holes in the right elbow was sitting at the kitchen island, a mug of coffee in his hand and a copy of the *Financial Times* in front of him. Suzie recognised him as Lord Harleyford from his appearances on television.

'Lord Harleyford?' Judith asked.

'Now what?' he drawled.

'We're from the Buckinghamshire police,' Suzie said and then turned to Lady Harleyford. 'Thank you, we've got this.'

'I very much doubt that,' Lady Harleyford said as she left the room.

'Sorry about all of the workmen everywhere,' Lord Harleyford said, not sounding apologetic at all. 'We're throwing our winter ball in a few days, and I'm damned if a police investigation is going to stop it. But how can I help? Haven't you had your pound of flesh?'

'As it happens,' Judith said, 'we're not here about your problems in Parliament. We wondered if you could tell us about your relationship with Mike Saxon.'

'What's that?' Lord Harleyford said, all of the colour draining from his face.

'Could you tell us about your relationship with Mike Saxon?' Judith repeated.

'Y-you mean that author who died?' he stammered.

'That's the one,' Suzie said.

'Terrible business,' Lord Harleyford said, hiding his confusion by taking a sip of coffee. He put the cup back down on the table. 'You understand I had no kind of relationship with him. I didn't know him at all.'

'But you know he's dead?' Becks asked.

'It was in the papers.'

'And you never met him at any of the swish events in Marlow I bet you go to?' Suzie asked.

'Absolutely not.'

'And never invited him to one of your balls?' Becks asked.

'Never,' Lord Harleyford said. 'I've never met him.'

'Then what about Gary Wise?' Judith asked.

Lord Harleyford gulped and then made a big play of trying to check his memory.

'No,' he said. 'Can't say I know the name.'

Lord Harleyford got up and took his cup to the sink.

'Oh, come on, you must have heard of him,' Suzie said. 'He's the footballer who was shot dead.'

'Don't follow football. I no more knew that footballer than I knew Mike Saxon.'

'Angela Gulliver says different,' Suzie said.

Although his back was to them, they could see Lord Harleyford freeze.

'Are you going to deny knowing her?' Judith asked.

'I am,' he said without turning around. 'I don't know who you're talking about.'

'You invited her to tea,' Becks said. 'There'll be a paper trail between your assistant and hers.'

'I meet a lot of people—'

'She said you were blackmailing Gary Wise and Mike Saxon,' Judith said. 'Why was that? And why did Angela also say you tried to blackmail her?'

'Is it related to you selling access to ministers in Parliament?' Suzie asked.

'That's not been proved!' Lord Harleyford barked as he spun around to face the women. 'And I can tell you it won't be. I'm fighting those allegations through the courts. Now I'm sorry, I appreciate you're here on official business, but I've a ball to organise, I can't possibly spare the time,' he said, heading over to a door in the corner of the room. 'You can see yourselves out,' he added. With that, he pulled the door open and stepped into a courtyard outside.

'Have you been blackmailing Gary and Mike?' Suzie shouted after him, but Lord Harleyford had gone.

'We can't let him get away,' Judith said and followed him outside, Suzie and Becks right behind her.

The women saw Lord Harleyford stride across the courtyard, so they set off after him.

'What's your connection to the victims?' Becks called out as they saw their quarry disappear down the side of some outbuildings.

'Why did you try and blackmail Angela Gulliver?' Judith shouted as they picked up their pace, but when they rounded the buildings, they saw that Lord Harleyford had vanished. All they could see was a gate that led into a grass paddock and, to the side of that, the beginnings of the wood they'd walked through to get to the house.

'Oh,' Becks said.

'Where did he go?' Suzie asked.

'Hold on,' Judith said, indicating some fresh footprints she could see in the damp grass in front of them. Letting out an 'oof' as she bent down to inspect them, she saw that they led across the lawn towards a low stone building a little way away. They went straight up to the front door.

'Got you,' Judith said.

Judith and her friends followed the footprints towards the building. As they arrived, Judith put her hand on the brass handle of the door.

'Are you sure we should do this?' Becks asked.

'He can't just run away,' Suzie said. 'We need answers.'

Judith pushed the door open and stepped into what looked like an old storeroom that had become a dumping ground for broken pieces of furniture and other artefacts from around the estate. There was an ancient Welsh dresser next to some old iron beds; a pile of wooden pallets next to a clump of fire extinguishers; a sit-on mower next to a neat pile of old wicker hampers.

There was no sign of Lord Harleyford.

'OK, he's not here,' Becks said. 'We can go.'

'Wait a moment,' Judith said as she moved through the room. 'The footsteps outside were fresh, I think he's in here somewhere.'

'Lord Harleyford?' Suzie called out.

There was no answer, so Suzie stalked over to an old wardrobe and yanked the doors open with an 'Aha!' There was no one inside. It just contained a row of oily overalls on coat hangers.

'Over here,' Judith said, beckoning to her friends from the centre of the room.

Suzie and Becks went to join Judith and saw that there was an open wooden trapdoor in the floor with old stone steps that led down into almost perfect darkness below.

'He went down there?' Suzie asked, trying not to sound too tremulous.

'He's not up here,' Judith said. 'Phones out, ladies.'

Judith reached into her purse, pulled out her phone and turned on the torch feature. Becks and Suzie did the same.

'Really?' Becks asked.

'For once,' Suzie said, 'I think I agree with Becks.'

'Don't be so feeble. Come on,' Judith said, and took the first step down into pitch black.

Chapter 25

The stairs were made of worn stone and Judith had to throw her phone's light directly onto the next step down just to see her way. As for the room she and her friends were descending into, there were no lights and the air was dank and damp. But there was also a stifling smell of something rotting. It was pungent and almost sweet. Judith pulled a hankie from her handbag to put over her nose. When she reached the bottom step, she shone her torch around and Becks and Suzie did the same on the steps behind her.

They seemed to be in an old cellar. It was hard to get a sense of its size, but there were pillars spaced evenly to keep the floor above them aloft. Shining her torch on the nearest pillar, Judith saw that it was covered in what looked like green algae.

She pointed her torch at the flagstone floor and thought she could see the faintest of footsteps in the dust. They led further into the darkness of the room.

'Come on,' she said, 'there are footsteps to follow.'

'We really shouldn't be doing this,' Becks said.

'If a lord of the realm can do it, I think we can too. It's one step at a time.'

'I'll stay back here,' Suzie said with a knowing nod. 'Make sure you both can find your way back to the stairs.'

'If you want to stay here on your own?' Judith asked.

'No, you're right,' Suzie said in a rush. 'I'll come with you.'

'Just make sure you don't think about what else could be down here beyond our lights and you should be fine.'

'Oh great, now that's what I'm doing,' Suzie said, but she got in line behind Becks and Judith and together they headed into the darkness.

From nowhere, a squeaking shadow flapped past their heads and the women froze.

'What was that?' Becks asked.

'I think,' Judith said, 'it was a bat.'

Her two friends inhaled sharply.

'Don't worry,' she continued. 'It's going to be more frightened of you than you are of it.'

'I wouldn't bet on it,' Becks said. 'Heavens, there are going to be mice down here, aren't there?'

'Don't tell me you're afraid of mice?' Judith asked.

'I know, I know! It's such a stereotype – the scared housewife – but I'm terrified of them getting up my legs.'

'Oh God,' Suzie said, 'what if there's a nest of rats?'

'Ladies!' Judith snapped. 'Let's show a bit of mettle. Follow me.'

Judith carried on into the darkness, her two friends keeping up with her if only to make sure they weren't left behind.

'Oh,' Judith said after a while. 'It's the end of the room. Hang on, what's this?'

Judith lifted her phone and used the torch to light the wall.

They could all see a faded mural. The paint was peeling, but it was possible to see three life-sized women dressed in togas and dancing in a forest setting. One of the women was holding an amphora, another a lyre and the third was playing a pan pipe.

'OK, that's creepy,' Suzie said. 'Why's there a painting down here?'

'I don't know,' Judith said as she held the torch up to look closer. 'It's been painted onto old wood panelling.'

'Look at this,' Becks said, throwing her light on the floor. The footsteps in the dust they'd been following went up to the wall and then stopped. 'Where did he go?'

'I know!' Suzie said. 'He's a vampire and he turned himself into that bat that flew past us.'

'Suzie!' Becks admonished.

'But he can't have come down here, can he?' Suzie said. 'Or we'd have bumped into him. These must be old footprints. There's no one about.'

'Do you know what I'm noticing?' Judith said. 'My ankles are cold.'

'Oh, OK,' Suzie said, 'we're in an underground cellar with a weird painting and a vanishing lord, but you want to talk about your ankles.'

'Hold on,' Judith said and started to feel more carefully along each section of the panelled wall.

'What are you doing?' Becks asked.

'There's a draught.'

'Please can we go now? This really couldn't get any worse.'

Judith put her palms to the wall and pushed.

A section of panelling hinged open, revealing a door. On the other side, there was a rough, rocky tunnel that sloped downwards.

'It got worse,' Becks said.

'We can't go down there,' Suzie said. 'It could lead anywhere.'

'It's where Lord Harleyford went,' Judith said, indicating the footsteps in the dust that stopped at the open door. It wasn't possible to see any footprints in the rock of the tunnel. 'The footsteps go right up to this door.'

'What if he turned around and left because he was – you know? – terrified?'

'He went down this tunnel,' Judith said, trying not to sound exasperated. 'We just have to follow him.'

Judith stepped into the tunnel and started to head downwards. The air became even colder as she moved away from her friends. She could see her breath in the spilled light from her phone.

Becks looked at Suzie, gulped once, and then followed Judith – with Suzie bringing up the rear.

'This is the bit in the film where we have to agree we aren't going to split up,' Suzie whispered.

'Shh!' Judith called back.

'Just trying to keep my spirits up.'

'Then can you do it more quietly?'

The corridor was dark and oppressive, and it was taking all of Judith's courage to pretend to her friends that she wasn't just as scared as they were. There were tonnes of cold rock above her and it took a real force of will to lift up her feet and put them down one in front of the other. Especially when it looked as though the corridor was heading towards a dead end. But when she reached it, she saw that there was an arch to her left that seemed to open onto a larger chamber. As she stepped through, lights came on and she was stunned by what she saw.

The room was broadly circular, had a large fire pit in the middle of it, and the rest of space was taken up with armchairs, sofas and occasional tables with lamps on them. It was these lamps that had lit up as she'd entered. And now she was looking more closely, there was a kitchen area off to one side with a double-height wine fridge and a washing-up area with what looked like a dishwasher next to it.

'Wow,' Becks said as she entered behind Judith.

'You can say that again,' Suzie agreed as she arrived last. 'How did you get the lights to turn on?'

'They came on automatically,' Judith said, walking to the centre of the room.

'What is this place?' Becks asked.

'It looks like an old cave,' Suzie said, looking up at the rough ceiling. 'That someone's dug a tunnel to. Aye aye,' she added as she saw a four-poster bed in a recessed alcove. 'With overnight facilities.'

Judith noticed that there were two further tunnels leading off from the cave. One, she could see, led downwards quite sharply. She went over to it and saw that a table to the side of its entrance had battery-powered torches on it.

'I'm not sure I ever want to know where this tunnel goes,' she said. 'It just heads downwards into darkness.'

Instead, she licked her forefinger, held her hand up and felt the chill of the thinnest breeze on her fingertip. It was coming from the direction of the other archway.

'This place gives me the creeps,' Becks said. 'Where did Lord Harleyford go?'

'If I were to guess, I think that tunnel on the other side of the room leads out of here,' Judith said. 'But I agree, this place is creepy. Come on.'

Judith went over to the other arch and, once Becks and Suzie had joined her in the tunnel, the lights behind them turned off and they were once again plunged into darkness.

'Huh,' Suzie said, impressed. 'That's a neat trick. Come on, let's see where we go next. Maybe it'll be the gift shop.'

Suzie pushed past Judith, the light on her phone shining brightly as she led them further along the passage. After a minute, there was a bend in the tunnel and they found themselves on another straight stretch that ended in another turn. They took it, all three women increasingly struggling with their feelings of claustrophobia. After rounding yet another corner, they found themselves at the base of a rickety wooden staircase that led upwards. There was a shimmer of light at the top.

'OK,' Suzie said. 'I think we know how Lord Harleyford got out.'

Suzie mounted the stairs first – the old wood creaked – and climbed upwards until she found herself looking at an old metal door, surrounded by stone. She turned the little handle; the staircase was suddenly flooded with light as she pushed the door open and stepped out into the fresh air. Blinking so that her eyes could get accustomed to the daylight, she looked about and saw that she was deep in the woods they'd walked through to get to the house. Making room for Judith and Becks's exit, she turned to look at where they'd come from and saw that the metal door was set directly into a rocky outcrop covered in little bushes.

The door was rusty, had an old 'Danger: Do Not Enter' sign on it, and she saw that there was a metal keypad immediately above the handle. Suzie pushed the door closed and the lock engaged with a heavy click.

'OK, what the hell was that?' Suzie asked.

'That's not the question we should be asking,' Judith said. 'What I want to know is, why did Lord Harleyford feel he had to escape from us like that?'

'That's obvious. He panicked the moment we mentioned Mike Saxon. And then he flipped out when we got onto Gary Wise and Angela Gulliver.'

'So what are we saying?' Becks asked. 'Is Angela right? Is he the killer?'

'I don't know,' Suzie said as she tested the idea. 'I reckon he's definitely involved. Somehow. Or knows something. But I just don't buy that someone that wealthy would need to resort to blackmail.'

'Someone that wealthy has already resorted to selling government access for money,' Becks said. 'For some people, enough money is never enough.'

'And I suppose a big house like that is going to eat the cash as well,' Suzie said. 'Let alone that sex dungeon – or whatever it was – we were just in.'

'There's something else as well,' Judith said. 'If he really was the killer, I can't help feeling he'd have had a story lined up to spin us the moment we started asking questions about Mike and Gary. Because you're right, Suzie. He completely fell apart almost instantly, didn't he?'

'Unless he was so sure of himself that he never thought anyone would ever come knocking,' Suzie said. 'Not that that sounds very plausible. His wife made it pretty clear to us that he's already had a heap of interviews with the police.'

'Can I suggest we get out of here before he comes back?' Becks said. 'And I want to look those caves up online, because I think I know what they are.'

'You do?' Suzie asked.

'Possibly. But can we focus on the "getting away from here" part of the plan first?'

'Good idea,' Judith said, and started to push through the scrubby bushes until she found the main track that led from the gardens back to the car park. They scurried down the path and were so keen on getting off the premises that they didn't even stop to get some of the freshly made crumpets that were advertised on a blackboard outside the orangery.

As Suzie drove her van back towards the main road, Becks pulled out her phone and started to type in some search terms.

'I was right!' she said.

'What have you got?' Judith asked.

'It was a memory I had from somewhere. I think a parishioner once mentioned it to me. Lord Harleyford comes from a notorious family. They made their money hundreds of years ago and have been as rich as Croesus ever since. Which means there was never anything for the family to do.'

'There's always *something* to do,' Judith said.

'Not if you were this guy – Francis, the seventh Lord Harleyford,' Becks said, indicating the screen of her phone. 'He set up a drinking society for his friends in London called the Hellfire Club. Wherever they went, their behaviour was so bad that they got banned from ever going back. But Francis knew there was a cave near his family home, so the rumour was that he got it fitted out for him and his friends to have their depraved parties in. Not that anyone ever knew what went on at them, but the motto of the society was "Wine, Women and Song", so I think we can guess.'

'Told you,' Suzie said. 'Sex dungeon.'

'It does sound rather grim,' Judith agreed.

'There were stories that they'd try and summon spirits,' Becks said, looking down at her phone. 'Or raise the dead. The whole club was shrouded in the occult. And the caves became known as the Hellfire Caves. But this was all supposed to have stopped in the nineteenth century.'

'The way the lighting came on automatically suggests it's still in use,' Suzie said.

'Is the Hellfire Club still going?' Becks asked. 'Is that what these murders are about? There's some kind of secret society with Lord Harleyford at the heart of it? And they get up to really bad things when they're together in the caves under his house.'

'Which could be why Gary and Mike were being blackmailed!' Suzie suggested in excitement as an idea overtook her. 'Someone found out what they were up to and was making them pay to keep their secret a secret!'

'But Gary and Mike were both paying their blackmailer, weren't they?' Becks said. 'So why did the blackmailer have to kill them?'

'Maybe Lord Harleyford found out that two members of his secret society were being blackmailed,' Judith said. 'So he killed them to make sure they didn't spill any of the secrets of the Hellfire Club.'

'You know what?' Suzie said. 'That sounds possible.'

As Suzie drove her van over Marlow bridge, a rowing eight appeared out of the mist below them on the water, flashed under the bridge and then was lost again in the mist on the other side.

'There's so much about this case we're still not getting,' Judith said. 'For example, how does Angela fit into this? Is she a concerned bystander trying to get to the bottom of what's going on? Or is she more involved than she's admitting?'

'Do we honestly think she could be the killer?' Becks asked.

'I don't know,' Judith said. 'I just don't know.'

The women fell into a contemplative silence as Suzie drove down the lane that led to Judith's house. As they passed the jagged stump of an old oak tree, Judith found herself remembering her first murder case. The huge oak had come down in a terrible storm, which had messed with her plans to catch her neighbour's killer. She'd nearly ended up with a bullet in her head because of it. She shuddered at the memory.

Suzie spun the wheel to her van and drove onto Judith's driveway. There was a cream Fiat 500 car parked by her door.

'Who's that?' Suzie asked.

'I don't know,' Judith said, as Suzie parked up and they all got out.

Approaching the car, Judith called out, 'Hello, can I help you?'

The driver's door of the Fiat opened and Eleni Paphides got out. She was dressed in a long black coat and black gloves.

Judith stopped in her tracks, Suzie and Becks stopping with her. Together they watched Eleni approach like an avenging angel.

'How dare you return to the scene of your crime!' Judith said, before Eleni could speak.

'I beg your pardon?'

'I know it was you who wrote that message on my mirror, but you need to know that you can't intimidate me – I refuse to play your game.'

'I've given all of my evidence to the police,' Eleni said.

The news caught Judith by surprise.

'I'm sorry?' she asked.

'Just like your friend suggested,' Eleni said, looking at Suzie.

'Woah,' Suzie said, as she realised how this sounded.

'You did what?' Judith asked her friend.

'It's possible we had a quiet word with Eleni,' Becks said. 'We wanted her to stop threatening you. And we sort of ended up agreeing that Eleni should perhaps take her evidence to the police.'

'Are you serious?' Judith said in mounting fury. 'We've got a killer to catch! I don't have time to deal with the police poking around in my life as well!'

'That's not my problem,' Eleni said. 'The police have all of my evidence. *All* of it, Judith Potts, not just what I showed you. This is your last chance to admit to what you did to my father. You go to the police of your own free will and make a full confession and they'll be more lenient. Because if you don't, then I can tell you, the next time there's a knock at the door, it will be the police arresting you for murder.'

Eleni turned on her heels, returned to her car and drove off.

Chapter 26

'I'm so sorry!' Suzie said as she and Becks followed Judith into her sitting room.

'What were you thinking?' Judith asked.

'I wasn't thinking, that's the problem. But I couldn't bear what she was doing to you, and I could see that she could have kept it up for days. For weeks! Just playing with you like a cat with a mouse.'

'So you told her to go to the police?' Judith asked.

'I didn't mean to – it just came out.'

Judith slumped into her armchair.

'No, it's all right,' she said. 'I suppose there's only one way to remove the plaster and that's to rip it off.'

'Is it possible she's bluffing?' Becks asked. 'About having definitive evidence? You know – beyond the photograph?'

'She's very definitely bluffing,' Judith muttered, as much to herself as to anyone else.

'But that means there isn't, in fact, any evidence that proves you were involved.'

'The police may still want to interview me, and they could whip me off to the police station at any moment. So we must redouble our efforts. And that means we need to focus on how Lord Harleyford fits into the case.'

'Are you sure we shouldn't be focusing on Eleni?' Becks asked.

'I'm done with her!' Judith snapped. 'There are two dead people who deserve justice, so I suggest we try and help them while we can, because I can't imagine Brendan's going to be able to catch their killer without us.'

As she spoke, Judith noticed the *Marlovian* magazines that Becks had earlier tidied into a neat pile. Seeing them all squared off irritated her. She felt it represented how both Becks and Suzie had interfered – straightening up the edges of her life when they really had no business doing so. But seeing the pile of magazines also gave her an idea.

'Lord Harleyford's ball,' she said to her friends' bemusement.

'What about it?' Suzie asked.

'It will have been covered by *The Marlovian*, won't it?'

Judith went over to the glossy magazines and picked up the top copy. The cover showed a red-jacketed man in a white-peaked cap with a swan's feather sticking out of it. The headline read 'Swan Upping Comes to Marlow'.

'It covers everything that happens in the town,' Judith said. 'And that includes photos from all of the posh events.'

'Oh, I get it!' Suzie said, her face lighting up. 'Like Lord Harleyford's ball last year!'

'Exactly. But it won't just be his ball, they'll have photos from every smart event in Marlow, won't they? I bet all of our victims and suspects appear in one photo or another.'

'Good thinking,' Becks said. 'Let me go and put the kettle on.'

As Becks left the room, Suzie chose the top copy of *The Marlovian.* The cover showed the Olympic rower Naomi Riches turning on the Christmas lights in the high street. She then flicked through the pages until she found a colourful spread of photographs. 'Oh God, these captions!' she said, indicating a photo that showed a woman wearing an enormous hat. '"The High Sheriff of Buckinghamshire, Lady Samara Wash." Very la-de-dah. But not currently a murder suspect.'

'Not yet,' Judith said as she picked up the next magazine on the pile and started to flick through it.

Becks soon returned and the women set to their task properly fortified with steaming cups of tea, although it was hard to keep Suzie focused on the task. She was too easily distracted by what the great and good of Marlow were wearing at every social event, and some of their more preposterous names.

'Barbara ffolkes,' she said with a delighted chuckle. 'Who has a surname that starts with two Fs? And why isn't it capitalised? Some people are weird.'

'What's the event?' Becks asked.

'Last year's Pub in the Park.'

'Are any of our murder victims or suspects present?'

'Not as far as I can see – oh, I see what you mean, you want me to stay focused. That's "focused" spelt with one F.'

Becks smiled and returned her attention to the magazine in her hand. The truth was that she was enjoying the task enormously. Her position as the vicar's wife meant that she'd come to know a lot of the people who were in the photographs, and she was getting a warm glow of satisfaction knowing that while she might have only come to Marlow a few years before, she had definitely been putting down roots.

'Got it!' Suzie suddenly announced, spilling her cup of tea as she clattered it back into its saucer on the table to her side.

'What is it?' Judith asked.

'Photos from the winter ball Lord Harleyford threw last year.'

'Fabulous!' Judith said.

'It says here it used to be held every year until the 1980s. Lord Harleyford decided to revive it a few years ago. And look, it's grand as hell,' Suzie said, indicating the photos that showed guests in black tie and ballgowns in front of braziers outside the house; fire-eaters performing; waiters serving champagne and dozens of photos of a ceilidh band in the main ballroom of the house, the hundred or so guests all dancing.

'Who's in the photos?' Judith asked hungrily.

'I've seen Lord and Lady Harleyford,' Suzie said as she turned her attention back to the beginning of the sequence. 'But no one from either of the murders is jumping out to me. Oh, hold on, yes they are!' she added, pointing to a photo on the other side of the page. It must have been taken later in the evening as it showed Lord Harleyford with his bow tie loose around his neck, the top button of his dress shirt undone. But it wasn't Lord Harleyford that caught Suzie's eye, it was the two men he was standing in between. One of them was Gary Wise and the other was Mike Saxon. Gary looked awkward, but Mike was grinning widely and there was a triumphant look to him. It was perhaps unsurprising, because he had his arm around the waist of a beautiful woman who was wearing a little black cocktail dress.

The woman was Jamilah Khalil, and she had a wide smile on her face.

'She lied to us!' Becks said.

'And not just Jamilah,' Judith said. 'Lord Harleyford told us he didn't know Mike Saxon or Gary Wise. And that they'd never been to his ball before. So what are the three of them doing together like this?'

'Stuff that,' Suzie said. 'I want to know what Mike's doing at the ball with Jamilah instead of Serena. And why's she letting him put his hand around her waist like that.'

'She's one of his women, isn't she?' Becks said.

'Of course she is!' Suzie said, slapping her forehead in a pantomime of comprehension. 'Why on earth did we believe her when she said she wasn't? We all said at the time that there was more to her and Mike than she was letting on.'

'Although . . .' Becks said, looking at the photo more carefully. 'He's so much older than her. Do we really believe she was his date?'

'Why else would she be there?'

'What if Mike received his invitation and told her he wanted her to accompany him? As his assistant, I'm not sure she'd have been able to turn him down.'

'She's having way too much fun in the photo for that to be an official engagement. But you know what? There's an easy way of finding out if Jamilah and Mike were ever an item, isn't there? We just have to ask her.'

'But she'll just lie to us again,' Becks said.

'You're right,' Judith said. 'Although there's still a way we may be able to find out the truth. Because we now know that if she and Mike were ever an item, he'll have taken her to the Holyport Hotel.' She went to her coat rack, plucked down her cape, swished it over her shoulders. 'I think we need to make a few enquiries,' she added, and then left.

Suzie and Becks joined Judith outside, and the three women

drove in Suzie's van to Holyport, where they parked up outside the run-down hotel. As they walked into the building, they found themselves in a draughty reception area. Suzie rubbed her hands together to get a bit of warmth into them, and then the three friends headed over to an antique desk, where an old man was sitting wearing a green waistcoat with a name badge on it.

'Hello,' Judith said, holding up her warrant card before smartly returning it to her handbag. 'We're with the Buckinghamshire police and have a few questions.'

The man coughed – a wet phlegmy expectoration that he swallowed before smiling in a way that bared his nicotine-stained teeth.

'I'll do whatever I can to help,' he said.

'Thank you,' Judith said, trying not to show her distaste. 'It's about the murder of Mike Saxon.'

The receptionist's eyes lit up at the name.

'It is, is it?' he said.

'Did you know him?' Suzie asked.

'You could say that.'

The women waited.

'Then could you say?' Judith asked, unable to keep the irritation out of her voice.

'He was one of those men who book a room, but never for the night, if you know what I mean. It was strictly by the hour.'

'That's a thing, is it?' Becks asked, surprised.

'If we're not running at full capacity, it's better to hire out a bedroom for a few hours than not at all.'

'You make this place sound like a knocking shop,' Suzie said.

'Aren't all hotels basically knocking shops?' the man asked with a laugh that became a wet cough. He got out an old handkerchief and wiped at his lips.

Judith had a sudden desire to be anywhere but where she was, so she got her copy of *The Marlovian* out of her handbag and showed the photo of Lord Harleyford, Gary Wise, Mike Saxon and Jamilah Khalil to the man. She asked him if he recognised Jamilah and the man made a great play of taking the magazine from Judith, peering closely at the photo and then shaking his head.

'Can't say I do.'

'Are you sure?' Suzie asked. 'We think she's one of Mike Saxon's girlfriends.'

'Oh, I've not seen *her* before,' the man said, but the way he leaned on the word 'her' made it clear that there was someone else in the photo that he recognised.

'Then who have you seen before?' Suzie said.

'Well, that would be telling, wouldn't it?'

'And it would be a great help if you did just that,' Becks said.

'I'm more than happy to,' the man said and then sat back in his seat and looked at the women with a leer.

'Oh,' Judith said, as she realised what was going on. 'You expect us to pay you for the information?'

'No, we don't need to do that,' Suzie said, stepping in front of Judith so she could look directly at the man. 'I'd like to book a room for two hours, please.'

The man's eye twitched as he tried to work out the angle that Suzie was playing.

'That's right,' Suzie said. 'A room for two hours. And then I'm going to go to Tripadvisor and list everything that's wrong with this hotel, starting with the man who works on reception.'

'Don't do that!'

'"I found the receptionist rude, dismissive and he kept coughing into a hankie – it was disgusting."'

'It's this woman!' the man said, jabbing his finger down on a photo on the other side of the page to the one that had Jamilah in it. 'Mike Saxon's been here dozens of times. Each time with a different woman, but I recognise this woman here. She came with him to the hotel about six months ago. And it was one of the times he booked a room for two hours in the middle of the afternoon. I remember seeing them together drinking champagne in the bar. I'm sure of it.'

Judith, Suzie and Becks crowded around the magazine and saw that the photo showed a group of revellers who were raising their glasses in a toast to the camera. The receptionist's finger was pointing at the person in the centre of the group.

It was Gary Wise's wife, Bethany.

Chapter 27

When Judith, Suzie and Becks arrived at Bethany's mansion in Hurley, they discovered that the lychgate had a large padlock and chain on it.

'Oh,' Suzie said. 'We're locked out.'

'Stuff that for a game of soldiers,' Judith said. 'We know there's a path through the woods to the back of Gary's house. Let's see if we can find it.'

Judith strode off by the flint and brick wall that marked the edge of Gary and Bethany's property, and Becks and Suzie followed. They kept the wall on their right-hand side as they walked up the track, a thick wood on the other side.

'It's creepy to think this is how the killer got in,' Becks said.

'Assuming it wasn't Bethany who killed Gary and she just pretended there was someone in the woods,' Suzie said.

'Do we really believe she killed her own husband?' Beck asked.

'Depends,' Suzie said. 'If she was having an affair with Mike Saxon, who knows what she might have done. Gary's a rich man. Divorce him and you get half of what he had. Kill him and you get it all. And I definitely got the impression, the last time we were here, that Bethany's a woman who likes the finer things in life.'

Judith found herself remembering the various vases of freshly cut flowers that were on display when they'd first met. And the four ovens.

'Let's not get ahead of ourselves,' Becks said. 'First, we need to find out why she was at the Holyport Hotel with Mike. Maybe there's an innocent explanation.'

As they walked, the woods on their left got thicker and the wall on their right remained impregnable.

'Bloody hell, their garden's big,' Suzie complained.

After a few more minutes, the wall turned sharply to the right and the women realised that they'd reached the furthest corner of the property. Beyond it, the woods thickened out on both sides of the track.

'OK, so there's no way into their house this way,' Suzie said.

'There must be,' Judith said and carried on down the track. After twenty yards or so, the path took a turn to the right and headed deeper into the woods. But it soon ended in a clearing that contained a large pile of stacked logs.

'Right, so the house is somewhere in that direction,' Judith said, pointing back through the woods. 'For the police to have believed the intruder got in this way, there has to be a route to the garden.'

Judith pulled back the branches of a tree, ducked down and started to push into the wood.

'And we're sure this is still a good idea?' Becks asked, pushing a branch to one side and following.

'Ow!' Suzie said, as the branch Becks had been holding snapped back into her face.

'Sorry!'

'Quiet, you two,' Judith said. 'We don't want anyone to hear us. Although I'll tell you this much. If the killer came in this way, in the dead of night, it can't have been easy to make their approach.'

'You can say that again,' Suzie grumbled.

'I can see the house,' Becks said and pointed ahead of them.

It was true. The trees were thinning out and it was possible to see the outline of Gary and Bethany's house. The women made better progress as they entered a clearing and could finally see across the lawn to the Tudor mansion.

'Do you think this is where he was killed?' Suzie asked, looking at the open ground around them.

'There's a clear line of sight to the upstairs windows of the house,' Becks said and then shivered. 'This could be where it happened. The killer came through the woods and Gary came from the house and met him here.'

'Hey!' a voice shouted from the direction of the house and they looked over to see Bethany approaching.

'We've been rumbled,' Suzie said.

'How on earth did she know we were here?' Judith asked.

'What's the plan?' Becks asked.

'We style it out,' Suzie said and then strode off to meet Bethany. She called out a confident 'Hello!' and then, with her next step, dropped like a stone out of view.

'Suzie!' Becks shouted, and she and Judith ran over to see what had happened to their friend.

There was a deep ditch that separated the garden from the wood and Suzie had fallen straight into it.

'Oh,' Judith said, 'a ha-ha.'

'It's not funny,' Suzie said, as she got heavily back onto her feet and began to climb out.

'I know it's not funny,' Judith said. 'But it *is* a ha-ha.'

'I swear to God—'

'No, the ditch is called a ha-ha,' Judith said, unable to stifle a laugh. 'It allows a garden to be separated from agricultural land without a big hedge getting in the way.'

'So why's it called a ha-ha?' Suzie asked as she held out her hand and Becks helped pull her out.

'I think because it's the sound you make when you fall into one,' Becks replied.

'Just what on earth do you think you're doing here?' Bethany said as she arrived.

'Just checking to see how funny your ha-ha is,' Suzie said. 'And I'll be honest, it's not funny at all.'

'You can't just come here like this. You're not with the police – you lied to me last time; you have to get off my land.'

'That's not what's going to happen,' Judith said.

'I spoke to Detective Sergeant Perry and he said—'

'You can first tell us why you were visiting hotels with Mike Saxon and *then* we'll get off your land.'

'What are you talking about?' she asked, but the women could see that her mind was scrambling to catch up with the question.

'The Holyport Hotel,' Suzie said, picking a dead leaf out of her hair. 'You and Mike Saxon. The receptionist remembers seeing you both together drinking champagne. On an afternoon when Mike had booked his room by the hour.'

'I don't have to explain anything to you.'

'You don't,' Judith conceded, 'but you will have to explain it to the police when we tell them.'

'You're just interfering busybodies,' Bethany said angrily. 'I knew it the first time you turned up here.'

'You were having an affair with Mike Saxon, weren't you?' Suzie said. 'So perhaps you can tell us where you got the gun from that you used to kill him and, before that, your husband?'

Suzie's words hit Bethany hard. She blinked a couple of times as she tried to make sense of what she'd just heard, and then the women saw the moment that all the fight went out of her.

'You honestly think I had an affair with that oaf?' she asked, apparently more hurt than upset.

'So then what happened?' Becks asked.

'OK, I admit I went to that hotel to meet Mike a few months ago. I found out why he chose the place soon enough. He was disgusting. Insisting we have a glass of champagne. And then, when I tried to leave, he said he had a room booked upstairs if we wanted to go up there "for a tumble". I was out of there in ten seconds flat.'

'Why did you even meet him?' Suzie asked.

'It was his idea. We'd met the Christmas before at a party.'

'At Lord Harleyford's winter ball,' Judith suggested.

'That's right,' Bethany said, unable to hide how impressed she was with Judith's knowledge. 'It was almost exactly a year ago. Anyway, Mike made a beeline for me, and I was kind of excited to meet him. My dad read his books when I was growing up, so I knew he was really famous. We chatted for a bit, but I got these weird vibes from him, so I told him I was married to Gary. And that's when he said Gary should write his autobiography. He said he knew Gary hadn't fulfilled his potential as a footballer, but that's what made him interesting. I told him he was being rude as hell, but he just laughed like it didn't matter. And the thing is,

I'd been thinking for some time that Gary should tell his story. I mean, the journey he's been on, and the things he's seen, it's kind of mind-blowing. So I kept the conversation going, but said that Gary wasn't too good at writing, so it wouldn't be easy for him. That's when Mike explained how he wouldn't have to write a word. All he'd have to do was talk to someone. And that person – the ghostwriter – would do the writing for him. And Gary's always been a good talker. Mike told me he'd find out who the best sports ghostwriter was if I gave him my number.

'So I did and didn't think any more of it. Just got on with my life. But a few weeks later, I got a text from him saying that he had just the guy for me. Would I go to the Holyport Hotel to talk to him about it? I didn't want to meet him. Not after how creepy he'd been at the party. But I figured, he'd gone to all of this trouble, I couldn't say no. I went to the hotel and he was there, with a bottle of champagne, expecting me to be impressed. It was just after he'd given me Harry Asquith's name that he suggested we go upstairs together. Apparently, Mike and Harry were doubles partners at his tennis club. He'd not known how good he was as a writer – which is why he felt he'd had to ask around. But, he told me, he'd been pleased to learn that Harry was considered to be one of the best in the business.'

'Harry and Mike were doubles partners?' Suzie asked.

'That's what he told me.'

'How interesting,' Judith said to her friends. 'Harry told us he barely knew Mike, didn't he?'

'Why are you so interested in Harry?' Bethany asked.

'Because before now,' Judith said, 'Harry was one of only two people who knew both victims. The other is Lord Harleyford – we've a photo of all three of them at the ball last year.'

'But now there's you as well,' Suzie said. 'That afternoon, when you went to the hotel, are you sure you didn't go upstairs with Mike?'

'How can you even ask me that?' Bethany said. 'He was a nasty old man, why would I be interested in him?'

'Even so, you're going to have to tell the police what you've told us,' Suzie said, and, as she spoke, she nodded to indicate behind Bethany's shoulder. 'Which you'll be able to do quite easily, as I see they've just arrived.'

Suzie's friends turned and saw that Brendan was approaching across the garden with two uniformed police officers.

'They're not here to talk to me,' Bethany said. 'Do you really think we don't have security cameras that cover the entrance to the woods? I saw the three of you the moment you turned onto the track that runs down the side of the house.'

'But the police said there wasn't any CCTV footage of the killer approaching the woods on the night your husband was killed,' Becks said.

'Whoever it was must have evaded the cameras.'

'In the middle of the night?' Judith asked. 'How did the killer get into the woods without being picked up by them?'

Before Bethany could answer, Brendan called out.

'What are you doing here?'

'Sorry,' Suzie said breezily, 'we got lost.'

'Seriously?' Becks asked. 'That's our line?'

'It's our line and we're sticking to it.'

'We were taking a walk through the woods,' Judith said, as Brendan and the two uniformed officers arrived. 'We got lost and Mrs Wise here is helping us off her property. And I know the three of us strike fear into the strongest of men, but I think turning up with two uniformed coppers for backup's a bit feeble, Detective Sergeant.'

Brendan flushed at the accusation – and at the reminder that he wasn't an inspector yet – and then pulled himself up to his full height.

'That's because I've been looking for you, Mrs Potts. New evidence has been handed in in relation to the unexplained death of your husband in 1976. I'd like to ask you to accompany me to the station to answer a few questions about what happened that day.'

'She's not coming,' Suzie said.

'And if you won't come voluntarily, I'll arrest you.'

'You can't do that!' Becks said.

'Don't you tell me what the police can and cannot do, Mrs Starling. Mrs Potts, will you come voluntarily?'

'Do I have any choice?' Judith asked, a tremor in her voice.

Brendan didn't reply.

'Then . . .' she said and crossed a little wooden bridge off to the side that spanned the ha-ha and started to walk towards the house. Brendan flashed a look of triumph at Suzie and Becks before turning to follow, his two police officers at his side.

Becks and Suzie watched their friend being marched off the premises and were utterly dumbstruck.

'I wasn't expecting any of that,' Bethany said. 'I only wanted you off my property.'

Just before Judith disappeared around the side of the house, she turned and called back at her friends, 'The man had red cheeks!'

And then she was gone.

'"The man had red cheeks"?' Becks said.

Why had Judith just shouted that at them?

Chapter 28

On the drive to the police station, Judith decided she wasn't, in fact, in a police car. And she most certainly wasn't being driven to a police interview. She'd been there before, and she wasn't going to go there again. When she arrived at Maidenhead police station, she only dimly heard the police officer ask her to follow him. Then, once inside the building, she barely heard the answers she gave to the questions she was asked as she was signed in. Only one question cut through.

'Do you wish to have a lawyer present for your interview?'

'No,' she said.

Judith knew that her best hope was to get her ordeal over and done with as quickly as possible. She hadn't been arrested. She hadn't been charged. She was a voluntary witness and she knew how the process worked. She just had to dead bat their questions. They didn't have any evidence. They *couldn't* have any evidence. And then they'd have to let her go.

The officer led her down a corridor into a small interview

room. There was a camera set into the ceiling that pointed down at the metal table and chairs.

Judith sat down in the chair that the man indicated and folded her hands onto her lap. She was good at waiting.

Five minutes passed, but it felt like half an hour.

Ten minutes passed.

The door opened and Brendan entered with a manila folder in his hands. He sat down opposite Judith with a tight smile. Judith smiled back. She wasn't going to give him the satisfaction of knowing how scared she was. As Brendan started the recording device and asked her to confirm that she didn't want a lawyer present, her mind flew back to the first time she'd been in a police interview room, on the day her husband's body had been found.

Brendan opened his folder and then leaned back and considered his witness.

'On the third of July 1976,' he said, 'your husband died in suspicious circumstances in the Ionian Sea. Just off the coast of Corfu.'

'It was dealt with by the Corfu authorities at the time,' Judith said.

'New evidence has come to light.'

'Evidence I dispute.'

'Of course you do. It puts your testimony in doubt. But first, I'd like you to tell me what you did with your police record.'

'I'm sorry?'

'You were interviewed under caution by the UK police when you returned from Greece on – ' Brendan looked down to his notes to check what he'd written ' – the fifteenth of July 1976. The Corfu police also sent over a hard copy of their file. As you're aware, all of those files were then stored by the Buckinghamshire constabulary in a repository just outside Maidenhead. Where you were last week.'

'Why's that of interest?'

'When I went to reference them before I brought you in, I discovered that they're now missing.'

'Are you accusing me of stealing my file?'

'I'd like you to tell me what happened while you were there.'

'My friends and I were signed in to the building, and then we went to the stack where the report on Gary Wise's car crash should have been, but we couldn't find it.'

'You went straight there?'

'All three of us went straight there.'

'How curious,' Brendan said, turning to another page in his notes. 'Because I've just spoken to Rebecca Starling and Suzie Harris and they told me – separately – that while they went to the stack together, you disappeared for at least five minutes.'

A cold fist clutched at Judith's heart.

'They said that, did they?' she asked in a quiet voice.

'They couldn't wait to help the police,' Brendan said with a smile. 'After I pointed out what would happen to them if they didn't, that is. They didn't have much of an explanation as to what you got up to in that time. So, what did you do?'

'I . . . ah yes, I remember now. For a short while, I was lost.'

'You, Mrs Potts?'

'I was confused.'

'Do you deny taking your old police files from the repository?'

'Why would you doubt me?'

'Because you killed your husband.'

'I didn't!'

'You were on his boat that day, I've photographic proof.'

'I was on the jetty – I'll admit that much – but I didn't get on his boat.'

'So you're already changing your story from your official statement at the time? Would you change your story about the repository if I told you there's CCTV footage from the stacks that I've requested.'

'Stop trying to throw me off balance,' Judith snapped.

'Stop trying to buy yourself time.'

'Then no, I wouldn't change my story about where I went in the repository.'

'Even though you lied about being with your husband on his boat just before he left?'

'I was upset when the police interviewed me; I was confused.'

'Just as you lied about going to the church. You never went anywhere near it that day, did you?'

'My husband had just died, I didn't know what was going on – have some pity.'

'Your husband hit you.'

Judith froze, overwhelmed by the sudden spike of hatred she felt towards Brendan. That he'd mention something that was entirely private to her. That he'd use her pain as an interview technique.

Brendan turned a page in his file and looked at a printout of an old, handwritten witness statement.

'My Greek counterparts digitised all of their records in the early 2000s,' he said. 'Even though a physical copy's no longer in our possession, they were happy to give me access to their copy of your file. It says here, you made a formal complaint against your husband three months before he died. You wanted out from a violent marriage. You had a motive.'

'The photo you have is a fake,' Judith said. 'It was given to you by Eleni Paphides. She's the illegitimate daughter of my husband. She's not a reliable witness.'

'The photo's not a fake.'

'It's so easy to manipulate images these days. Have you checked the paper it's printed on? It will be modern paper.'

'It was the first thing I did,' Brendan said, looking squarely at Judith. 'I gave the photo to forensics, and their report says the paper it's printed on is at least thirty years old. The photo is authentic.'

Judith's heart started to pound, adrenaline coursing through her.

'But you don't have the negative it came from, do you?' she asked, unable to keep a note of desperation out of her voice.

'I'm not going to divulge to you what evidence we may or may not have.'

'Which suggests to me you don't have the negative,' Judith said, clinging to what she felt was a critically important point. 'I insist you either charge me for a crime or you let me go,' Judith said.

A smile twitched at the corner of Brendan's mouth.

'You're refusing to cooperate?' he asked.

'I've cooperated fully with you.'

'But you've not told me all the secrets you keep padlocked up. It's time to confess, Mrs Potts.'

Brendan's mention of a padlock sparked a thought for Judith. It was barely a flicker, but she stilled as she considered what it might mean.

'Mrs Potts?' Brendan asked, irritated by Judith's sudden silence.

'Not now, Brendan,' Judith said, her mind lassoing loose thought after loose thought and corralling them into order. But for once, what she was considering was so overwhelming that she couldn't even begin to comprehend it.

'For the record,' Brendan said, 'the witness is refusing to respond.'

Judith realised that she had to get home, and at any price. There was a piece of evidence she had to check.

'Charge me or release me,' she said.

'I beg your pardon?' Brendan said.

'I'm happy to admit that when I was interviewed by the Corfu police, I forgot to mention that I briefly went down to the boat with my husband that morning. But I didn't go on his boat when he left for sea, and my testimony after that point remains the same. I went to the church and prayed for him. Unless you'd like to produce any other evidence?'

'I think I've got more than enough.'

'Really?' Judith said, hope blossoming in her heart. 'Eleni really was bluffing when she said she had more than that one photo?'

'Will you admit that the photo we're talking about is of you and your husband, and that it was taken on the day he died?' Brendan said, ignoring the question.

'I'm not admitting anything. However, I'm happy to sign a statement that says I briefly went down to the cove that morn-ing. Which is possibly when the photo was taken. But spit spot, Brendan, I need to get on.'

'"Spit spot"?'

'If all you've got is one dodgy photo, then I really think this interview is over.'

Brendan sat back in his chair, his brow furrowed. Judith

thought that he looked like a small child who'd just had his favourite toy taken away from him.

'You have nothing else you'd like to add?' he asked.

'Nothing,' Judith said and folded her hands on her lap. 'And I'm sorry to say that I don't have time to write out a new statement for you right now. I'll come in to the station in the next forty-eight hours to do that – which I'm sure will be fine for you, seeing as it's such a minor addition to my file. Don't you think?'

Brendan could see the resolve in his adversary, so he told Judith that he was happy to agree to her terms as long as she did indeed come back to the station to update her statement. Before he'd even finished speaking, Judith had scraped her chair back and was striding out of the room. Nor did she break stride when she passed PC Merchant on reception – not even when he called out a good afternoon to her. Instead, she hurried to Maidenhead station and got onto the Marlow Donkey.

As the train clattered towards Marlow, the Thames shining like a silver ribbon, she found herself thinking of all the times she'd taken walks along the river's banks. The picnics she'd had on her own. The dozes she'd had under the weeping willows. This stretch of the river represented peace and tranquillity for her, but now she knew that she was hurtling towards chaos. It felt no less to her than that she was going into battle, and it wasn't long before she was banging the front door to her house open and marching inside, removing her grey cape and throwing it onto a sofa as she headed for the staircase.

Going upstairs, she entered her bedroom, went over to the mantelpiece above the little fireplace and picked up the letter opener she'd put there years ago solely for this purpose. Then she went over to her four-poster bed and got down on her knees.

Lifting the edge of the duvet, she ignored the thick layer of dust on the floor and instead used her hands to feel to the third floorboard along. It had been loose when she'd first moved in and she'd told the builders who'd helped her fix the house up not to mend it.

Using her fingers to find the edge of the board, she inserted the letter opener into the gap and tried to prise it open. It resisted, but then the board popped and she was able to lever it up until she could remove it with her hands.

She reached into the void and pulled out an old manila folder. It contained the Corfu police files on the investigation into her husband's death that she'd stolen from the police repository. Just as Brendan had surmised. Flicking through the old, dried pages, the sellotape that was holding some of it together now dark amber with age, she found the witness statements that had been taken from the other village members at the time. Before she got too engrossed, she closed the file and put it to one side.

She reached into the cavity again and felt around until her hand found a thick piece of ribbon. She grabbed at it and pulled out a fabric-wrapped package. The material was one of her great-aunt's old Hermès scarves, and the design of nautical knots and flags had always made Judith smile. Not on this occasion. She undid the ribbon that was holding the package together and let the scarf fall away.

A mobile phone, three bundles of money and a maroon passport were revealed.

The bundles of money were in euros, dollars and pounds, and amounted to about £6,000 in total. As for the passport, it had been issued by the government of Malta. She opened it and looked at the photo of herself that stared back. That version of

Judith – eight years younger – had known that one day she might need a passport that the British government didn't know about. Judith reflected that she was eternally grateful to her younger self for her foresight.

She creaked back to her feet, dusted down her knees and carried the money, phone, passport and files back down the stairs to her sitting room. Putting them on her desk, she approached the incident board behind her desk.

On the wall were all of the photos of the clues, victims and suspects from the two murders. She reached up and carefully took the pins out of one of the witness photographs and lifted it from the wall. She now knew, if her theory was correct, that the photo revealed who'd killed both Gary Wise and Mike Saxon.

She put it down on her desk.

It was of Angela Gulliver.

Chapter 29

The following day, Becks and Suzie were in a tizzy. Or rather, Becks was in a tizzy; Suzie was in a blind panic. They'd not seen Judith since she'd left with Brendan and they'd been phoning her ever since. Their calls were going straight through to voicemail. But they didn't manage to get hold of her at any point that day. The next morning, Becks went to Suzie's for an emergency meeting.

'She's still being held by the police, isn't she?' Becks said as she paced up and down Suzie's sitting room. 'She's been charged with something, put in the cells and they've thrown away the key!'

Suzie was sitting in her armchair, rolling herself a cigarette. Emma had picked up on her distress and was sitting to her side, her head on Suzie's lap. Having rolled the cigarette, Suzie put it behind her ear for later, not realising that it was joining three others she'd already rolled and forgotten about.

'And what did she mean, "the man had red cheeks"?' Suzie asked for the hundredth time. 'What sort of comment is that?'

'It's a crossword clue, isn't it?'

'But how can it be? She said crossword clues have to have two halves – with one half being the basic clue.'

'That's "the man" – meaning we're looking for a man. She's telling us the identity of the killer, I'm sure of it.'

'But what did she mean, "had red cheeks" – how can that be the cryptic part of the clue? I don't think it means there should be an anagram. Or that the answer's hidden within the words. Or any of the other tricks crosswords use.'

'But it must be a crossword clue,' Becks said as Suzie picked up her phone and speed-dialled Judith's number. 'Or why did she go to all of the effort of giving us those crossword books? You know what Judith's like. Everything she does is for a reason.'

Once again, the call went straight through to voicemail.

'Where are you?' Suzie called out in frustration and slapped the phone down.

As she did so, Emma lifted her head and looked out of the window, suddenly alert.

'What is it, Emma? Is it Judith?'

Becks went to the window and looked down the driveway in front of Suzie's house.

Tanika was on the pathway looking at her.

Becks and Suzie went to the front door to meet their friend.

'You've got news on Judith?' Becks asked.

'I do,' Tanika said. 'Not that I should know, and I very definitely shouldn't be telling you, but I really don't know what to do with what I've been told.'

'What's happened?' Suzie asked.

'I got a call from a friend at the station. Apparently, Brendan interviewed Judith the day before yesterday about her ex-husband.'

'Has she been charged with anything?' Suzie asked.

'I don't believe so. But when she was released, she was asked to stay in the country. It's standard procedure. You put the witness's name on a watch list.'

'Why are you telling us this?' Suzie asked.

'That evening, Judith got on the last ferry to France. Have you any idea why?'

'*France?*' Suzie said, utterly nonplussed.

'Has there been any sight of her since?' Becks asked.

'According to Alice – sorry, I mean my "contact" –' Tanika added hurriedly, 'as soon as she arrived in Calais, she vanished. She's not used any bank card to buy anything in the last forty-eight hours. Or used her passport to hire a car or any other form of transport.'

'She's stuck in Calais?' Becks asked.

'If I know Judith, I very much doubt that,' Tanika said.

'No, wait,' Suzie said, holding up her hands as though about to stop a charging bull. 'Are you saying she's skipped the country?'

'It's how it's looking.'

'No, this is impossible,' Suzie said, going back into her house and fetching a coat. 'Not that she'd skip the country,' she added, 'but that she wouldn't have told me and Becks. I refuse to believe that. Come on,' she said as she closed her front door behind herself and pushed past her two friends.

'Where are we going?' Becks asked.

The answer to Becks's question was Judith's house, and when she, Suzie and Tanika arrived, they got out of their vehicles and approached the front door.

'I can't let you break in,' Tanika warned Suzie.

'Don't worry,' Suzie said. 'We know where the spare key is.'

Suzie reached up above the porch and felt along the gutter.

After a few attempts where she only pulled out wet leaves, she finally grabbed hold of a couple of rusting keys that were held together with a bit of string. She used them to open the front door and pushed it open.

'Don't worry,' she said to Tanika as she entered. 'Judith doesn't have an alarm.'

'What are we doing here?' Tanika asked.

'There's no way Judith bolted without leaving us a message,' Suzie said as she entered the sitting room and started to look along the mantelpiece. 'There'll be a letter or note to us somewhere. Telling us where she's gone. And why. We just have to find it.'

'You're right,' Becks said, going over to Judith's card table to see if there was anything left on it by the finished jigsaw of Burgh Island.

Tanika was drawn to the incident board behind Judith's desk and paused as she looked down at the surface. There was an open tin of travel sweets. The lid to it was placed to the side.

'Look,' she said to the others. 'She didn't even put the lid back on her sweets. It suggests she left in a rush.'

'Or maybe she just forgot to put the lid back on,' Becks said as she and Suzie started to search through the loose papers on the desktop and hunt through the drawers. As they did so, Tanika turned back to study the board. As ever, she was impressed with all of the information the amateur sleuths had been able to collate. And also, as ever, she didn't want to inquire too closely about where they'd got their information.

'There's nothing here,' Suzie said in frustration and moved over to start checking the bureau to the side of the room. Becks went over to the bookcases.

'Maybe she left a note here,' she said as she started to look from shelf to shelf.

'There's something missing,' Tanika said, tracing a red piece of wool that went from a location on the map of Marlow to a red pin with nothing attached to it. 'Look,' she said to Suzie and Becks as they approached. 'All of the red wool goes from locations on the map – or from one of the index cards she's put up on the wall – to a piece of evidence. Always. But this piece of wool just goes from the centre of Marlow and then finishes out here on the wall. There was something pinned to the wall here, wasn't there?'

'Hold on,' Becks said, looking at the gap on the wall. 'This is where Angela Gulliver's photo is supposed to be.'

'You're right,' Suzie said. 'Judith had a photo of Angela Gulliver at the end of that piece of wool.'

'Where's the photo now?' Becks said, looking around.

'I've not seen it,' Suzie said.

'Is Angela Gulliver a suspect?' Tanika asked.

'Possibly,' Becks said. 'She arrived here in pretty suspicious circumstances. And she gave us a tip-off about Lord Harleyford. But we've never been able to directly tie her to either of the victims – except for a brief encounter she had with Mike Saxon at a party.'

'It doesn't matter why she took the photo down,' Suzie said, heading for the stairs. 'We aren't going to be able to work anything out until we find Judith's note. I'm checking upstairs.'

Suzie clumped up the wooden stairs and disappeared into Judith's bedroom. Becks suggested that she and Tanika go and have a hunt in the kitchen. Once there, Tanika stopped in surprise.

'She definitely left in a hurry,' she said, pointing at the heaped pile of unwashed plates, mugs and cutlery in the sink.

'No,' Becks said with a smile. 'It always looks like this. If anything, it's possible she had a good clear-up before she left, seeing as it's all in the sink. Let's see if there's a note for us anywhere.'

'So . . . why the mention of Lord Harleyford?' Tanika asked as she started to open drawers. 'Isn't he the government minister who's just had to resign?'

'He is. And he seems to be at the heart of these murders somehow. Him and the secret caves he has under his house.'

'There are secret caves?'

'There are, and it's possible he's the person who's been blackmailing Gary Wise and Mike Saxon. Or, if not that, he maybe killed them because they were being blackmailed and he didn't want them spilling the secret. Whatever it is, it could be connected to a secret drinking society that he runs.'

Becks opened the fridge and gasped.

'You've found something?' Tanika asked eagerly.

Becks closed the door to the fridge, her eyes glazed over in horror.

'You don't ever want to look in there.'

'It's bad?'

Becks nodded slowly, and then she moved over to a dresser that was up against the wall opposite the fridge.

'Then what have you got on the other suspects?' Tanika asked.

'OK,' Becks said as she started to search through a pile of cookbooks. 'Gary Wise's wife Bethany seems to be your typical grieving widow, but there's a question mark over her relationship with Mike Saxon. She was seen going to a hotel where he takes his lovers, but she says it was because he was recommending that Harry Asquith ghostwrite Gary's autobiography.'

'The recommendation came from Mike Saxon?'

'It did. And he, Harry Asquith and Lord Harleyford all belong to the same real tennis club. But this being Marlow, that could just be a coincidence. However, it suggests the three of them could all be in Lord Harleyford's Hellfire Club together.'

'That's what it's called?' Tanika asked, surprised.

'If it exists. We don't know for sure. But if Harry's our killer, it's possible his motivation is money.'

'I remember. He's up to his ears in debt.'

'Since Gary died, he's bought himself a smart new car.'

'Is that so?' Tanika said, inspecting a small bottle that seemed to have oozed black tar out of its lid. Reading the faded label, she asked, 'What's gravy browning? Actually, I don't want to know,' she said and put the ancient artefact back on the shelf with a grimace. She moved on to another cupboard.

'Were you ever able to find the police report on Gary's car accident?' she asked.

'No,' Becks said, 'we've not found any record of what happened that night. Maybe it was pulled. Maybe it never existed. We just don't know. There's quite a lot we don't know.'

'What about Mike Saxon?'

'We've only talked to two people close to him. His wife, Serena, who is happy to admit she hated him. Not least because he was a terrible philanderer. But we also discovered that it's been her writing his books for however many years, so she loses out on being able to make money now he's gone. After all, he can't very well publish from beyond the grave.'

'Although if she'd already got enough money . . .?'

'The same thought occurred to us. She might have taken the view that his serial adultery meant it was time for him to die. Although, I'm not sure she'd have so readily admitted to hating him if she were the killer. And, if she killed Mike, it seems unlikely that she'd be the person who was also blackmailing him.'

'Do you know who that person could have been?'

'No idea. Although it's very definitely the same person who was extorting money out of Gary. It was the same phone number contacting both men.'

'Then why was Mike being blackmailed?'

'We still don't know. Possibly it was his adultery. Perhaps it was something else. It's so frustrating not having you running the case! It's like trying to do this with one hand tied behind our backs.'

Tanika smiled sadly.

'If it's any consolation, I feel the same,' she said. 'I've missed working with the three of you. I've missed working with my team. But you said there are two people close to Mike Saxon who you've spoken to?'

'We've also spoken to his personal assistant,' Becks said. 'A woman called Jamilah Khalil. She told us she wasn't in any kind of relationship with Mike, but we've seen a photo of the two of them together at Lord Harleyford's winter ball last year. It could mean something. It could mean nothing. But it brings us, once again, back to Lord Harleyford. He's at the centre of all of this – he has to be – but we just don't know how.'

'You also mentioned Angela Gulliver?'

'Her presence in the case makes the least sense of all. Although, the fact that Judith's removed her photo from the wall suggests she's possibly our killer – or, at least, that's what Judith thinks.'

'Judith's never wrong.'

'I agree. But I can't see why she'd be blackmailing either man. Or why she'd want to kill them. If only Judith was here!'

Becks put down the last recipe book and looked about herself. She and Tanika had run out of locations to search.

'Are you *sure* Judith would have left you a message?' Tanika asked.

'The three of us are a team,' Becks said. 'She wouldn't run away like this without telling us why.'

Becks and Tanika searched the remaining downstairs rooms, but they still didn't find anything that could be a message. And from the sound of the angry clattering that was coming from upstairs, Suzie wasn't finding anything, either.

Becks and Tanika were back in the sitting room when Suzie stomped down the stairs.

'I can't find anything!' she announced. 'Here, let me try her again,' she added as she pulled her phone out of the bum bag around her waist.

Suzie jabbed her finger at the screen of her phone and listened. A man's voice announced that the phone number she was calling wasn't available, but she could leave a message if she wanted to.

'I'm not having this!' Suzie said as she hung up the call. 'She must have left a message for us!'

The three friends were at a complete loss. But then, they all heard the rattle of the letterbox as something was delivered.

'Bet that's it!' Suzie said and sped out of the room, followed by Tanika and Becks.

When they arrived at the front door, they stopped in disappointment. All that had been delivered was that day's copy of the *Marlow Free Press*.

Chapter 30

Suzie led Becks and Tanika back into the sitting room and plonked herself down in Judith's favourite wingback.

'She left no message for us,' she said, despondently.

'Although there is the last thing she said to us: "the man had red cheeks",' Becks said. 'Which is obviously a crossword clue, but we can't work out what it means.'

'Hold on,' Tanika said. 'What's that?'

Becks explained Judith's remark as she'd been led away by Brendan.

'And you're sure it's a crossword clue?'

'It's the only thing that makes sense,' Suzie said.

'Then that's the message she left for you.'

'I don't think it can have been,' Becks said. 'She said her red cheeks comment to us before she was taken off and interviewed. What we're looking for is the message she left for us *after* Brendan had finished with her but *before* she skipped the country.'

'OK, that seems fair enough. Then what's the answer to her crossword clue?'

'We've tried every trick we know,' Suzie said. 'We've even checked through the books she gave us, but we can't make head nor tail of it.'

'It doesn't seem to behave like a crossword clue at all,' Becks said. 'She didn't even say how many letters the answer would be.'

'Then perhaps you're making this harder than it needs to be,' Tanika said. 'If it doesn't make sense as a crossword clue, maybe it isn't. And instead, it just means what it means. Judith wants you to look for a man who's got red cheeks.'

'You mean she wasn't being clever–clever?' Suzie asked sceptically. 'That doesn't sound like Judith.'

'Seeing as Brendan turned up when you weren't expecting, maybe she didn't have time to be clever–clever. So what might she have been referring to?'

'We've no idea,' Suzie said. 'That's why we think it's a crossword clue. If it isn't, it could be any of the men in the case.'

'Do they all have red cheeks?'

'Well, not Harry Asquith,' Becks said. 'His face is completely pale. Like he's recently died.'

'Then what about Lord Harleyford? I've seen him on the TV and I'd say he has a pretty ruddy complexion.'

'You're not wrong there,' Suzie said, realising the truth of Tanika's words.

'But she didn't say his name out loud,' Tanika continued. 'So it's not his name she wanted you to hear. She didn't even call him a lord, so it's not his status, either. It's just the colour of his cheeks. That suggests to me there's some other element of the murders where red cheeks are important. Or someone saw someone with red cheeks.'

'But that's not the case,' Becks said, before she stopped herself.

'Actually, that's not true. When we spoke to Jamilah, she said that on the day that Mike died, she saw someone with ruddy cheeks arguing with him that morning by his home office.'

'You're right!' Suzie said. 'She said the man was wearing a flat cap and a green coat. Is Judith saying that that was Lord Harleyford?'

'There's an easy way to find out,' Tanika said. 'If you're saying this Jamilah woman saw him, you only have to go and show her a photo of Lord Harleyford and see if she recognises him.'

'But why's it even important?' Suzie said.

'Maybe she was telling you in her own way that he's the killer.'

'In which case, why did she remove Angela's photo?' Becks asked. 'Although you're right, Tanika. We should talk to Jamilah. After all, we now know that she went to Lord Harleyford's winter ball last year with Mike Saxon.'

'Which she kept from us,' Suzie said.

'And if it really was Lord Harleyford who argued with Mike on the day he died, it's deeply suspicious that she didn't recognise him. Seeing as she met him last year.'

'And that's where I leave,' Tanika said. 'I need to make sure I'm nowhere near you when you do any actual investigating.'

'Are you sure?' Suzie asked.

'Quite sure, thank you. See you later.'

'Thanks for all of your help,' Becks said as Tanika left the room. 'We wouldn't have got there without you.'

Tanika paused in the doorway to look back at Becks and Suzie.

'Yes, you would,' she said, and then she was gone.

'How long do we give it before we can leave without it looking like we were together?' Suzie whispered to Becks.

'I'd give it five minutes,' Tanika called back from the front door.

'Oh,' Suzie said, surprised. 'She heard me.'

'Yes, she heard you,' Becks said with a smile. 'But I'm still not sure we've decoded Judith's message right.'

'I know what you mean. It's weird that she'd go on about crosswords so much and then, when she gives us a clue, it *isn't* a crossword.'

'I think we maybe have to conclude that her giving us those crossword books has ended up having nothing to do with the case. It was just Judith being . . . eccentric.'

Suzie frowned as she considered whether Becks was right, but she couldn't see any reason to disagree with her. As soon as five minutes was up, the women left Judith's and drove to Jamilah's house. When they rang the doorbell and asked if they could come up, Jamilah buzzed them in without a word.

When they arrived at the top of the staircase, Jamilah opened the door in a fluster.

'Now is not a good time,' she said.

'Did you get your job?' Becks asked.

'As it happens, I did,' Jamilah said. 'But how can I help you?'

'It's a quick question. We just want you to look at a photograph and tell us if it is the person you saw outside Mike's office on the morning he died.'

'OK, as long as it's just that.'

'Hold on,' Becks said as she fished out her phone and got up Lord Harleyford's Wikipedia page. She zoomed in on his photo before showing it to Jamilah.

'Do you recognise this man?' Suzie asked, hoping that Jamilah didn't realise the trap that she was setting for her.

'I'm not sure. I didn't get a good look at the man's face. I'll be honest, I'm not even sure it was a man. It could have been a woman in trousers and wearing a flat cap.'

'Hold on,' Suzie said, taking Becks's phone and doing a quick internet search for Lord Harleyford. She chose a different image of him. 'How about this photo of him?' she said as she enlarged the image. It showed Lord Harleyford at a local shoot with a shotgun under his arm, surrounded by other men with guns. He was wearing a flat cap, a green Barbour coat, brown corduroy trousers and green wellies.

'No – sorry, I still don't recognise him.'

'It's Lord Harleyford. But you know that because you went to his ball last year.'

At the mention of the ball, Jamilah flashed a glance at the mantelpiece above her fireplace.

'And don't think about denying it,' Suzie continued. 'We've seen a photo of you there with him and Mike Saxon.'

While Suzie was speaking, Becks drifted over to the mantelpiece to see what had made Jamilah look in that direction and saw a stiff invitation to Lord Harleyford's winter ball. Jamilah's name was handwritten in the top left-hand corner in blue ink.

'And you're going again this year, aren't you?' Becks said as she picked up the card and handed it to Suzie.

'I think it's time you told us what's going on,' Suzie said.

'I know how this is looking,' Jamilah said, 'but I've not done anything wrong.'

'How about you tell us what you've done, and we can be the judge of that.'

'How did you find out I was there?' Jamilah asked, before realising the answer to her question. 'You've seen the photos in the *Marlovian*, haven't you? I should have known better than hoping you wouldn't come across them. But there's actually not much to say. Mike told me he had an invite for two to the ball last year, and that his wife was refusing to go with him. So would I like to go as his plus one? I obviously didn't want to, but it was such a fancy ball, I was tempted. I told him I'd be happy to go as long as he didn't think it was a date. He always liked it when people were blunt with him. And he said he'd honour my wishes. It would be strictly platonic.'

'The photo didn't look platonic,' Suzie said.

'You're right. The moment we arrived, he wanted to dance with me and show me off to his friends. I'd escape from him for a few minutes, realise I didn't know anybody, and then he'd find me and offer me another drink. I think he thought that if I got drunk enough I'd let my guard down. As for that photo, you go back and look at it again. I'm not smiling in it, that's a grimace – I was in a hostage situation.'

'Why didn't you tell us about this when we first talked to you?' Becks asked.

'Because, believe it or not, I want his killer caught. And I know I didn't have anything to do with his death, so I didn't want you wasting your time.'

'You could have told us that you recognised Lord Harleyford when you saw him arguing with Mike on the day he died.'

'But that's the thing, I didn't recognise him. Honestly. I just saw a man with red-faced cheeks. It could have been anyone as far as I was concerned. And remember, I only met Lord Harleyford once, and that was last year. On the day Mike died, I saw the person's rough body shape, the colour of their face, and the fact that they were wearing a flat cap. As I said before, it could even have been a woman.'

'I don't buy it,' Suzie said. 'If you don't know Lord Harleyford, how come he's invited you to his ball again?'

'I've no idea!' Jamilah said. 'The invitation only arrived this morning. But it's such a grand event, and I didn't want last year's experience of it to be my only memory of it. I figured that with Mike no longer here, if I went again, I'd be safe to enjoy myself. Make some happier memories.'

'Hang on,' Suzie said, taking in the details on the card. 'The ball's tomorrow night.'

'That's why I'm in such a rush – I'm trying to work out if I've got an outfit. And I've got to get my hair and nails done. Or at least that's what I thought. Are you saying he could be the person who killed Mike?'

'It's definitely a possibility,' Becks said.

Jamilah shuddered.

'Then there's no way I'm going,' she said, taking the invitation from Suzie and going over to the corner of her room, where she put it in the bin. 'That's made my day a lot easier. Thank you so much for coming round.'

'Yeah, sure,' Suzie said.

'And I'm sorry about not telling you the full story about me and Mike. But I've told you everything now. It really was just that one time that I went to an event with him. It was over a year ago, and it never happened again. I only didn't tell you about it because I didn't think it had anything to do with his death. I promise you.'

Suzie and Becks realised they weren't going to get any more out of Jamilah, so they thanked her for her time and let themselves out of the house.

'That woman!' Becks announced as soon as they were on the street outside.

'Who?' Suzie asked. 'Jamilah?'

'She *never* tells us the truth until she's forced to.'

'Forget about her,' Suzie said. 'Lord Harleyford's the killer, isn't he? That's what Judith was telling us with her comment about red cheeks. It was he who argued with Mike Saxon on the day he died. And he's the person who killed him later on. Come on, it's always felt like it had to be him. After all, it was he who pressed Angela about blackmailing Mike and Gary six months ago. He's our man!'

'I just don't know,' Becks said. 'We're basing a lot of this on Jamilah's testimony and I'm not sure we can trust her. And there's something else as well. If Lord Harleyford's the killer, why did Judith take the photo of Angela Gulliver with her rather than his?'

Suzie scoffed at her friend's question and suggested they go to her house, as it was just around the corner. They needed to try and work out the meaning of everything they'd just learned.

When they arrived, Suzie unlocked her front door and pushed it open to reveal that that day's post had arrived while she'd been out. She picked it up as she led Becks into her kitchen.

'It's just retirement home flyers,' she said, dumping the post on the countertop and putting the kettle on. 'I remember the days when my junk mail was for credit cards and fancy holidays. Now it's all hearing aids and funeral homes. It's so depressing.'

'What's this?' Becks asked as she picked up a thick cream envelope with Suzie's name and address handwritten on it in blue ink.

'Let me see,' Suzie said, tearing open the envelope.

She pulled out a stiff invitation that proclaimed 'The Harleyford

Winter Ball' in raised black ink. In the top left-hand corner, the name Suzie Harris had been handwritten in blue.

'Oh God,' Suzie said, and showed the invitation to Becks, 'I've been invited as well. What the hell is going on?'

Chapter 31

'Hold on,' Becks said as she fished her phone out of her pocket. Before Suzie could ask her what she was doing, she speed-dialled a number.

When the call connected, she said, 'Hi, Colin. Are you home? Can I ask a favour? Today's post should have arrived. Can you get it and see if there's a cream envelope with my name and address written on it in blue ink? Thank you.' Becks waited a few seconds in silence. Suzie, realising what her friend was checking, didn't say anything either.

'Oh, I see,' Becks said. 'Yes, thank you. No, there's no need to open it. Thanks. I'll be home later on.'

Becks hung up.

'I've got a cream envelope as well,' she said to her friend. 'I've also been invited to the ball.'

'OK, this is now seriously weird,' Suzie said. 'What's Lord Harleyford playing at? What's so important about the ball that means we've got to be there? And Jamilah as well for that matter.'

'I suppose there's only one way to find out. We could go to the ball, couldn't we?'

'I want to know if someone else has been invited.'

'Who?' Becks asked and Suzie explained that they should see if Judith had received the same invitation.

When they arrived at Judith's house and let themselves in with the spare key, they picked up her post and saw that there wasn't a heavy cream envelope with her name and address on it.

'That makes no sense,' Suzie said. 'You and I got invitations, but Judith didn't?'

'Maybe Lord Harleyford knows she's out of the country?'

'How can he possibly know that?'

'But what do you think we should do? Go to the ball?'

'What would Judith do?'

'Go to the ball.'

'Then let's go to the ball.'

'But is that the right thing to do? And since we're here,' Becks added, looking about herself to check they definitely were on their own, 'maybe we need to address the elephant in the room. What if she really was involved in her husband's death? You know, really quite *actively* involved.'

'Oh,' Suzie said. '*That* elephant in the room.'

'Because I'm sure she didn't do it. Of course not. But if she did do it – *if* she did, as I say – she'd behave pretty much like she has done. As soon as the police started to move in, she'd drop everything and flee the country.'

Suzie didn't speak for a few seconds as she considered her friend's words.

'It's what I'd do,' she admitted. 'If I knew I was about to be arrested. I'd feel I had no choice.'

'So is that what we're saying? She's . . . guilty?'

'It doesn't feel right. Not Judith. Although, I wouldn't mind too much—'

'You *wouldn't* mind her committing murder?'

'Sure. We know her husband was a wrong'un. If Judith did him in it's because the world's better without him in it. That doesn't bother me. But I draw the line at her leaving the country without telling us where she's gone.'

'You really are an extraordinary person,' Becks said as they returned to the front door.

'Thank you,' Suzie said, not realising that the comment wasn't quite the compliment she thought it was.

Becks picked up the copy of the *Marlow Free Press* that had been delivered that morning, but as she put it on the side table, she paused, the paper in her hand.

'You OK there, Becks?' Suzie asked.

'Shh!' Becks said, her mind racing.

'What do you mean "shh"?'

'I mean *shh*, Suzie. Is this it?'

'You're talking in riddles – it's like Judith's with us right now. What do you mean, "is this it"?'

'I think this could be the message we've been looking for.'

★

The following morning, Tanika was watching her mixer whizz up a homemade soup and trying not to think too closely about the Wise and Saxon cases, when there was a knock on the door. Clicking the off switch, she wiped her hands on a tea towel and moved to the front door. When she threw it open, she was surprised to see that Becks and Suzie were standing outside.

'We need to borrow a set of handcuffs,' Suzie said.

'I'm sorry?'

'Why don't we come in?' Becks said.

'I think you'd better stay exactly where you are,' Tanika said, squaring up in the doorway. She wasn't going to let Becks and Suzie railroad her.

'We know who the killer is and we need to make the arrest.'

'You *what*?'

'We almost definitely know who the killer is,' Becks said, correcting her friend.

'*Almost* definitely?'

'Close enough to make no difference,' Suzie said with a waft of her hand that suggested it really wasn't a biggie. 'If he isn't the killer, he's hand in glove with the killer. And he's planning something tonight at the winter ball. Whatever it is, we have to catch him at it.'

'No, no, no,' Tanika said. 'Back up here. Who are we talking about?'

'Lord Harleyford,' Suzie said.

'And you think he's going to do something tonight?'

'Oh, he's definitely up to something,' Suzie said. 'But don't worry, we're going to stop him. We're going to make a citizen's arrest using a pair of your handcuffs.'

'Have you informed the police?'

'What – you mean *Brendan*?' Suzie said.

'It doesn't have to be Brendan. But he is the SIO on the case. If this Lord Harleyford is the killer, you need to hand your information over to the police. Because I won't help you. I *can't* help you.'

'But we're good at this!' Suzie said.

'You don't have to tell me that, but you don't have me to protect you anymore. And considering Judith's position at the moment, you could get into real trouble if you try and do this on your own.'

'Are you being serious?' Suzie said, affronted. 'You won't help us?'

'I'd go further than that. If you know who the killer is and try to deal with him on your own, I'll be forced to report you.'

'All we asked for was a set of handcuffs!' Suzie huffed.

'Are you going to report Lord Harleyford to the police?' Tanika asked.

'No way! I'm not having Brendan get his size twelves all over this. He's been behind us in the investigation every step of the way. He's not getting the glory at the end. But if you won't help us, then we'll do it ourselves. Won't we, Becks?'

Suzie returned down the path and headed towards her van.

Becks hovered and then took her courage in her hands.

'I agree with Suzie,' she said. 'This is too important to leave to Brendan. We're going to the ball tonight. We're going to confront Lord Harleyford. And we're going to accuse him of killing Gary Wise and Mike Saxon.'

Tanika watched Becks turn and leave, and felt overcome by a deep weariness. Didn't her friends realise the impossible position they'd just put her in? She went back into her kitchen and tried to pretend that Becks and Suzie hadn't just visited her. But it wouldn't work. The fact that she was currently suspended meant that she didn't have the luxury of turning a blind eye to anything.

In fact, she realised with a sinking heart, she would have to follow correct procedure and report them. If it ever came out in her tribunal that she'd known what they were planning and not told anyone in the investigation, she'd never get her job back. It would be a career-ender. She couldn't do that to Shanti. Or Shamil. Or her father for that matter. Becks and Suzie really had put her in the most invidious position.

She went to her phone and picked it up. Scrolling through the names in her contact book, she found the details she was looking for. For the briefest moment, her finger hovered over the screen, knowing the terrible consequences of what she was about to do. But she had no choice, she told herself.

She stabbed her finger down on the screen, her decision made.

The call connected and started ringing.

'What do you want?' a man's voice barked as he answered.

'Brendan, it's Tanika here,' Tanika said before she changed her mind. 'I need to tell you that Becks Starling and Suzie Harris are planning to take the law into their own hands tonight. At a ball in Marlow. I need you to stop them.'

Chapter 32

Brendan gritted his teeth as a teenager in a high-viz jacket directed him to park in a field just beyond Lord Harleyford's stables. He found a spot in among the BMWs and Audis and – what's that he could see? – a Rolls Royce, if he wasn't much mistaken. He slammed the door on his Ford Mondeo, blipped the lock shut and then headed up the torchlit path towards the mansion. To his eyes, the house was offensively large. As far as he was concerned, the overlit statues above each window wouldn't have looked out of place in a shopping centre. He all but snarled at the security team who asked to see his invitation before they let him proceed.

Brendan got out his warrant card.

'Detective Sergeant Brendan Perry,' he snapped. 'I'm here on official business.'

'Of course, sorry, sir,' the guard said and stepped aside to let him pass.

As Brendan approached the house, he only had one resolution. He was going to find Suzie and Becks and he was going to arrest them for interfering in a live murder case. He didn't see why it shouldn't end in a custodial sentence for them both. Especially if it could be proved that they'd helped Judith skip the country. Either way, he'd make sure their lives in Marlow were ruined. Suzie wouldn't be able to run a dog-walking business with a criminal record. And it would be even worse for Becks. Her husband wouldn't be able to continue as the town's vicar with a criminal for a wife.

But first he had to find them.

*

At the same time that Brendan was arriving at the house, a hooded figure was scurrying through the woods near the house, heading towards the secret entrance to the tunnels of the Hellfire Caves. The house glowed just beyond, shafts of darkness stabbing through the woods where the trees broke up the blazing light. The hooded figure stopped and looked around, their breath frosting in the cold night air, their heart racing. Had they just heard a branch snap nearby? It was so hard to tell over the noise of the party.

The figure left the path, pushed through the bracken and reached the secret door that led into the caves. Their black-gloved hand pressed a sequence of five numbers on the keypad, twisted the knob sharply and then pulled the door open.

They looked about themselves one last time to check that no one could see them and then stepped into the darkness. The door closed with a heavy click as the lock reset.

They were inside.

*

Only a few minutes later, Suzie turned her van onto the driveway of Lord Harleyford's estate and almost immediately saw a young woman wearing a high-viz jacket who directed her to the parking area by the stables. Suzie wound her window down to say thank you, then drove into the field and allowed another teenager to point her to the spot where she should go. Suzie smiled a thank you and made sure she parked as carefully as possible. Her van seemed almost to be dwarfed by the two Porsche 4x4s she parked in between. In fact, as she got out, she couldn't help noticing that all of the cars she could see were extremely expensive, although she smiled as she saw an old Ford Mondeo parked nearby. At least there was one other person at the party who drove a normal car.

'How do I look?' Becks asked, straightening her midnight blue velvet jumpsuit.

'A million dollars,' Suzie said with a smile.

'Thank you,' Becks said. 'So do you.'

'I look like a barn door in nice shoes. You're too kind, Becks Starling.' Before Becks could disagree, Suzie barrelled on. 'So what do you reckon? Shall we go and catch ourselves a killer?'

The women joined a stream of black-tied partygoers as they walked towards the house along a path that was lit by flaming torches. When they reached the house, Suzie let out a quiet whistle at how it had been lit up in gold with strings of lights around the windows and doors. It looked like a fairytale palace.

A man in a suit and tie ushered them over to a gazebo where two female security guards checked through Becks's and Suzie's evening bags and removed their mobile phones.

'Can't we take them in with us?' Suzie asked.

'I'm sorry,' the woman said as she put each phone in a little ziplock bag. 'His lordship wants his guests to enjoy themselves without feeling they're going to appear online. You can get your phones back when you leave.'

The woman handed over two tickets so Becks and Suzie could recover their phones later on, and then she turned and placed the bags into a large metal locker behind her.

'But we need our phones,' Becks said.

'If you want them, you can't attend the party,' the woman said, hardening her smile. 'You choose.'

'No, of course,' Becks said, before turning to Suzie. 'We'll just have to do this without them.'

'Is that wise?' Suzie asked.

'Is any of this wise?' Becks replied.

'No – good point,' Suzie conceded.

The two friends approached the main door and Suzie was quick to pluck two glasses of champagne from a waiter in a dark green tailcoat and bow tie. Knowing that Suzie always liked to have one drink on the go at social events and another "as backup", Becks also took a glass of champagne for herself.

They went through the front door and stepped into what felt like a winter wonderland. Silver-sprayed branches were tied up in bundles, the ancestral portraits on the walls had white fabric swags draped across them like snow and everywhere was covered in candles, the flames guttering in the draughts of the ancient hall.

There must have been two hundred people milling about while a string quartet on a raised dais played an arrangement of 'In the Bleak Midwinter'.

Becks stopped dead in her tracks as she looked across the room.

'Brendan's here!' she whispered to Suzie and then turned her back so she wasn't facing him.

'Seriously?' Suzie said, before also turning her back on the room. 'Tanika must have tipped him off. Just like you said she would. We can't let him see us. Not yet. We need to blend in with the crowd.'

'That could be difficult,' Becks said, nodding at an approaching figure. 'I think we've been spotted.'

Lord Harleyford approached. He looked uncomfortable, as though he'd been forced into a dinner suit a few sizes too small for him, which the women noticed was very much the case. There was a sheen of sweat on his top lip.

'You came,' he said by way of an opening.

'You invited us,' Suzie said. 'And thanks,' she added, raising one of her champagne glasses in a toast. 'Because it gives me the chance to ask you where you vanished to the last time we were here.'

'I didn't vanish anywhere,' Lord Harleyford said.

'You did. And then you invited us to your party at the last minute. What's going on?'

'I suppose the late invitation needs a bit of an explanation,' Lord Harleyford said with a smile that just managed to make him look even more anxious. 'The party's for the great and good of the county. The pair of you are very definitely that, so I'm pleased to have you here.'

'I don't doubt that Becks and I are both great and good,' Suzie said. 'But why did we only get the invite yesterday?'

'No, good question. The truth is, I only recently thought of inviting you.'

'And what made you have that thought?'

Before Lord Harleyford could answer, they heard a self-satisfied voice call out, 'What are you two doing here?'

The women turned and saw Harry Asquith approaching.

'Do you know Harry Asquith?' Lord Harleyford asked, relieved at the interruption. 'Top chap.'

'We've met one or two times,' Becks said with a neutral smile. 'You two know each other through real tennis, don't you?'

'Maybe a little,' Harry said.

'A little?' Lord Harleyford said. 'Harry was at school with my son all the way through – from pre prep onwards. I've watched him grow up. It's why I'm asking him to write my autobiography. I need someone I can trust to tell my side of the story. Now if you'll excuse me, I see that Mayor Muriel has just arrived.'

Lord Harleyford moved off, but the women kept their eyes on Harry.

'What?' he asked.

'You've known Lord Harleyford your whole life?' Suzie asked, raising an eyebrow.

'So what?' Harry said, trying not to sound defensive.

'And now you're writing his autobiography?'

'It's like I said the last time we met. I have to eat. And after Gary died, I was in a mess, I'm happy to admit it. I needed the money from that book. If only to pay off some of my debts. But then, I was playing tennis at the club, and I realised William was the answer I was looking for. I could use his problems to solve mine. So I suggested to him that the best way of dealing with his recent . . . difficulties . . . was to get his story out there first. Before the police charge him with selling access to ministers.'

'And you came up with this plan *after* Gary died?' Suzie asked.

'I just said, didn't I?'

'And it was Lord Harleyford's money that allowed you to buy a new car?' Becks asked.

'That's none of your business.'

'We'll take that as a yes. What do you know about the Hellfire Caves?'

'God – people are obsessed with that place. It's just where William and a few of his friends go for drinks. You have a chance to unwind knowing you're among like-minded individuals.'

'So you're admitting you're part of that crowd, are you?' Becks asked.

'I wouldn't call it a "crowd". And before you ask, I've never seen Mike Saxon or Gary Wise down there. Really, it's all quite innocuous. Just men complaining about how the world's gone to hell in a handcart.'

'Then why's there a four-poster bed down there?' Suzie said.

'No idea, but don't think for a second that it gets used. It's no more or less than a gentlemen's club – or private drinking club – that's all. Now, talking of drinks, I'm going to get a top-up,' Harry said, lifting his empty glass to show the women.

'Before you go,' Becks said, 'can I ask one last question? In the caves under the house, there's a third tunnel that leads away from the main chamber, isn't there? The one that has some torches on a table next to it. Where does it go?'

'Nowhere,' Harry said, thrown by the question. 'It just heads downwards to a little cave that's even deeper underground. Really, the pair of you ask the most irrelevant questions,' Harry added and then melted back into the party.

'Wow,' Suzie said. 'That was clever of you, Becks. It's good to get that confirmed.'

'Thank you,' Becks said. 'I guessed we'd be able to ask someone.'

'Good grief, look who it is!' Suzie said, pointing at a woman at the edge of the room who was wearing a dark green ballgown.

It was Serena Saxon.

Becks and Suzie manoeuvred through the crowd. As they crossed the room, Suzie downed one of her glasses of champagne and swapped it out for a fresh glass from a tray that was being held by a waiter.

'Serena, what are you doing here?' Becks asked as she and Suzie reached her.

'Is that any of your business?'

'No – of course not. It's just odd.'

'If you must know, I'm slaying some ghosts. Mike was invited last year, but told me he didn't have a plus one, so I didn't come. This year, now he's dead, I saw the invite on the mantelpiece and decided to come on my own. Seeing as I hadn't made the cut last time.'

Becks could see an undercurrent of anger swirling through Serena's words and realised she could guess what was really driving her.

'You know he brought Jamilah last year, don't you?' she said.

Serena took a sip of her champagne and then finished it in one.

'Congratulations,' she said to the women, bitterly. 'You win a prize. You're right, my husband was bedding his beautiful personal assistant.'

Becks could see that Suzie was about to say that they hadn't known for sure that that was what had been going on, so she dug an elbow into her side to keep her quiet.

'How did you find out?' Becks asked.

'I was at the dentist, of all places. Idly flicking through a copy of the *Marlovian* when I saw him with her – bold as brass, the pair of them together. Him with his arms around her and her grinning like the cat who'd got the cream. That's when I realised what had been going on. The reason why, every time Mike went to a book festival last year, I was no longer invited. Jamilah went with him instead, didn't she? And I'd known she'd been interested in him from the start. She had a way of looking at him I recognised. But I genuinely believed he wouldn't make a move on her. Not if there was a chance I'd find out.'

'But you *did* find out,' Suzie said. 'As you've just admitted to us. So tell us, what did you do?'

'I did . . . nothing,' Serena said, her voice full of self-reproach. 'I kept telling myself I'd confront him, but I just let it slide. He continued to lead his life and I continued to lead mine. Two separate people rattling around that huge house. Hating each other and not saying anything. The English way.'

'Were you ever going to tell him you knew?' Becks asked.

'I genuinely don't know.'

'You liked your lifestyle too much, didn't you?' Suzie said. 'That was the problem.'

'I was a coward, you're right. I didn't want to lose what I had. And, believe it or not, I enjoyed writing Mike's books. I know they're male fantasy clap-trap, but I loved doing the research, and there's still an art in putting together a good plot. I knew that if I confronted him, Mike would leave me for her, and I could hardly carry on writing his books if I became wife number three of four.'

'You really think he'd have married Jamilah?' Becks asked.

'That was always her endgame. It's like I said. I recognise the type. The only mistake I made was that I didn't realise just how cunning she was.'

'I have to confess,' Becks said, 'she's been running rings around us as well.'

'But why didn't you tell us any of this before?' Suzie asked.

'And admit that I'd been discarded for a younger model?'

'Didn't you ever want to catch your husband's killer?'

'Not really. It will have been one of his exes who did this to him, and I really don't want to know about it. You mark my words. It will have been a floozy of his who he dumped when he took up with his new assistant.'

'Is it possible he ever dumped Jamilah?' Becks asked.

Serena looked at Becks carefully before she replied.

'What makes you say that?'

'It's just I can't help noticing we only have her word for why he sacked her on the day he died. She told us it was because he didn't like the notes she gave him on his latest book.'

'A book we now know you wrote,' Suzie interjected.

'But who's to say their bust-up wasn't for a far more personal reason than that?' Becks continued. 'After all, he manhandled her that day. That suggests there was more going on than literary criticism.'

'Oh God, why won't she leave me alone?' Serena said, a sob catching in her throat as she looked across the room. 'What's she doing here?'

Serena then turned and disappeared into the crowd, and Suzie and Becks peered across the room to see what had caused her so much distress.

'Bloody hell,' Suzie said, as she realised what she'd seen.

Jamilah Khalil was standing on the other side of the room looking directly at Suzie and Becks. She raised her glass of champagne in a silent toast to them.

'Little minx,' Suzie said. 'Come on, Becks.'

Suzie pushed off back through the crowd, once again managing to swap out an empty glass of champagne for a fresh refill by the time she'd arrived on the other side of the room.

'Ladies,' Jamilah said with a knowing smile as Suzie and Becks arrived.

Jamilah was wearing the same tight black dress she'd worn at the ball the year before. But this time she'd added a pair of black gloves that stopped just above her elbow.

'You said you weren't coming,' Becks said. 'I saw you put the invitation in the bin.'

'I changed my mind.'

'No you didn't,' Suzie said. 'You were always coming. You lied to us.'

'Oh dear, you've caught me out,' Jamilah said, sarcasm dripping from every word. 'What am I going to do?'

'Just like you lied to us about your relationship with Mike,' Becks said. 'Serena's just confirmed that you and he were an item.'

'And finally you get to the truth. It took you long enough. Very well, I'll admit it. I was having an affair with Mike. Just like you guessed the first time you spoke to me. But do you really think it was ever going to be in my interest to tell you?'

'You're as bad as Serena!' Suzie said.

'That old cow? Whatever I was up to with Mike, at least we had fun together.'

'You should have told us,' Becks said.

'Why? It's like I said to you before. I had nothing to do with Mike's death. And my private life is my private life. If I'd told you about Mike, my boyfriend could have ended up finding out.'

'You want to stay with him?' Becks asked, amazed.

'Just because I'm in a steady relationship, doesn't mean I can't have a little fun on the side. And that's what Serena never understood. Mike was fun. He was spontaneous, he'd say things he shouldn't and he *loved* spending money.'

'But he was seeing other women,' Becks said.

'I was seeing another man. You really are a prude, Mrs Starling. It's what's called an open relationship.'

'But we asked at the Holyport Hotel – the receptionist didn't recognise your face.'

'That was the one thing I drew the line at. I only met Mike in my flat – that was the rule. Or at the Ritz when we were in London. You know what your generation always say about young people like me? That youth is wasted on the young. I've always taken the view that it wasn't going to be wasted on me.'

Jamilah looked at Becks and Suzie, enjoying how much she was irritating them.

'He dumped you on the day he died, didn't he?' Becks said.

Jamilah took half a step back, as though she'd just been slapped in the face.

'You didn't argue with him about his book,' Becks continued, pressing home her advantage. 'He didn't care about his book.'

'He didn't even write his books,' Suzie said. 'His wife did.'

Suzie and Becks were thrilled to see that, for once, Jamilah looked unsure.

'That's right,' Suzie said. 'We've learned that he didn't write them. So he wouldn't sack you over your opinions of them. And he definitely wouldn't have manhandled you.'

'You're right,' Jamilah said. 'He said he was going back to his wife. That's what really happened. That morning, he told me he was going to mend his ways. That's the phrase he used. "Mend his ways". And I was to get off his property. I couldn't believe it. He was an old walrus. A boring, old man, with bad breath. I was supposed to be the one who'd dump him, not the other way round.'

'You were hurt.'

'I was furious. If you must know, it's the other reason I didn't admit to being in a relationship with him. Because, by the time you asked me about it, I wasn't in one. Now, if you don't mind, I've got business to attend to.'

'What sort of business?' Becks asked.

Jamilah beckoned Suzie and Becks closer and they bent their heads to her.

'Some of the richest men in the UK are here tonight,' she whispered into their ears. 'I'm hunting.'

She then raised her glass of champagne in a grim salute and moved off.

'Wow,' Suzie said.

'And to think I thought Serena was the cynical one,' Becks said.

'Yeah,' Suzie said, agreeing with her friend. 'But what does it mean? Does it change our plan? If only Judith was here, she'd be able to tell us what it all meant.'

'But she isn't here,' Becks said.

'I know. I know,' Suzie agreed. 'We've got to do this on our own. Although it's really unsettling everyone else is here, isn't it?'

'How do you mean?'

'Well – there's us for a start. And then there are all of the suspects for both murders. Harry Asquith, Serena Saxon and Jamilah Khalil. Not forgetting Lord Harleyford.'

'It's not quite everyone,' Becks said. 'I can't see Bethany Wise.'

'But has she ever really been a suspect?'

'I know what you mean,' Becks agreed. 'I've never seen why

she would have killed her husband. Let alone Mike. And there's someone else who isn't here. Someone who fits into these murders in a way that only Judith understands – if only she were here to tell us how. Angela Gulliver.'

As she spoke, Suzie saw a woman enter the main door wearing a petrol-blue gown, her hair a cascade of grey above her head, silver hoops dangling from her ears.

Angela Gulliver had arrived.

Chapter 33

'What on earth are you doing here?' Becks asked Angela as she and Suzie converged on her.

'Why shouldn't I be here?' Angela said, offended by the question.

'Lord Harleyford invited you as well?' Suzie said.

'As it happens, my invitation arrived this morning. But better late than never, I say. This is, after all, the party of the season – it wouldn't be complete without me. But tell me,' she added conspiratorially, 'did you manage to speak to Lord Harleyford after I tipped you off about him?'

'We did,' Suzie said, 'but he ran away from us.'

'Into the Hellfire Caves,' Becks said. 'And we lost him.'

'You know about the caves, do you?' Angela said, impressed. 'If you ask me, I think they could be the key to unlocking the whole case. In fact, if you pushed me, I would say that I think Lord Harleyford is the ringleader of some sort of cult. Like his forebears. I think it all started out innocently enough as a male drinking club. I can't be the only one who's noticed it's only men who've died so far. But put men with power and money in a secret society and what do you think they'd get up to? It's probably best if you don't answer that question.'

'This isn't just some fun escapade,' Becks said, stung by the gossipy tone in Angela's voice.

'Of course not, it's deadly serious.'

'Are you trying to save your show, is that what this is about?' Suzie asked.

'I beg your pardon?'

'The last time we talked, you admitted that your TV show was in trouble.'

'And that you've not got much else going on professionally,' Becks added, picking up on her friend's point. 'It would be front page news if you solved these murders. Which would really boost your TV show.'

'Basically,' Suzie said, summing up the situation as she saw it, 'if your show got cancelled, you'd stop being famous, and I think that would kill you.'

'You really think I'm that shallow, do you?'

'Yes,' Becks and Suzie both said at the same time.

'How could you?' Angela said, hurt by the accusation. 'The next thing you'll be suggesting is that I killed those two men just so I could then be seen to catch their killer.'

'You said that,' Suzie said. 'Not us.'

'You know what I think?' Angela said with a sniff. 'I think that you're one Judith Potts short of a crime-fighting trio.'

'Excuse me?'

'I know you're having to do all of this without her. And I have to say, I can see that the two of you are way out of your depth.'

'How can you possibly know that we're doing this on our own?' Becks asked.

'You're not the only one with contacts in the police,' Angela said with a sweet smile that was utterly deadly. Having issued her put-down, she sashayed off into the crowd.

'Well!' Becks said.

'I know,' Suzie agreed. 'But that means you're right. Apart from Bethany, that's a full house of suspects here.'

'And I can well believe that any of them are capable of murder. They're not the nicest of people, are they?'

'I think it's why Bethany's the only one of them who stayed away. She's the only one of them who doesn't have her head turned by an invite to a fancy ball.'

As she spoke, an alarm went off on Becks's wristwatch.

'It's time?' Suzie asked, downing the remainder of her champagne.

'It's time,' Becks said and then she took a deep breath to steady herself. 'Can you see him?'

'He's over by the string quartet,' Suzie said. 'I've kept him in view ever since we got here.'

'And Brendan?'

'He's on the other side of the party. I don't think he's seen us yet.'

'I can tell you that he hasn't, because if he had, he'd have confronted us.'

'Which means we're all systems go. Let's do this.'

Suzie led Becks over to the string quartet. When she arrived, she stepped in front of Lord Harleyford.

'You're both looking very serious,' Lord Harleyford said.

'That's very much part of the plan,' Suzie said. 'Because we're done with pussyfooting around. We know that you're the person behind the blackmail. And that means it's you who killed Gary Wise. And Mike Saxon as well.'

'I beg your pardon?' Lord Harleyford said, his ruddy face turning an even deeper shade of red.

'And it all came about because Gary Wise contacted an investigative journalist, didn't it? That's what set off this terrible sequence of events.'

'I didn't kill anyone!' Lord Harleyford said, barely containing his rage.

A few nearby guests turned their heads at the sound of raised voices.

'You've lived a life of privilege, but inheriting a fancy title and house has never been enough for you. Which is why you've been selling access to ministers for cash.'

'That won't be proved,' Lord Harleyford spat at the women, but they could see fear mixed in with his fury.

'I think it will. And in the meantime, Becks and I are making a citizen's arrest.'

'We've got an audio recording of your last encounter with Mike Saxon,' Suzie said.

'What?'

'You heard me.'

'It's not true.'

'Wanna bet? Basically, you'd better come quietly, because if you don't, we can do this noisily.'

Before Lord Harleyford could answer, Suzie grabbed a glass of champagne from a passing waiter and banged her forearm against the tray he was holding so that it fell to the floor, where it rang out like a cymbal. Everyone at the party turned to see what had caused the commotion and the string quartet stopped playing.

'Oh,' Suzie said. 'Butterfingers.'

Becks reached into her little evening bag and pulled out a USB memory stick.

'This is a recording of your conversation with Mike on the morning he died. Which is full of choice revelations and would put you in prison for a long time.'

'You want to keep all of this?' Suzie said, indicating the finery of the great hall. 'Then you should make a full confession, before we take proof of your wrongdoing to the police.'

'Give that to me,' Lord Harleyford said as he grabbed for the little drive, but Becks pulled it out of his reach.

Lord Harleyford leaned forward so he could get closer to the women.

'You give that to me right now,' he said with a snarl. 'Or, God help me, I'll kill you.'

Horrified, Becks and Suzie both stepped back, but Lord Harleyford took a step towards them to close the gap.

'You want this memory stick, you come and get it,' Becks said, but there was a tremor in her voice as she spoke.

And then she turned on her heels and she and Suzie strode out of the party as fast as they could. Flashing a glance over her shoulder, Becks could see Lord Harleyford following them. They sped up as they entered the corridor with all of the stone busts in it, until they were all but running past them to get away from Lord Harleyford, who appeared at the end of the corridor as they ducked through the door into the kitchen.

'Come back here!' Lord Harleyford shouted and broke into a run.

As Becks and Suzie crossed the kitchen, they heard the clattering of approaching feet and they threw the door open and raced across the yard at the back of the house, Lord Harleyford tearing after them.

The women ran around the corner of the outhouse and sprinted off across the lawn, a full moon hanging low over the building they were heading towards. As they arrived and yanked the door open, Lord Harleyford appeared behind them and hollered, 'You can't go in there!'

He started to lumber across the lawn like a charging rhino.

The women slipped inside, lit only by moonlight through the window; the broken furniture looming darkly, the air ice cold.

'We don't have our phones,' Suzie said.

'We can do it from memory,' Becks said as she went over to the trapdoor that led downstairs and stopped at the top of it. *Could they really do this?*

The door banged open, Lord Harleyford arriving in a snarl of rage, and the women disappeared down the steps as fast as they could, both of them stepping heavily onto the floor of the basement as it rushed up at them.

'Where's the door?' Suzie asked. 'I can't see a bloody thing!'

'It's over to the left!'

Becks led the way between the pillars, trying to feel where they were with her hands so she could orientate herself.

When they arrived at the wooden panels, she and Suzie started pushing at them, trying to find the secret door.

'Where is it?' Suzie said as footsteps clattered down the stairs and Lord Harleyford – his phone torch lighting his way – started running towards them.

'Got you!' he shouted, but as he arrived, Becks found the edge of the secret door, pushed it open and, as they slipped through it, Suzie slammed it back into the face of Lord Harleyford as he ran into it. He let out a roar.

The women were now in a jet-black tunnel.

'We just need to get to the main room,' Becks said as she started to run down the tunnel, keeping her hand against the wall so she could stay on the path.

Suzie followed. As they reached the end of the tunnel, Lord Harleyford's footsteps ringing out behind them, they turned into the main chamber, the lights finally turning on.

'OK, now what?' Suzie said, taking deep gulps of air to get her breath back.

'This isn't the deepest part of the caves,' Becks said, and went over to the middle tunnel that led from the main chamber. This was the route they'd not taken the first time they'd been in the caves. She grabbed up one of the torches that were on the side table and turned it on. Suzie did the same.

'This isn't even close to a good idea,' Suzie said.

'This has *never* been a good idea,' Becks said, running into the tunnel. Suzie followed.

This was a far rougher passage, with rocks and other debris underneath their feet as they ran. The tunnel got even colder and narrower as it curved, twisted and dropped ever deeper. And then it tapered to the thinnest of gaps and they stopped, throwing their torchlight light on the space that was far too slender for either of them to get through.

'No . . .!' Becks said, the sound of Lord Harleyford running down the tunnel behind them getting ever nearer. 'We can't get through that. It's a dead end.'

Chapter 34

'We know it must be possible to get through,' Suzie said to Becks as she pushed past her friend and turned sideways so she could insert herself into the rough gap.

As she did so, Suzie saw that the opening was at its narrowest at head height, but it got wider nearer the floor, so she dropped to her knees and carefully wriggled her shoulders. The wall pressed against her head, almost touching her nose, but she managed to scrape through to the other side.

Becks looked over her shoulder as she heard the sound of footsteps pounding closer, the tunnel beginning to glow with torchlight as Lord Harleyford approached. Before she lost her confidence, she turned sideways and pushed through the gap, but then she realised she'd left her torch behind. As she reached back to get it, Lord Harleyford arrived, his hair and eyes wild; his torch throwing crazed shapes onto the walls.

'Come back here!' he hollered, but Becks grabbed her torch, pulled it through the gap and turned to face Suzie.

'Suzie—' she said.

'Stick to the plan,' Suzie said as she turned and strode down the tunnel. 'We have to get to the lowest point of the tunnel.'

Becks used her light to look at the bloody graze she'd given her knuckles and then she followed. Suzie only walked now and Becks fell in behind her. They knew that they must be near the end and they were still just ahead of Lord Harleyford. As they carried on, the tunnel widened until it became a little chamber that contained rocky outcrops and loose boulders.

This time it really was a dead end. The only way out of the chamber was the way they'd come in. They turned as they heard Lord Harleyford enter the chamber from the tunnel, breathing hard. There was a cut to his forehead; blood slicking down his face and making him look like a terrifying ghoul.

'You're trapped,' he said as he regathered his breath. 'Give me that USB.'

'We know you're not the killer,' Suzie said.

This brought Lord Harleyford up short.

'*What?*'

'We know you're not the killer,' Suzie repeated.

'Then why the hell did you tell me I was?'

'We needed you to follow us.'

'Why?'

'Because we knew that the real killer would follow you.'

'Are you serious? This was all a set-up?'

'I'm afraid it was,' Becks said.

A shot rang out – *whip-crack!* – and Lord Harleyford spun sharply and dropped to the floor with a sickening thump.

'No!' Becks shouted and went to Lord Harleyford, falling to her knees as she saw blood start to pool on his white shirt front from a bullet wound just below his left shoulder.

'No, no, no, this wasn't supposed to happen,' she said as she looked up and saw the dim outline of a figure standing by the entrance of the chamber.

Smoke curled from the muzzle of a pistol.

'He was innocent!' Suzie called out, dropping to her knees to inspect Lord Harleyford. His eyes were closed and it didn't look as though he was breathing. *Was he dead*?

Becks looked at Suzie, both of them terrified, and both of them knowing they had to try and stall for time. It was the only option they had.

'You might as well step into the light,' Suzie said. 'We know who you are.'

The figure didn't move, their gun hand rock steady as it pointed in the direction of the two women. Becks's whole body was shaking, but she refused to be intimidated. She pushed up from her knees and rose to her full height.

'Didn't you hear?' she said. 'We know who you are.'

Suzie got to her feet at her friend's side, reached for her hand and took it firmly in hers. They would face the killer together.

'Becks is right,' she said, red-hot fury in her voice. 'And you don't need to worry about us recording this encounter or anything. We had to hand in our phones at security. It's just us two and you, Brendan.'

The figure didn't move.

'That's right,' Becks said. 'We know it's you, Detective Sergeant. It was you who killed Gary Wise. And who then killed Mike Saxon.'

'And Lord Harleyford,' Suzie added.

The figure stepped forward. It was Detective Sergeant Brendan Perry. His eyes were wild and his jaw clenched and unclenched as he desperately tried to work out what options he had.

'You're next,' he said.

'Don't you want to know how we worked it out?' Suzie asked.

Brendan banged the palm of his left hand against the rock wall in frustration, but his gun hand barely wavered as it pointed at the women.

'You've got to be curious,' Becks suggested. 'Although it wasn't us who worked it out. It was Judith, of course. She realised you were behind the killings before she left the country. And then she left us a message telling us.'

'Shut up about that woman!' Brendan shouted. 'If it wasn't for her, I wouldn't have had to do any of this. It's all her fault!'

'You're going to blame Gary's murder on her?'

'Damned right I am – the meddling bitch.'

'And Mike Saxon?'

'I had to stop him going to the police.'

'Because you were blackmailing him.'

'He thought he was the big man, but he wasn't – not at the end. And it will be the same for you two. It's like you said. It's just the three of us down here. And no one followed me, I made sure of that – I was checking behind me the whole time. It's just us and thousands of tonnes of rock above us. When you vanish tonight, I'm not sure anyone will even know to come down here to look for your bodies.'

'You don't want to do this,' Becks said.

'I've got no choice! I've not had any choice at any time. But – finally – I'm going to be able to make the pair of you shut up.'

'You idiot!' Suzie said, madly improvising.

'*What?*'

'You've fallen into our trap. Isn't that right, Judith?' Suzie said, looking dramatically over Brendan's shoulder.

Brendan spun around, only to realise that Judith wasn't, in fact, standing behind him.

He turned back to face the women; his mouth curled into a sneer.

'Nice try,' he said. 'She's not even in the country. We've got a watch on all the ports and airports. But it's good to know that, when it came down to it, the great Judith Potts let you down.'

'Never!'

Judith ran out from behind an outcrop of rocks and swished her grey cape over Brendan's head, knocking him to the ground with all of her weight, which allowed Suzie to step forward and stamp her foot down on his wrist. Brendan screamed in pain and let go of his gun and, as Becks jumped onto his back and wrenched his other arm up, Suzie dropped all of her considerable heft onto him so that all three women had him pinned to the floor.

Brendan writhed under the women's weight, but he couldn't shift them.

'Tanika's handcuffs?' Judith asked through her gasps of breath.

'Wouldn't give them to us,' Suzie grunted as she ripped the leather strap from her evening bag and started to wrap it around Brendan's wrists. She then passed it in between his wrists and wound it around a couple of times to tighten it off.

As Brendan continued to struggle, Becks and Judith followed their friend's example. They ripped the straps from their handbags and used them to tie Brendan's feet together.

Finally, Brendan was bound tightly enough and they rolled off him.

As he continued to fight against his bonds, the women took

a minute to regather their breath and check over their bruises and grazes. Suzie had deep scratch marks on her right arm from where Brendan had grabbed at her. Becks had banged her forehead on the stone floor and felt it gingerly as she got to her feet. She'd have a bruise there tomorrow, she knew. As for Judith, she peeled off the black woollen gloves she was wearing and checked her hands. A nail on the index finger of her right hand had bent back and she knew it would throb for a while. Other than that, she was mercifully undamaged.

'Sorry ladies, that didn't go quite as I planned,' she said.

'"Didn't go as planned?"' Suzie wheezed. 'It didn't *remotely* go to plan! Tell me you at least recorded everything he said?'

'Don't worry, I've got my phone on a tripod behind that rock over there. It videoed the whole encounter.'

The women looked down at Brendan.

'You know what?' Suzie said, indicating the leather straps that now bound Brendan by his hands and feet. 'We handbagged him.'

Lord Harleyford stirred and then drew in a rasping breath as he regained consciousness.

'Someone help me!' he gasped through the pain of his bullet wound.

Chapter 35

An hour later, Judith, Becks and Suzie were sitting on the tailgate of an ambulance, silver foil heat preservers over their shoulders, steaming cups of tea in their hands.

Once he'd come to, Lord Harleyford had discovered that he'd been able to walk, so they'd left Brendan tied up in the chamber and headed back to the surface as a four. As soon as they'd left the caves, Becks used Lord Harleyford's phone to call for an ambulance and the police. After that, the party had broken up quickly, but there had been doctors present among the guests, so they'd been able to attend to Lord Harleyford while he'd waited for the ambulance. Fortunately for him, the bullet had passed straight through his shoulder.

'I knew you'd get my message,' Judith said to her friends as she took a sip of warming tea.

'You didn't make it easy,' Suzie grumbled.

'If it had been easy, anyone could have intercepted it. And I disagree. I think I made it perfectly clear how I'd be communicating with you.'

'But how on earth did you work out that Brendan was the killer?' Becks asked.

'Yes, good question. I suppose my thoughts had already begun to turn to the killer being a police officer, even without me consciously knowing it. After all, right from the start we've suspected a police officer got rid of the records of Gary Wise's car crash. I was focused so closely on trying to imagine who could have had a police officer in their pocket that I didn't consider that it was actually a police officer who was behind all of this. I wonder if Brendan was perhaps the first responder to the scene when Gary had his drunken car crash? Or maybe he heard about it from a friend afterwards? In the staff canteen, perhaps? Or by the proverbial water cooler. Either way, I think Brendan approached Gary and told him that he could make the problem go away. And we all know how desperately Gary loved Bethany – and how angry she'd be if she found out he'd smashed up his car while drunk. Let alone what the newspapers would say. So Gary did the easy thing and agreed to the deal. Brendan made the police report disappear.

'But he wasn't done. Because Brendan now had leverage he could use against Gary. After all, Gary had just colluded in a crime, and Brendan decided to exploit that. He started to demand money from Gary to keep quiet. And Gary paid up. As Brendan had guessed, the sums were significant to him, but hardly too taxing for someone on a footballer's wages.

'But for my theory to be correct, I also had to then find a link between Brendan and Mike Saxon. Seeing as how he was also a victim of the same blackmailer. And that's when I remembered a comment that Brendan made on the one occasion he came to my house. He let slip that he was a big fan of Mike Saxon's writing and had even been to a few of the talks that he'd given. Which reminded me that, quite early in our research, we discovered that Mike had got into a punch-up with a fellow author at the Henley Literary Festival. A fracas, we learned, that had only been resolved when an off-duty police officer stepped in. I began to wonder if that off-duty police officer had been Brendan. After all, Henley's the nearest literary festival to Marlow. If Brendan went to any talks that Mike had given, it would make sense that he'd have been at that one.

'And I remembered that Mike's Wikipedia page said that the fight broke out when he told another author that he should get a ghostwriter to write his books for him. Which was quite a risky statement to make when you think about it, considering how Mike's books were ghostwritten by Serena. Then let's add one other piece of information to this – the fact that Serena told us that some people in the publishing industry knew that she wrote Mike's books for him. All we have to do is imagine that the author Mike attacked that night knew that Mike didn't write his own books and we can see how insulted that writer would have been. It certainly doesn't feel impossible to imagine that this writer would have hit back by saying that while *he* didn't employ a ghostwriter, he knew that Mike did. If Brendan was the person who broke up the fight that night, he could have overheard the author saying that Mike used a secret ghostwriter for his books – his wife.'

'Which is why he blackmailed Mike Saxon next,' Becks said. 'It wasn't anything to do with the women he was sleeping with.'

'Not even his affair with Jamilah,' Suzie said.

'Exactly,' Judith said. 'Mike's self-image would have been destroyed if it got out that his wife wrote his books. And, once again, Brendan asked for enough money for it to be meaningful for him, but not so much that a rich man like Mike wouldn't pay up.'

'Then how does Lord Harleyford fit into all of this?' Suzie asked.

'Well,' Judith said, 'we've known for some time what his crime is. He's been selling access to government ministers to the highest bidder.'

'He's claiming he's innocent,' Becks said.

'Nonsense!' Suzie said. 'He's guilty as charged. That's why he resigned his seat in the House of Lords.'

'Quite,' Judith said. 'And while I don't know how Brendan managed to find out Lord Harleyford's secret, we know his modus operandi now. He offers to keep your dirty secret out of the press in return for regular payments.'

'You think that's what happened?'

'I don't just think it, I know it. You see, before I left the country, I came here to see Lord Harleyford. I explained that I knew he was being blackmailed by Brendan and offered him a deal. All he had to do was send invites to his party to all the key players of both murders – and to the two of you – and tell me the code to the woodland entrance to the Hellfire Caves. And then I'd catch and expose Brendan for him.'

'Why did you want the other witnesses here?' Suzie asked.

'To put extra pressure on Brendan. He would have been panicking as it was, seeing as Tanika would have told him that you were about to accuse Lord Harleyford of murder. As only Brendan knew, if Lord Harleyford was challenged like that, he'd almost certainly end up revealing the name of his blackmailer. And once the police started to look into Brendan, what was to stop them discovering that he was the person who'd killed Gary Wise and Mike Saxon? By the way, did all of the suspects turn up at the ball?'

'Everyone was there except Bethany Wise,' Becks said.

'Obviously she decided she didn't want to come. Quite sensibly.'

'No wonder Lord Harleyford was so shocked when we accused him of murder just now,' Suzie said with a chuckle. 'He thought we were all on his side.'

'We *were* all on his side,' Judith said. 'But I could only get so much information to you in my message.'

'Have you any idea how hard it is to lure someone to the lowest point of a load of tunnels?' Suzie asked.

'I knew you'd come up with something. By the way, how did you do it?'

'We told Lord Harleyford we knew it was him who'd argued with Mike on the morning he'd died. Which we knew to be true – once we'd worked out your "ruddy face" comment.'

'Not that we got there quickly,' Becks said. 'It took Tanika to point out that your comment wasn't in fact a crossword clue.'

'And we then told Lord Harleyford that we had a recording of his argument with Mike on a USB stick. Which was a lie. We didn't.'

'But it had the desired effect,' Becks said. 'He got so wound up that he threatened to kill us. Horrible man, frankly. But once we'd accused him and caused enough of a commotion, he followed us when we left.'

'And Brendan followed him,' Suzie added. 'Just as you said he would. It was then just a matter of getting us all down to the spot where you said you'd be hiding. In a place so remote that we'd be able to get him to confess to the murders.'

'I'm so sorry that it all ended up being far more dangerous than I'd planned,' Judith said.

'It all came out in the wash I suppose,' Suzie said. 'And it adds to the charges the police can bring against Brendan. Attempted murder of Lord Harleyford as well as the actual murders of Gary and Mike.'

'And I did tell Lord Harleyford that the plan was risky,' Judith said. 'But he told me he'd been trapped by Brendan for so long that he felt he had no choice but to go along with it.'

'But I still don't get how you worked out it was Brendan in the first place,' Becks said.

'To answer that, I first have to explain how I worked out that the photo Eleni showed me was a fake. Or rather, it was you, Becks, who worked it out for me. Because you pointed out that I was wearing my wedding ring in the photo.'

As Judith spoke, she held up her left hand to show off the gold band that she wore on her wedding finger.

'Of course you were,' Becks said. 'You'd been married for some time when the photo was taken.'

'And yet, something only I know is I only started wearing this ring *after* Philippos died.'

'You didn't wear a wedding ring when you were married?' Suzie asked.

'Philippos wouldn't wear one, so I didn't either.'

'Then why did you start wearing one afterwards?' Becks asked.

'That's a story for another time. The fact that I was wearing a wedding ring in the photo meant that it must have been taken after Philippos's death. But he was in the same photo as me, so how could that even be possible? And that's when I had the creeping feeling I'd seen the photo before. To be more precise,

I had a memory of having seen that photo of Philippos on the jetty before. Not with me standing near him wearing my wedding ring of course. That was still impossible. But I had a memory that it was me who'd taken the picture of him. So I got out my old photos and started looking through them for all of the pictures I had of Philippos on the jetty.

'And the thing is, I couldn't find a single one. Which was surprising. Philippos went down to his boat every day. I remember taking quite a few photos of him there. They were all missing. It was peculiar to say the least. But then I realised I still had all of the negatives of the photos.

'I started going through the hundreds of strips of negatives I owned. It was extremely demanding, holding each negative up to a bare bulb so I could see it properly. But I eventually found it – the original negative of the photo that Eleni had given me. It showed Philippos standing on his jetty, the boat in the water and the sun in the sky, in exactly the same position. I was stunned. But I refused to think what it could possibly mean until I'd finished hunting through all of my negatives. The existence of the first negative implied the existence of a second negative. And I eventually found it.'

'A photo of you on your own on the jetty wearing your wedding ring,' Suzie said.

'Exactly so,' Judith said. 'As I say, it must have been taken after his death, seeing as I was wearing my wedding ring. And that's when I remembered. The Corfu police took photos of me on the jetty – wearing the clothes I was wearing on the day Philippos died. At the exact same time as Philippos had gone out. I'd buried the memory so deep I didn't even remember it until I saw the photo.'

'But why would they do that?' Becks asked, confused.

'They circulated it across the whole island, appealing for witnesses to come forward to say they saw me with Philippos either on the jetty or on his boat on the day that he died.'

'They were gunning for you,' Suzie said, appalled.

'It's how they managed to flush out the local farmer who then said he'd seen me on the boat. When the police were taking their photo of me down at the jetty, I remember asking them to take a photo of me with my camera. I wanted a record for myself. Ironically, I was worried that if I didn't, they'd doctor their photo somehow. As it turned out, they didn't, but – many decades later – it would be doctored by a different police officer in a completely different country.'

'Hold on,' Suzie said. 'Back up a bit, would you? You *didn't* wear a wedding ring when you were married? But within a few days of your husband dying, you'd started wearing one?'

'The point is,' Judith said, sidestepping the question for a second time, 'with the negatives of the two photos – one of Philippos and one of me – I now had proof that Eleni had broken into my house, found my old photos in the box room upstairs, gone through them and used a photo-editing programme to put the photos together and make it look as though they were taken at the same time. I felt so shocked. Violated.

'Although, I couldn't help wondering, did it really ring true that Eleni was behind it? This remained a fair question even when I later found out that the fake photo had been printed onto photographic paper that was at least thirty years old. After all, if there's a place in the world where you're going to be able to find unused photographic paper from decades ago, it will be an island like Corfu. The place has always been full of the most ancient shops down the dustiest backstreets. But I'd met Eleni a few times by this point and she'd struck me as fiery and passionate rather than cold and calculating. The way those photos had been chosen and put together demonstrated a level of planning that I didn't naturally equate with her. And also an understanding of how forensics worked. Getting the new photo developed onto old paper was really very clever, really, and one that I felt was beyond her.

'So the question of whether she'd in fact been behind the original theft was one I hadn't entirely resolved. Even though I had no idea who could have done it if it wasn't her. And then we come to Brendan's interview of me.

'During it, he referred to me keeping my secrets "padlocked" away, which struck me as an odd phrase. You know – linguistically. I'd have expected him to say I kept secrets *locked* away. That's what you do with secrets. You lock them away. So why the sudden mention of a padlock? And that's when I asked myself the simple question: what if it had been Brendan who'd broken into my house?

'You see, when I'd first gone to get my photos out of my box room, I'd noticed that the padlock on the door had been forced and left on the floor. I presumed it had been me who'd broken it the last time I'd looked at the photos, as I knew I'd have been a little "under the influence", as one might say. But what if it wasn't me who'd forced the padlock? What if it had been Brendan? It was an impossible thought, but I couldn't escape the feeling that the theory of Occam's razor – that the simplest solution should always be considered first – was suggesting to me that Brendan was behind the break-in. And the thing was, I realised there was a way I could prove it. I ended my interview with him as fast as I could, went home and I took the photo of Angela Gulliver down from the incident wall in my sitting room.'

'Which now makes even less sense than it did before,' Becks said. 'It made us think Angela was the killer.'

'Yes, I suppose it would have done. But I knew it possibly proved that Brendan was the killer. Don't you remember? When he came to my house, he took the photo of Angela from the wall, meaning *it was covered in his fingerprints*. Just as I hoped the broken padlock upstairs also had his fingerprints on it. So I went upstairs and brought the padlock down to my study. I blew icing sugar onto it and revealed that there were four clean fingerprints. It was then a relatively easy matter to lift the prints with Sellotape and put them on black paper.

'Using a magnifying glass, I discovered that three of the fingerprints belonged to me, but the fourth one didn't. When I then compared it to the prints of Brendan's that I'd lifted from the photo of Angela, I found a match. He has a rather distinctive scar on the forefinger of his right hand. And with the discovery of Brendan's fingerprint on the padlock, there was only one conclusion. It was Brendan who'd broken it. Logically then, he was the person who'd taken the two photos that were now missing. He was also therefore the person who'd mocked up the composite photo of me and Philippos on the jetty. And also the person who'd got it printed onto old paper and into the hands of Philippos's mother so that she could show it to Eleni the next time she visited.

'How could he have done all of that?' Becks said.

'I wasn't sure at first, but then I remembered there was a time we were talking to Tanika about Brendan. She told us that there was one brief spell when he stopped trying to undermine her, and it was when he'd gone on holiday earlier this year "to the Med". I think that that's when he went to Corfu and won the confidence of Sofia. I realised that if that's what he did, the whole case starts to fall into place. That feeling I'd had bubbling under the surface that perhaps it had been a police officer who'd been involved became a certainty. Detective Sergeant Brendan Perry was the blackmailer, and the killer, and he was also trying to set me up.'

'Why?' Becks asked.

'Here I think I have to blow my own trumpet. I think Gary had been talking about going to the press for some time. Which I think made Brendan realise that he was going to have to stop Gary – permanently. And, if you were Brendan, and you were mixed up in blackmailing a footballer, a lord and a thriller writer, but you were beginning to get out of your depth, and the whole thing was beginning to fall apart, where might you have seen the greatest threat to you staying out of prison?'

'Judith Potts,' Suzie said in appreciation.

'Indeed. Brendan thought that if I was embroiled in trying to clear my name, I wouldn't have the capacity to concentrate on him, which – let's be clear – I didn't. But then I didn't need to, because he made one fatal mistake. He didn't realise that the pair of you would be just as effective at catching the killer without me as you are with me.'

'That's not entirely true,' Becks said. 'Without your message to us, we wouldn't have known what to do.'

'But you got the message, that's all that matters. And it wasn't just us that Brendan didn't want working the case. He also made sure that Tanika got officially suspended as soon as possible after his first murder. After all, what better way to make sure the killer isn't caught than to be the person who's put in charge of investigating the murder?'

'It's kind of clever, really,' Suzie said.

'I'd rather you said that with less admiration, Suzie,' Becks said.

'I don't care,' Suzie said with a shrug, 'it's still clever. But it explains why the police never made any real progress, doesn't it? He didn't want the killer caught. The killer was him.'

'Although it doesn't explain why you left the country,' Becks said.

'No, I suppose not,' Judith said. 'But now I'm back, I can tell you all about where I went and what I did after I arrived in Calais.'

Chapter 36

'I hired a car from what I can only call a very "local" company,'
Judith said. 'It didn't look as though they'd process my paperwork
any time soon, and I also paid for the car in cash. Then I drove
to Corfu.'

'I beg your pardon?' Suzie said.

'It took two days.'

'Sorry,' Becks said, still not sure that she'd heard correctly.
'You drove for two days straight?'

'Not entirely. I only had to get to Ancona in Italy. From there
I was able to sleep on the ferry to Corfu. I needed to know for sure
where Philippos's mother had got hold of that fake photo. I was
gratified to see she recognised me the moment I walked through
the door. Even after all of these years. But I was less pleased to
discover that although she is now over a hundred years old, she
hadn't softened in the intervening time. Her hostility towards me
remained the same. But I'm much older now too – it's water off
a duck's back. And before she could refuse to offer me a drink – or
a chair to sit in – I showed her the photograph Eleni had given

me and asked where she'd got it from. She didn't immediately say. I think she was working out what angle she could play to cause me the most aggravation. In the end she shrugged and said a man had given it to her.

'I got out my phone, went to the Maidenhead police station website and showed her a photo of Detective Sergeant Brendan Perry. That shook her. She accused me of being a witch. How could I possibly know that that was the man who'd given her the photo of me and Philippos?

'It's all I needed to know. Brendan had given her the photo and dripped poison into her ear that it had been taken on the day her son died. Which, of course, confirmed her long-held belief that I'd lied to the police. I bet she couldn't wait to show the photo to Eleni – the daughter of the woman she'd always wished her son had married. And then began a chain of events that ended with Eleni in this country accusing me of murdering my husband.

'Which also explains something Eleni said to me when I asked her where she'd got all of her evidence from. She had all of the various witness reports and so on from the investigation into Philippos's death. She said they were all given to her by a friend in the police force. At the time, I presumed she must have been referring to the Corfu police, but she wasn't. I think Brendan was once again behind it – either knowing that Eleni would come to Marlow to accuse me, or suggesting to her that she come here and confront me. It should be easy enough to find out. We just have to ask her.'

'That's how she got your phone number as well!' Suzie said. 'Brendan gave it to her.'

'And it's how she knew where you lived,' Becks said. 'And where I lived for that matter.'

'He fed her all she needed to harass me and keep me off balance.'

'I still can't believe it,' Becks said.

'I know,' Judith agreed. 'It's quite a lot to take in.'

'Aye aye,' Suzie said, 'Lord Harleyford incoming.'

The women looked over and saw that Lord Harleyford was walking towards the ambulance, a paramedic at his side. His black dinner jacket was draped over his shoulders and his arm was in a sling. He glared at the women as he approached.

'I suppose I should thank you,' he said without a hint of gratitude.

'You're welcome,' Suzie said with a smile that was similarly frosty.

'Can I have that USB drive now?' he asked.

'There was nothing on it,' Becks said. 'Sorry.'

'What?'

'We needed to lure you away from the party. To where Judith was already waiting in the shadows. Ready to record our encounter with Brendan.'

'You knew he would follow?'

'He wouldn't have any choice. This afternoon, we spoke to one of his colleagues and told her that we were going to make a citizen's arrest. Knowing how honest she is, she was always going to have to tell Brendan that that was what we were up to. Although, I'm sorry our plan didn't quite go to . . . well, plan,' Becks added, indicating Lord Harleyford's shoulder.

'I'm told it's just a flesh wound,' he conceded.

'But we still got the confession out of Brendan,' Suzie said. 'As Judith knew we would. We just had to look like we were trapped, in the deepest cave beneath your house, and he'd feel he could say anything to us and it would just be our word against his.'

'After all,' Becks said. 'How could Judith be in the shadows filming his confession on her phone if she was last seen on mainland Europe? Although that rather begs the question,' she said, turning to her friend. 'How did you get back into the country without the police finding out?'

'That was easy enough,' Judith said. 'I used my normal passport to leave the UK. It was important Brendan found out I'd left the country. Then, to get back in, I flew from Corfu to London on a second passport I have. From Malta.'

'You have a second passport?' Becks asked.

'It's all above board. There was a scheme for a while where, as long as you invested an amount of money in Malta, they'd give you a Maltese passport. And since I'd not used it before, I figured it would get me back into the country without the authorities realising that the Maltese Judith Potts was the same as the British one. And I couldn't imagine that customs would put two and two together quicker than I could get to the party tonight.'

'Amazing,' Suzie said.

'Tell me, Lord Harleyford,' Judith said. 'There's one part of this case I've not worked out. How did you find out that Brendan was also blackmailing Gary Wise and Mike Saxon?'

'Because he was an idiot,' Lord Harleyford said. 'Cunning – don't get me wrong, he was definitely that. And naturally devious. But an idiot. Last year, on one of the occasions I was handing money over to him to keep him silent, he bragged that I wasn't the only celebrity in Marlow he had under his thumb. As it happened, I was holding my winter ball a few weeks later – an event that has its fair share of local celebrities. I realised I could use it to my advantage. During the party, I went up to every famous person I could find and quietly told them I'd heard about their blackmail and did they want to talk about it? Understandably, most people I spoke to were thrown – or got angry – and I just laughed it off as a bad joke. But when I spoke to Mike Saxon, he started blustering in a way that I recognised all too well. He was guilty. Even though he denied it. But I wanted to be thorough. So I started getting other famous people around to afternoon tea. When you've got a house like mine, most people say yes.'

'Which is why you invited Angela Gulliver to visit!' Suzie said.

'When I spoke to her, she didn't respond positively to my questions at all. But I'd already picked up another one of Brendan's victims by then. Gary Wise. When I'd suggested to him that he was being blackmailed, he broke down right there and then. He couldn't wait to make a full confession. He even said he was considering going to the press, although I soon talked him out of that idea. After all, Brendan had made my little difficulty go away. I didn't want any of that coming out in a courtroom. But, not long after, Brendan started to get more and more erratic. Making more and more demands, and my patience snapped. I told him I wouldn't give him another penny. Brendan was furious and immediately told the press all about . . . well, that I had what I believe my grandchildren would call a side hustle.'

'Selling access to government ministers,' Suzie said, not wishing to let Lord Harleyford sugarcoat his crime.

'It made no sense,' Lord Harleyford said, ignoring Suzie's interjection. 'By dropping me in it like that, Brendan no longer had any kind of leverage over me. Then Gary Wise wound up shot dead. That terrified me. And made it clear how high the stakes were. A bit of "cash for questions" was small beer compared to what Brendan was now prepared to do. I take it Gary went to the press after all?'

'You're right,' Becks said. 'He contacted a crime journalist. He was going to make a full confession – that he'd let a police officer remove his police record following a car crash after a night of drinking. And that he'd then allowed himself to be blackmailed ever since.'

'But he wanted to give Brendan one last chance,' Suzie said. 'To stop what he was doing. Gary really was a good man in the end. And he offered Brendan a chance to stop. But when they met up in the woods behind Gary's house, Brendan shot him dead.'

'And took his phone in the hope it wouldn't be discovered that Gary was being blackmailed,' Becks said.

'Exactly so,' Judith said. 'It also explains why the killer was able to get to the back of Gary's house without appearing on any of the CCTV cameras. It was Gary who'd taught Brendan how to take a route through the woods that avoided them. But can you tell us what happened the day after Gary died?' Judith asked Lord Harleyford. 'When you argued with Mike?'

'There's very little I can say,' he said with a sigh. 'He was still denying that he was being blackmailed by Brendan. Even when I told him that his and my lives were at risk. What if we were next? I suggested we should go to the police together and make a full confession – that's how much of a state I was in. But I got the impression Mike felt he was a tough guy like one of the heroes from his books. He sent me away with a flea in my ear and said he'd sort it out for himself. The next day, I discovered that Mike had been shot dead as well. I was now in a blind panic. And then I got a message from Brendan telling me that if I went to the police, I'd be next. It was all too much. I was being chased by the press, I was having to pretend that everything was OK as my wife organised the ball, and Brendan was threatening to kill me. Which explains why I panicked like a startled mare that first time the three of you turned up at my house. I couldn't let you near me.'

'You could have told us the truth,' Judith said.

'I know that now. I suppose I should thank you, Mrs Potts. And you, too, Mrs Starling and Ms Harris. You got me out of this predicament and all it's cost me was a bullet in the shoulder. The more I consider it, I can't help feeling I got away lightly.'

'I wouldn't be so confident,' Judith said. 'You're still being investigated for corruption. And I know the person I hope leads the case. Come on, ladies.'

Judith put her cup of tea down on the tailgate and took off the foil covering from her shoulders. After thanking the paramedic for his help, Judith led her friends over to where she'd seen a car arrive. It was a white Peugeot.

Tanika got out of it.

'I've just heard what happened, are you all right?' she asked, rushing to her friends.

'Just a few grazes and bruises,' Suzie said. 'No lasting damage.'

'And if you think we're bad, you should see the other guy,' Becks said with a smile.

'Is it true? Brendan was behind . . . everything?'

'It explains why he's been making so many official complaints against you. And Judith. You were the two biggest threats he faced.'

'But you know what this means?' Suzie said. 'There's no way they'll be able to keep you suspended when the only person who ever brought any grievances against you has just been arrested for murder.'

'I don't know if it will be that simple,' Tanika said.

'Who was it who rang you this evening to tell you that Brendan had been arrested?' Judith asked.

'My superintendent,' Tanika admitted.

'Then I think it could well be that simple,' Judith said with a smile. 'You'll have your job back. And better than that, the first criminal you put behind bars will be Detective Sergeant Brendan Perry.'

The four friends looked at each other and couldn't help but smile.

'I'm sorry we asked you for your handcuffs,' Becks said. 'We had to get Brendan to the ball without him realising he was being set up. And we knew you'd have to tell him what we were planning to do.'

'I don't care about that,' Tanika said. 'But how did the pair of you know what Judith was planning?'

'She left us a message after all,' Suzie said.

'That's not possible, the three of us went through her house together – there was no message.'

'Oh, there was a message all right, it was there all along.'

'Where was it?'

'In the *Marlow Free Press*,' Becks said. 'As we should have remembered sooner, Judith was still setting the crosswords in it. But that's why she'd been so keen to make sure we were up to speed on solving cryptic crosswords.'

'I had an instinct, quite early on,' Judith said, 'that I'd maybe have to vanish suddenly. There had to be a way for me to communicate secretly with my friends. I couldn't leave them in the lurch.'

'Just like we said,' Suzie said. 'Although things weren't helped when Judith gave us that message about the man with ruddy cheeks.'

'I felt I had no choice. All I'd worked out at that stage was that Lord Harleyford was very possibly the person who'd argued with Mike Saxon on the day he'd died. I had to give you what I had. It was then, during the long hours of my drive to Corfu, that I compiled the crossword that was my real message to you. Where I revealed who the killer was and how I wanted you to trap him.'

'Not that it was even close to easy trying to solve it,' Becks said. 'It took us all day.'

'And evening,' Suzie added.

'I had to make it work as a real cryptic crossword,' Judith said.

'It was about the hardest thing I've ever done!' Becks said.

'How on earth could you pass on messages in a crossword?' Tanika asked.

'It was amazing!' Suzie said. 'My favourite bit was when we had to "lure" "killer" "perry" "deepest" "tunnel". I didn't know that "perry" was a type of drink made from pears, so I learned something as well.'

'We nearly gave up when we realised she was saying that Brendan Perry was the killer,' Becks said. 'It was just so impossible to believe.'

'I never found it impossible to believe,' Suzie said, correcting her friend.

'No – wait,' Tanika said, wanting to make sure she understood correctly. 'The three of you caught a killer by communicating with each other through a cryptic crossword?'

'You know what?' Judith said with a broad smile. 'We did.'

Chapter 37

The following morning, Judith woke late. As happened most days, it took her a few seconds to realise that she'd survived another night and that this wasn't in fact a hangover, she just felt this terrible *every* morning. She looked at the alarm on her bedside table and was surprised to see that it was just before nine o'clock. Why was she awake so early?

There was someone banging at the front door.

Judith threw back her duvet, went over to her thick curtains and peeked through a gap to see who was outside.

There was a Fiat 500 car on her driveway.

Judith's heart sank.

She put on her embroidered dressing gown and left the room, picking up a shoe box from her dressing table as she went. She knew there was no rush. The person outside wasn't going to be going anywhere anytime soon.

Once she'd unlocked and opened the front door, Judith smiled at the woman standing outside.

'Hello, Eleni,' she said.

Eleni Paphides looked unsure – and so young, Judith thought. In her hands she was holding that morning's *Marlow Free Press* and Judith could see that the headline screamed 'Detective Double Killer' next to a large head and shoulders photograph of Brendan.

'I'm so sorry,' Judith said, her heart going out to the younger woman. 'You trusted him.'

Eleni was still too bewildered to respond.

'The photo he gave your grandmother was a fake,' Judith said as kindly as possible. 'He mocked it up out of two different pictures he stole from me.'

'Why?'

'His life was falling apart and he couldn't have me and my friends on his case. Literally. So he used you and he used your grandmother, Sofia.'

'She can handle it,' Eleni said and Judith couldn't help but smile. Eleni wasn't wrong.

The younger woman looked at Judith as though for the first time.

'I know we probably won't meet again,' Judith said. 'I don't think that would suit either of us. But I'd like you to have this,' she added, handing the shoebox over.

Eleni nodded, taking the offering. But she also knew that there was nothing she could say that would make up for the ordeal she'd put Judith through. She was relieved to see that Judith wasn't demanding any kind of apology. She turned and started to leave.

'When your father smiled it was like the sun coming out,' Judith said and Eleni stopped in her tracks. 'He was the most charismatic man I ever met. You remind me a lot of him.'

Eleni turned to look at Judith.

'If he'd known you, he would have loved you with all of his heart,' Judith continued. 'And he had so much heart.'

Judith knew that she was varnishing the truth, but she also knew that Eleni had suffered enough in her life. This was a gift she could give the younger woman that cost her nothing in return.

'Thank you,' Eleni said, and then she turned and got into her Fiat.

Before she drove off, Eleni popped the lid off the shoebox and saw that it contained a number of old photographs. Each and every one was of her father. In his house. With his friends in the bar. His family. Sunbathing, his body taut and mahogany-tanned. There was even a photo, taken in the village square, that showed him with Michaela, her mother. And in every picture, her father's vitality shone through.

Eleni looked back to thank Judith, but she was gone.

Inside her house, Judith went into her kitchen to put the kettle on. Really, she told herself, no one should have to meet their illegitimate stepdaughter first thing in the morning before they'd even had a cup of tea. As the kettle came to the boil, she realised there was something she wanted to do. She went through to the sitting room and sent Becks and Suzie text messages. Then she went upstairs to wash, change and get ready for the day.

When she came downstairs, she could smell fresh croissants and saw that Becks was in the sitting room laying out a tray of breakfast things in front of a guttering fire that Suzie was attacking with bellows.

'You're blowing too much air on it,' Becks said.

'I'm not blowing enough,' Suzie said as she smashed the handles of the bellows together and was instantly engulfed in a cloud of ash.

Suzie fell about laughing and then giggled even more as Becks complained that the ash was now getting into the cups of tea.

The fire had finally caught, though; flames licking up the logs.

'Told you it needed more air,' Suzie said, rubbing ash out of her hair.

'Good morning, ladies,' Judith said as she entered.

She let Becks and Suzie fuss over her as they made her comfortable in her favourite wingback and brought her a steaming cup of tea and a fresh croissant, butter and raspberry jam. It went without saying that the jam had been made by Becks.

Judith realised that she didn't want to tell her friends about Eleni's visit that morning. But for once it wasn't because she wanted to keep it a secret, it was because she felt it was something that didn't need mentioning. It was a situation that had been resolved entirely to her satisfaction. And the contentment she was feeling gave her confidence to follow through with her decision.

'I want to tell you what happened,' she said.

Becks stopped stirring her tea and Suzie paused mid-munch.

'What *really* happened, the day Philippos died,' Judith continued.

'Of course,' Becks said, and Suzie finished her mouthful as quickly and discreetly as she could.

'Don't worry,' Judith said, 'I'll wait.'

'There – all gone!' Suzie said as she picked up a napkin and wiped some butter from her chin.

Judith took a moment to decide how to begin, but then she realised how simple the task was. She'd just tell her friends the truth.

'Philippos had gone out for a morning ouzo with his friends in the village square. Which was never good news. It never ended well when he started drinking early, and that day was no different. When he got back a few hours later, he'd drunk too much and was spoiling for a fight. I don't know what came over me, but by George, I gave him one. I pointed out his failings. Said he needed to grow up. Take responsibility. Get a job. I don't know where it came from, but a storm had been forecast that day and the air was so hot and muggy – it was like something had to break. Which is what happened. He hit me – struck me to the floor.' Before her friends could offer their sympathy, Judith said, 'You don't have to say anything, it wasn't the first time, but that was the day I decided it would be the last.

'I told Philippos he'd better not go out sailing because a storm was coming in. He hated being told what to do – and doubly so if that person was me – so I had a fair idea how he'd react. He said he'd go out on his boat, storm or no storm. And then I followed him all the way down to the jetty, telling him he couldn't go out while knowing that it was the one thing that would make him go. I baited him. Even when he slipped and fell onto the foredeck. He really was very drunk. I just stood there, telling him how it was too dangerous for him.

'But I needed to know I'd be free of him. Truly free. So when he pushed past me to fill up a canister with water, I got onto his boat and went below deck. As you deduced many years ago, Suzie, I've always been a competent sailor, and I knew that boat inside and out. The engine was underneath some boards in the cabin and that was also where there was a little hose that ran from the bilge pump to the hull.

'Making sure I kept an eye on Philippos as he filled up with water back on the jetty, I pulled the board up so I could see the engine and all of the pipes and cables that led to and from it. That was when I saw him head back with the canister and I knew I only had seconds before he discovered me. So I reached down to the hose and tried to unplug it. But it was attached to the hull with a brass hose nut that was screwed too tight for me to undo. And no matter how hard I twisted it, it wouldn't come loose. I'll never forget how my stomach lurched as he stepped back onto the boat. I was in so much danger. God knows what he'd do to me if he found me.

'But I wasn't going to back down. I kept on twisting, the skin of my fingers rubbing raw against the metal, my heart thundering as he realised I was below decks and called out. What was I doing? And then the hose nut gave just a tiny fraction and I had to bite back the pain as I twisted and twisted as fast as I could. The nut finally released and the end of the hose popped free from the hull. As Philippos started to come down the steps into the cabin, I just had time to see water seeping in through the hole in the hull as I slipped the floorboards back into position and stood up.

'I remember so clearly the look of suspicion on his face. He knew I'd been up to something, but he was too befuddled with booze to know exactly what it was. Even so, I wasn't in the clear. I was still holding the hose nut, so I put my hands behind my back.

'"What's that in your hand?" he said to me,' Judith whispered, now entirely lost in the past. '"Nothing," I lied.

'And then he came towards me, with this look in his eyes, and there was only one word to describe it. Violence. As he grabbed my arms to find out what I was holding, inspiration came to me. I slipped the brass hosenut onto a finger. It's been on my hand every day since then.'

Judith held up her left hand, the single golden ring on her wedding finger glinting in the firelight.

'It's not a wedding ring?' Becks asked. 'It's *never* been a wedding ring . . .!'

'It's brass, not gold,' Judith said. 'And threaded on the inside. But when Philippos inspected my hands to see what I was holding, he only saw my empty palms and didn't notice the new ring on my finger. And in his confusion, I was able to get past him and onto the jetty. Then I waited, knowing that his boat was very slowly shipping water. It wouldn't remotely be a problem for a sailor like Philippos as long as he wasn't drunk. And as long as there wasn't any bad weather. As he hoisted his sails and set off, he didn't look back at me. But then, I wasn't looking at him. I was looking at the dark clouds that were already massing on the horizon.

'I went to the village, just as I later told the police. I did go into the church – although that didn't quite work out as I'd hoped. The priest, who I knew was there, either didn't see me, or pretended that he didn't. And then it was just a question of waiting until Philippos's body washed up two days later.'

Becks and Suzie didn't know what to say.

'Years ago,' Suzie eventually managed, 'I remember asking you why you still wore your wedding ring, and you said you wore it so you'd remember. But it wasn't your wedding day you were remembering. It was the day you . . . became free.'

Judith realised she felt a lightness that she'd not felt for decades. The feeling of release was startling. Exhilarating, even.

'Come on,' she said, standing up and going over to the peg where she kept her cape. 'You can help me do something I should have done years ago,' she said as she threw it over her shoulders and walked out of the house.

Becks and Suzie followed their friend, but struggled to keep up with her as she strode through the long grass. Although there was a chill in the air, it was a day of bright sunshine, the sky a clean blue – not a single cloud to be seen – and Judith smiled as she reached the edge of the Thames and started to twist at the ring on her wedding finger.

'The threading isn't helping,' she said when Suzie and Becks joined her. 'And my finger's not as thin as it once was,' she added as she gave the ring a particularly hard twist and then finally managed to pull it off.

She held it up and it glinted in the sunshine.

'Can I see?' Becks asked and, after the briefest of pauses, Judith handed it over.

Now she was looking at it closely, Becks could see that it really was just a little brass ring with a threaded inside, as could be used to screw a hose to a fitting on a boat's hull.

'All of this time . . .' she said as she passed it to Suzie. 'I just thought it was a wedding ring.'

'You're amazing,' Suzie said.

'Thank you,' Judith said. 'But if I am, it's only because I found the pair of you.'

The women looked at each other and realised, as they stood in the warmth of the winter sun, that they'd always have each other. Through thick and thin. Good times and bad.

'Shall I?' Judith said as she took the ring back from Suzie, before turning to face the river.

'I think that's a *very* good idea,' Becks said.

'Yup,' Suzie said. 'Do it.'

Judith threw the ring as high and far as she could. It landed with a satisfying plop, and then she saw it wink once in the sunlight – and twice – as it spun down into the depths, where it was lost forever.

★

Acknowlededgments

This story benefited hugely from the help of my editor, Manpreet Grewal. She stepped in with crucial notes at a time when it might have all gone a bit wonky (or wonkier still, depending on how you feel it eventually turned out). Every writer should have an editor as smart and sympathetic as Manpreet. My literary agent, Ed Wilson, also made vital interventions at key moments, and I'm indebted, as always, for his help.

While on the subject of literary agents, I'd like to thank Hélène Butler, Anna Dawson, Kroum Valtchkov and Magdalena Guzdziol. If it takes a team to get a book out, it also takes a team to keep a writer washed, scrubbed and out of debtors' prison, and I'm very lucky that everyone at Johnson and Alcock is so very, very brilliant.

I want to thank Hannah Boursnell for her extraordinary attention to detail when she did the copyedits. More than that, Hannah was so smart about the finickity details that mattered and those that didn't, and I can guarantee that if there are any factual or grammatical errors in the text, it will be because I didn't follow her advice. (This would therefore be a good point to say that while the Hellfire Caves are real, I've never actually visited them, even though they're located only a few miles from Marlow. What's more, as far as I can tell from their Wikipedia entry, they're not at all like how I describe them in the book either. So, I should start by apologising to the Dashwood family, who own the caves, for taking their tourist attraction – and somewhat racy family history – and then running fast and loose with the truth of both.)

I also want to thank Amal Ibrahim for her patience as she kindly pretended that I wasn't disregarding delivery deadlines as they whizzed past (even up to and including these acknowledgements, which I'm writing quite a while after I said I would – sorry Amal).

I also want to thank my wife Katie Breathwick, and our two children, Charlie and James. When I created the TV show *Death in Paradise* in the far distant past, our children had only recently been born, and I named two of the characters in episode one Charlie and James as an in-joke. Now, as I write this almost two decades later, both children are at university, and I can't believe that I've spent the intervening years coming up with ways of killing people and then catching their murderers. Thank you, all three of you. I couldn't have done it without you.

Finally, there's one last person to thank . . . and that's you! At the risk of coming over all schmaltzy, I only get to write books because they're bought and read. Publishers are funny that way. They only seem to publish books if more people buy them than they cost to print. And seeing how the world of *The Marlow Murder Club* has always been an elaborate love letter from me to my mother and her wonderful friends, all of whom were such an influence on me as I grew up (plus all of my batty and oftentimes terrifying great aunts and grandmothers), it's such a thrill to know that Judith & Co. have found a readership who enjoy their company as much as I do. Thank you.

Robert Thorogood
Marlow
September 2025

Discover the gripping and funny Marlow Murder Club Mysteries from the *Sunday Times* bestselling author. Now a major TV series!

The Marlow Murder Club are on the case . . .

From serial killers to dead mayors and deadly drama clubs, the Marlow Murder Club are there to succeed where the police fail. So, join Judith, Suzie and Becks as they investigate crime throughout Marlow and come face-to-face with some of their most challenging cases yet.

ONE PLACE. MANY STORIES

Bold, innovative and
empowering publishing.

FOLLOW US ON:

@HQStories